Chloe Does Yale

Chloe Does Yale

Natalie Krinsky

HYPERION New York

"The Wapshot Chronicle" © 1954 by John Cheever, reprinted with the permission of the Wylie Agency, Inc.

From *Anna Karenina* by Leo Tolstoy, translated by Constance Garnett. Originally published by P.F. Collier & Son, 1917, later published by Modern Library and Random House. Public domain.

Andy Warhol quotations © 2004 Andy Warhol Foundation for the Visual Arts/ARS, New York

Copyright © 2005 Natalie Krinsky

Library of Congress Cataloging-in-Publication Data

Krinsky, Natalie.
    Chloe does Yale / by Natalie Krinsky.
      p. cm.
    ISBN 1-4013-0107-X
      1. Women college students—Fiction. 2. Journalism, College—Fiction.
3. Advice columnists—Fiction. 4. New Haven (Conn.)—Fiction.   5. Sex customs—Fiction. I. Title.

    PS3611.R55C47 2005
    813'.6—dc22

                                          2004047302

Designed by Lorelle Graffeo

FIRST EDITION

10   9   8   7   6   5   4   3   2   1

To my Mom and Dad, who have grinned the entire way.
I don't know how you do it.

Chloe Does Yale

1

*E*XOTIC EROTIC IS YALE'S answer to Hugh Hefner's Valentine's Day party. Granted, EE, as it is called, takes place in September, while Hugh's bash appropriately occurs in mid-February. Hugh Hefner's party is filled with well-endowed scantily clad Playboy Bunnies, while Exotic Erotic is populated by well-read scantily clad undergrads.

Exotic Erotic is also the best party at Yale. Its motto: The less you wear, the lower the fare.

Being only slightly more modest than cheap, I shelled out the requisite three dollars at the door. I could have avoided the fee by showing the freshman manning the entrance my left breast, but to his great disappointment I passed up this once-in-a-lifetime opportunity.

Why he asked to see my *left* breast is beyond me. Of course, now I'm wondering if there is anything wrong with the right one . . .

Once inside, it occurs to me, as it does every year, that being nearly naked in front of four thousand other people who are nearly naked is quite an interesting, if not jarring, experience. It's the kind of experience that takes a generous amount of Jack (as in Daniel's) or Johnnie (as in Walker) to justify. Neither Jack nor Johnnie has made an appearance in my night quite yet.

I look down at my outfit. No bubble-wrap bra here (unlike the two girls I see ahead of me), just a pink string bikini and four-inch heels. Every time I move, the bikini bottoms wedge themselves a little higher, and I am stuck trying to extract them from their chosen crevice. As if this effort, combined with sucking in my stomach to hide the freshman-sophomore-and-junior fifteen doesn't have me sufficiently occupied, when I check over my shoulder to make sure that no one is witnessing this spectacle, I come face-to-face with the entire men's lacrosse team.

Uh-oh.

They are a rather unforgiving bunch, as I found out following a botched hookup with the star goalie, and in typical fashion begin chanting my name, graciously sending over a willing delegate with the mission (impossible) of removing my top. All of a sudden, Exotic Erotic has become a twisted game of capture the flag. My face is hot and I am certain that it has turned the same bright shade as my bikini.

Attractive.

Mortified, I quickly move into the crowd to avoid said delegate. All of a sudden I feel like a finalist at the Special Olympics version of a Miss America Pageant. And I have totally abandoned sucking in; escaping the clutches of an entire varsity team is enough of a workout.

Once I'm out of sight, I step up onto a bench in the Timothy Dwight courtyard, the site of this annual bash, muttering profanities as I frantically scan the crowd for the friends I came with. Unfortunately they are nowhere to be found among the sea of heads bopping to Biggie Smalls. The scene is sort of humorous, actually, and I wish I were in better spirits to enjoy it, as all the naked kids from privileged Greenwich are shakin' what their mama gave them to the hardcore sounds of gangsta rap. Granted, I'm no exception. My Upper East Side roots mean I'm not exactly down with the 'hood either. Tired of searching and rather disheartened, I climb down from my post on the courtyard bench and resign myself to smoking a cigarette in the hopes that something interesting will happen.

Lung cancer, skin cancer, wrinkles—I don't care. I am from the shrinking group that continues to believe that smoking is sexy. Especially in a pink string bikini (wedgie or no wedgie).

As I inhale my future demise, taking in my surroundings, I am realizing that Yalies shouldn't be naked. That's what the University of Miami is for. We are smart. Smart people are not attractive people. Stephen Hawking—smart, not attractive. Einstein, same deal.

Except that I hear he was a freak.

All these Nietzsche-reading girls should have picked up some Nair before the party. Smack in front of me, there's a hairy cellulite-dimpled junior in a scanty Cleopatra costume. Even back in the day, Cleopatra knew where it was at—queens don't have armpit hair.

I need a drink. Where are my drunken friends when I need them?

Just as this thought passes through my mind, I look up to find, sauntering toward me, two handsome young drunks who have lived on the floor below me for three years running—Activist Adam and Hot Rob.

Women at Yale distinguish various guys by nicknames: Just-an-Idiot Justin, Pretty Jim, Flaming Philip, Biting Brandon, El Señor Pequeño Rick . . . the list goes on. It's how we tell one Mike from another. There is a monumental difference between Magic Mike (the first guy I dated at Yale) and Mole Mike (whose affliction was discovered during an impromptu game of strip poker).

In any event, Activist Adam and Hot Rob are making their way toward me. They are the kind of guys who get more action than G.I. Joe in the eighties, but because I have lived with them since we were freshmen, I refuse to enlist with their troops. A feat that is not shared by most of my friends—or of the female population at Yale, for that matter.

Activist Adam is the kind of kid who grew up in the trenches of prep school, specifically Hotchkiss, the crowning jewel of them all.

His parents are über-wealthy, with houses in Vail, Southampton, and Palm Springs. Yet after a semester spent at the Mountain School (a place where rich kids milk cows), he has turned to Greenpeace and "fighting the man" to ease his insurmountable guilt. Ask Activist Adam what his father does, and he will tell you he is an artist. Actually Adam's dad is an investment banker who doodles on a legal pad during meetings and is a member of the board of the Museum of Modern Art. Adam himself specializes in the fine art of bullshit, a skill that comes in handy both in his major (English) and minor (Lying to Women). He will participate in any protest as long as it involves a sit-in. Showers only occasionally so as not to waste water or soap—both of which, according to Activist Adam, we should use sparingly. He can be forgiven only because of the adorable blond curls that swing over his green eyes (he cuts his own hair), his broad shoulders, and of course, his irresistible charm.

Hot Rob is of a different breed, and without a doubt is the most attractive man I have ever met in my life. He is tall and dark-haired, with piercing blue eyes and a dimple on each perfectly tanned cheek. When he introduced himself to me freshman year, he extended his hand and in an even voice said, "Hi, I'm Rob. I'm from Baltimore. We have the highest incidence of gonorrhea per capita in the United States."

Though I have yet to confirm that statistic, Hot Rob himself has a good chance of contracting the disease. He is a soccer player and an equal opportunity employer. By that, I mean that all it takes is a vagina and a pulse (not necessarily in that order) for him to try to get a woman into bed. Most people think that Hot Rob gets only the most attractive girls. This is a myth; he doesn't discriminate.

As the two come into view, I burst out laughing. Activist Adam has only a fig leaf covering his (I've heard) sizable member, while Hot Rob is wearing a zebra-print thong and a blue wig cut into a blunt bob. He looks like a Mod Squad drag queen.

"Hey, guys," I say, suppressing my giggles.

The two of them grin at me as if they're up to something and nod their hellos as Activist Adam hands me a flask full of a mysterious concoction. I take a sip to test it out, and when it doesn't make me gag, I begin imbibing like Michael Jordan in a Gatorade commercial.

Life's a sport. Drink it up.

Soon, if I'm lucky, I won't be able to see straight, and I will be convinced that this pink string bikini was actually a good idea.

"Chlo," Hot Rob says, "you must love this party. It's like sex central. This is your *domain*."

Hot Rob is referring to the column I write weekly for the *Yale Daily News*. It's called "Sex and the (Elm) City," New Haven being the (Elm) city. And sex being the most hotly pursued commodity on college campuses nationwide.

Activist Adam sniffs under his arm and makes a face.

"Do you want to play chuck, fuck, or marry?" he asks. This has been our favorite pastime since we were card-carrying freshmen. We choose three people from the crowd and we have to chuck one, fuck one, and marry another. Exotic Erotic is an ideal setting for this game; it's when everyone lets it all hang out and the naked truth is revealed—which is not necessarily a good thing. Personally, I'd rather have my truth masked in a flattering pair of jeans.

"Definitely," I say.

I choose the first three. A swimmer dressed only in a swim cap who looks like she could pummel the two boys, Hulk Hogan style. Second, Hot Rob's ex-girlfriend—to make things interesting. She's a nameless blond from California who has the personality of a dish towel, but according to Rob, she fucks like a banshee. I look around. Who is going to be my third?

"Ahh! I got it!" I say as I lay my eyes upon my final choice. "Breastopalous."

Breastopalous has the biggest breasts in the world. Well, in our insular Yale world. Hence her nickname. Hot Rob and Activist Adam each give her the fuck rating—you can't compete with breasts the size of your head. Or a small farming town in North Dakota.

All of a sudden my friend Cara comes barreling toward me, grabs my hand, and pulls me away from the boys. *"Chloeeee!"* she screeches, her Texas drawl cutting through the crowd.

"Maxwell Lyons wants to meet you," she exclaims breathlessly.

"Who?" I reply. I have no idea who Maxwell Lyons is.

"Maxwell Lyons," she says, sounding annoyed. "You know, Fifty Most Beautiful People Maxwell Lyons."

"Fifty Most Beautiful People Maxwell Lyons?" I repeat slowly.

Hmmm. Long adjective.

The Rumpus, Yale's monthly humor magazine (and I use the term *humor* liberally), has the annual tradition of choosing the fifty most attractive undergrads and publishing an issue devoted solely to making the rest of the student population feel bad about themselves. Apparently Maxwell Lyons is pretty.

Mazel tov, Maxwell.

"You know him. Senior in Branford," Cara continues, more exasperated than before. "He used to date Breanne."

I look at her blankly. I am still clueless as to why this stranger with a name that makes him sound as if he should be on *Days of Our Lives* has any interest in conversing with me. At this point, I am far more intrigued by the thought of a pepperoni slice and a vanilla milk shake from Yorkside Pizza.

"How did my name come up, and why on earth does he want to meet me?" I ask.

"Well," says Cara dramatically, and she begins speaking a mile a minute, her words spilling over one another. "See, we were standing over there next to the DJ talking about superstar dick and then he said—"

"Cara," I say, interrupting here, "what is superstar dick?"

"It's when you find someone, like, only decently attractive but because they're famous they're, like, really hot, and you want to hook up with them. You know, like Adam Sandler. Or that fat guy with the mustache from 'N Sync."

For someone with a GPA higher than my waist size, Cara sounds like a complete idiot when she's been drinking. I'm not quite under-standing where this speech is going, but I let her continue. Because I'm polite like that.

"So anyway, we were talking about superstar dick, and then your name came up, because of the column and everything, and well, Max was saying that he thought you were cute but made even hotter be-cause you're sort of like a celebrity around here."

I am trying to process all of this. Does this Max guy think I'm at-tractive? I have the sneaking suspicion that Cara just insulted me.

"So what you're saying," I begin slowly, "is that he wants to hook up with me because I'm a Yale B-list celebrity." (Only B-list because I am merely a sex columnist, not in movies or the daughter of a gover-nor or a president. Or a billionaire.)

"No!" she exclaims. "Will you just meet him?" Without waiting for my response she pulls me toward this nonintriguing character.

I am always fascinated by the way people behave when they meet someone that they are being set up with. Most people, like me, pretend that they don't have the faintest idea of what's going on. I decide that this will be my Maxwell Lyons tactic. Although, as I am later to dis-cover, he really never *does* have the faintest idea of what's going on.

Cara and I link arms and saunter (or at least try our best to saunter in four-inch heels on grass) over to Maxwell, who is still standing near the DJ booth surrounded by a group of guys, all quite average looking in comparison to him.

All of a sudden his superstar genitalia theory seems pretty unim-portant.

Cara, unfazed as usual, pushes through the guys and heads straight toward Maxwell. We are now standing smack in the middle of the circle the guys have formed, like two helpless lambs among lions.

"Max!" Cara is screeching again. "Do you know my friend Chloe?" she says, turning toward me.

He smiles.

All I can think about is how badly I have to pick my wedgie.

"Hi. It's nice to meet you," Max says. "I read your column every week. It's really funny."

"Thanks," I reply with a half-smile.

Wow, I am smooth. It's no wonder that I write a dating and relationships column each week. I'm quite the guru.

About three hours later, I find myself sitting in Max's living room. He lives in a house on Lynwood Avenue with six other guys, plus a middle-aged man who rents out the basement and brings home hookers on the weekend, but is a "really cool guy."

Needless to say, the place is filthy; beer cans litter the floor, and every once in a while I detect rustling noises emanating from the walls. When I inquire as to their origin, Max assures me that it's only a family of mice that also live in the house.

"No big deal," he says.

Phew. I was nervous it was something serious. Good thing it's only rodents.

The two of us are sitting in his crack den of a living room staring at one another. No one really has anything interesting to say, as we've already exhausted the "what's your major?" and "where are you from?" conversations.

We both know we're going to hook up. It's inevitable. Why would I be here otherwise? Why *am* I here? Do I *really* want to be doing this? It's three in the morning. I could be sleeping right now. Christ, I could be knitting myself a sweater. I am nowhere near drunk enough for this.

The funny thing about meeting someone at a party and going

home with him/her is that all along it seems like a stellar idea. After all, Max is considered attractive by the general Yale population, and I'm sure kissing him would be fun at first, but then there come all the other questions that follow the initial lip-on-lip contact. Am I going to see him again? Well, of course I'm going to *see* him again, but is he going to speak with me again? Does he want to date me? What do I know about him? How far am I willing to go with this person? How far will he try to go with me?

Actually, scratch that last question—I know exactly what's on his mind. You see, I have a theory about men at Yale. Twenty percent of them are gay; that leaves eighty percent available to the female population. So far the numbers seem good, right? Wrong. From there, ten percent are involved in fulfilling long-term relationships that are not with me. Thirty percent have little clue as to how to interact with women, so they forgo the trouble. They interact with books. The remaining forty percent have gotten laid a few times and are actively pursuing the next time. I bet Maxwell falls into that last forty, mostly because he's not gay.

"Do you want a tour of the house?" Max's voice snaps me out of my overanalyzing.

"Sure, that would be great," I respond.

As he begins to show me around, I ask him a slew of questions that lead me to believe he is not a rapist. This is positive, so I revert to the weather. I have a way of making typical weather conversation very funny and interesting for everyone involved. (This is of course a lie.)

Finally he concludes the tour in his bedroom.

"And this is my room," he announces proudly. As if he just led me into the Taj Mahal. It's your typical college-male room. Computer. Navy blue sheets and a plaid cover. Pile of dirty laundry in the corner. *Maxim* magazines strewn here and there, and a few *Playboy*s, which he casually kicks under the bed and out of view. A Miles Davis poster.

Max sits on the bed and I begin exploring, secretly looking for evidence of a girlfriend back home/at another school among the various pictures and books that line his shelves. I am suddenly very aware of the fact that I am wearing only a pink bikini.

He gets up and walks toward me. He *is* really cute.

"Wow," I say, scrutinizing his bookshelf and stalling, "have you read *The Two Koreas*?"

"Yes. But do you know what I'd rather do than talk about *The Two Koreas*?" he asks sweetly.

That's a line if ever I heard one. And I can think of at least three things he would rather do.

"What?" I ask coyly, playing along and tilting my head to the side. I can't decide if this is cute or if I just look like I'm trying to get water out of my ear.

And without a word, he leans in and kisses me. It's good. He's a goooood kisser. For just a moment I lose myself in it.

Even my mind is giving a little sigh.

But the moment of enjoyment is fleeting and my mind begins racing again. The good kiss is lost and now he's doing something very odd with his tongue. I hate it when men kiss as if they are having intercourse with their mouths. They make their tongue erect and move it in and out of your mouth like a power tool. Maxwell has suddenly developed a severe case of Black & Decker. I try to pull back to make it stop, but he persists.

The hookup progresses rather quickly, as we both started out half naked courtesy of the good folks on the EE planning committee. (I have to remember to write them a thank-you note.) This is when things get tricky; it's the big bad hookup decision. Am I going to let this relatively complete stranger see me naked? Hooking up with college guys is like playing a sordid game of cat and mouse. They are after the mouse, and you need to hold them off as best you can. I am fending Maxwell off like a warrior princess. Hand moves to the bikini bottoms. *Whop!* I smack it away. He tries the left hand—tricky. *Whop!* I got that one too.

And then, in an unprecedented move, Maxwell gets off the bed and gets completely naked. This is unheard of! I have no reaction. I look at naked Maxwell and think of my next move. How do I extract myself from this situation? Suddenly, horror of horrors, I realize that Maxwell has *no hair down there*. Maxwell's somewhat sizable Maxwell is shaven clean. Bald eagle. He's got nothing. What possesses a guy to shave below the belt is one of life's great mysteries, rivaled only by the fact that Michael Jackson has children of his own. Maxwell has thrown me two curveballs (pun intended).

As Maxwell climbs back into bed, looking rather pleased with himself, I assess my next move. Who knew hooking up was so strategic? But back to the question, or rather penis, at hand. What am I supposed to do here? I am at a loss. I am supposed to be the Charles in Charge of sex advice, and I feel about as out of place as Tammy Faye Bakker at a Snoop Dogg concert. I don't like this guy. I mean, I don't *think* I like this guy. So far the only information I have gathered is that he's from Southern California (exact location unknown) and is a political science major. He has really nice brown eyes and no hair on his balls. I guess the no-hair part is a clue about something, but about what, I am not exactly certain. How does he expect me to react to this move? Sleep with him? And not that I don't like sex, because believe me—I mean, BELIEVE me—I like sex as much as the next girl. And so what if I write about doing it—I'm merely an observer, a commentator on human (or maybe even subhuman) behavior. I don't know more or less than anyone else.

"Uh, are you okay?" Maxwell is looking at me. This stream-of-consciousness stuff takes up a lot of time.

"Oh. Um. Yeah. Me? I'm great. Sorry, just, you know, a little ummm—distracted! Yes, I'm distracted," I stutter apologetically, but I'm not sorry. Well, I don't think I am.

"I'll distract you," he says, leaning over to kiss me.

"Yes, well, you're doing a very good job," I say, followed by an uncomfortable laugh.

How am I going to get out of this without doing something I regret? Scratch that—without doing *more* things that I regret?

I can't just get up and walk out. He's naked. I'm nearly naked. Okay, *fine*, I could get up and walk out . . . but what's he going to think? A sex columnist who is afraid of sex?

No sex. Definitely no sex. My numbers just couldn't bear it. I think women are constantly weighing the benefits of sex with someone against adding another notch on the bedpost. I don't think Maxwell is worth another notch. Especially not after his bald-eagle shenanigans.

So how can I get out of here with just something minor—I'm talking no exchange of bodily fluids? Maybe I'll just . . . maybe I'll just give him a hand job.

But the truth is that in college, no one gives hand jobs anymore! I've asked around. Athletes, artisans, intellectuals, communists—no one gives hand jobs! I find this highly alarming. What about the sweet innocent dating sequence that takes place in syrupy teen movies? The one where you make out in someone's car after catching a Saturday-night flick? The hookup progression has several steps, and with the removal of the hand job, we go from kissing one thing to, well, kissing another. If blow jobs have become the hand jobs of our twenties, how do good girls take a walk on the wild side without compromising their DJ-from-*Full-House* status?

Maxwell and I are kissing. He's back to the Black & Decker tactic. I reach over and rather awkwardly begin to deal with Maxwell's bald Maxwell. He reaches for a bottle of lotion sitting on his nightstand.

"Uhh . . . usually I use this for dry skin," he stammers.

"Yeah. Me too."

Finally I finish tugging at his member and he comes with a groan. After a moment he opens his eyes and the two of us look at each other silently. I gather my belongings up off the floor.

"Well," he says.

"Well," I reply.

"It was really nice meeting you, Chloe. I'd love to get to know you better."

Good sign. I guess.

"Soo . . . ," he continues, "I guess I'll see you around."

Ummmmm. Excuse me? "I'd love to get to know you better" and "I guess I'll see you around"? In the *same* sentence?

What . . .

The . . .

Fuck?

And with that, my night ended/morning began—in utter confusion. Yet despite the awkwardness of the evening, I was certain about one thing—I know that I want him to pick up his phone and call me to tell me that he had a great time the other night. It is this thought that occupies me as I make my way through the streets of New Haven on this warm September morning, wearing nothing more than my pink string bikini. There is something satisfying and hopeful about the post-hookup phone call, something that retroactively dignifies drunken collegiate Saturday-night romps in the dark.

But dignity, it seems, is lost on me. Maxwell does not call. Monday. Tuesday. Wednesday. No call. Thursday. Friday. My phone remains silent.

THE YALE DAILY NEWS

SEX AND THE (ELM) CITY
BY CHLOE CARRINGTON

Afraid I'll Miss Your Third-Day Call?
Don't Worry, I'll Dial Star Sixty-Nine

So . . . you spent one night this weekend figuring out how to turn a drab hand job into a fab hand job by using a li'l lube.

Way to go.

As for me, I'm stressed and I'm sweaty and I can't find my problem set, nor have I figured out how to balance my cup of nonfat granola mixed with my nonfat yogurt along with my nonfat life. I'm clutching my cell phone hoping it will ring and THE PHONE CALL will come as I'm doing this awkward run-walk because I'm one of only five morons on this campus who wear heels when they have four miles and three and a half minutes between classes.

You all know the phone call I'm talking about. The post-hookup phone call. The one that comes three days after you hooked up. Or at least is *supposed* to come three days afterward. Not one day, that's too desperate. And not a week later because that leaves *me* desperate, but is two days okay? How about four?

This means that if you met at Toad's on a Saturday, your phone should ring somewhere around ten or eleven P.M. on Tuesday. Or if it was at SAE late-night on Thursday (where your shoes were ruined by the delightful weekend entrée of beer, with a side of mud in a lovely vomit sauce), your phone call should come Sunday afternoon, preferably after brunch, where you sat for an hour and a half discussing whether the phone call was actually going to come, and if it did, were you going to do the coy flirty voice, or were you instead going to be cool and aloof and "very busy, can't really talk, but I'll call you later."

Monday morning screws this whole process up because when you're running to Macro (on Hillhouse) from History in LC (far away from Hillhouse) you make eye contact with THAT person from THIS weekend who's seen you NAKED and who's supposed to make the phone call. There's a "Hey," followed by a "S'up," to which you respond, "I'm good," then you realize that's an answer to a question that person didn't ask, so you say, "I mean, nothing." Then there is an awkward pause that lasts approximately seventy-five minutes, and then you walk away quietly. Great.

That encounter is always the most terrible one. You both walk away wondering. Wondering about what the other is thinking, and what's going to happen with the phone call now. Who's supposed to do it? And why did they look so much better in the dimly lit Toad's coat-check room after six beers?

Six beers do wear off. Eventually.

Once again, we're back to the phone call. Will it come (let's hope as quickly as he did)? And what's it going to be?

There are several types:

The obligatory phone call. You don't really like the other person. You regret that you've seen their body after three months of not going to the gym and two rounds of the freshman fifteen. You just want to get it over with. You'd rather be on the phone with your grandmother. With anyone. There's chitchat, it's uncomfortable, and when you hang up, you both realize there's no hope.

Then there's the I'm-a-little-too-happy-to-call call. This one comes a little too early. Why? Because that guy hasn't gotten ass in six months and he's really—no, make that *really*—excited that you came through in the clutch. Then again, he might actually like you. We all know that beautiful life-long relationships can develop from a romantic encounter at Zeta Psi.

There's the maybe-if-I-call-right-now-you'll-come-over-and-get-naked-with-me-again call (MIICRNYCOAGNWMA for short). This person is really optimistic. It's eleven-thirty on a Wednesday, he or she doesn't have any work, and you need to write a twelve-page paper about the pottery of ancient southwestern Eritrea. No one is coming over. No one is getting naked. Thanks for nothing.

There is, of course, the slight variation on the MIICRNY-COAGNWMA call, which is the you-give-really-good-hand-jobs-let's-see-what-you-can-do-with-your-mouth call. This one means he's really interested in getting to know you . . . next weekend. You have so much in common!

Finally there's the no-call. This means they don't call. Let's be honest, this is rude. Okay, kind of rude depending on how either party looked Monday. But regardless, I have to say, that no matter what kind of call it is, it's better than no call. No call sucks, and there's no reason for it. You don't even have to dial more than five numbers if you're calling from on campus. There are blue phones everywhere. This college is TELLING you to call. After all, maybe her roommate will pick up, and she's cute . . .

2

LISA, MY SMARTEST FRIEND, and I are having lunch. It is exactly one week after Exotic Erotic and everything is going wrong. Lunch is taking place at Commons—the most offensive of all Ivy League dining halls. Commons is the size of a small basketball stadium and seats about as many people. It always smells like mushroom barley soup and is filled with athletes and super regulars. Athletes are people who go to Yale because they row crew or have a way with balls. Super regulars are people who go to Yale because they invented the board game Cranium or discovered the cure for Tourette's.

I am having browned field greens and an assortment of deli meat. This is what I have eaten every single day at every meal for the past two and a half years. It is the only dining hall meal, I have discovered, that ensures minimal caloric intake while guaranteeing optimal nutritional value. Everything else served in the dining hall is inedible (shepherd's pie), unidentifiable (chana masala), or 31 grams of fat per serving.

Lisa and I are dining between shopping the classes "Local Flora" and "Physics for Poets"—the sciences of champions, taken not by choice, but out of a necessity to graduate. Shopping period occurs

twice a year at the beginning of the semester. Though it sounds enticing, as in Barneys semiannual warehouse sale, it pales drastically in
comparison. For two weeks, neurotic Yale students attend every class
that seemed remotely alluring when they anxiously ripped open their
blue books (course lists) in mid-July. This averages out to about 247
classes over two weeks. When the fortnight is up, students settle on
those classes that most tickled their pickles. It's an exhilarating
process—really it is—that allows no time for lunch, a stipulation Lisa
and I have decided to ignore in our third year of this academic hell.

We have congregated to discuss, among other things, Maxwell's lack of a phone call and the pros and cons of fucking her
newest professor—make that *professors*. Lisa does not fornicate
with mere twenty-year-old mortals. She prefers men who are tor-
tured by the threat of imminent academic destruction (i.e., are
approaching their thirteenth year of dissertation writing); who take
her to see movies like *Hiroshima, Mon Amour* in Milford, lest they
be seen with her in New Haven; and present her with works by Jean-
Paul Sartre for Valentine's Day. *Les autres* are, after all, hell—unless
they are fucking you on your desk in the Hall of Graduate Studies.

"I hate my life," she says, plopping down and strewing her stack
of books and syllabi all over the table.

"Oh, yeah?" I reply, barely looking up from my wilted vegetables.
"I hate mine, too. You can go first. Your problems are always exponentially more interesting or scandalous."

"The Philosophy Department is my new lair. I find it so . . .
so . . . *intellectually* stimulating," Lisa begins.

"Is *intellectually* another word for clitoris?" I ask her with a smirk.

"No," she replies indignantly. "It's just that this new hangout of
mine has two lovers and I'm in somewhat of a bind. I have been given
so many roads. Down which should I trek?"

"You're going to have to be a little more specific."

"I am dating *two* assistant professors in the Philosophy Department," Lisa states.

"Mazel tov."

"Seriously," she continues, "I need to choose one. And fast."

"Why?"

"Because dating two is far too much existential thought for my brain to handle."

"Can we back up?" I ask.

Lisa nods impatiently and takes a bite out of her 600-calorie chicken Caesar wrap. It's all right because this is a time of severe crisis.

"Are you going to name your Kantian love child Immanuel? And then go on Maury Povich to find out who the real father is?" I can't take Lisa seriously because she's always seeing at least two guys.

"Chloe," she says in a warning tone, "I am going to wring your neck. Just because you think I'm crazy does not mean that this isn't a problem."

"Okay, okay." I relent. "I have a real question, then."

"Proceed."

"How did you get yourself into this predicament? I thought you weren't going to do this anymore."

"Well," she begins dramatically, "see, I took 'Death' with Shelley Kagan last semester ['Death' is an honest-to-goodness class], and two of the TAs were very attractive—you know, in that dark, brooding philosophical sort of way. Anyway," she continues, "I flirted, asked for their help on my papers, stuck around after class . . . you know, engaged in all of that highbrow bullshit, discussed the veil of ignorance. I was on like an Easy-Bake oven."

"You're easy like an Easy-Bake oven," I remark.

As you can tell, Lisa is no stranger to the art of professor-luring. Though having a cerebral capacity the size of the tristate area certainly helps.

"So, as I was saying, I worked my game as best I could."

"You just used the word *game*. How contemporary of you."

"Chloe!"

"Okay, okay, go on. I'm listening. Two TAs, 'Death,' flirting, go on." I take a bite of my turkey and chew thoughtfully for emphasis.

"So, incidentally, the Philosophy Department has been going through a serious intellectual drought over the last few years and has been desperate for some new blood."

"Unlike yourself."

"Yes. And they picked both of my fine young gentlemen to fill available assistant professorships this year."

"So now you're dating two men who earn a combined salary of thirty thousand dollars a year."

"Yes. Moving right along, I ran into Stuart last week outside of Koffee Too as I was picking up a decaf double-skim mocha latte on my way to class, and we got to talking about Hegel's theory of contradiction, and well, to make a long story short, he asked me out."

"You're dating a guy named Stuart? Don't you remember that book *Stuart Little*? Is he? You know, little?"

"Actually, Chloe, Stuart is *unusually* well endowed."

"Unusually?"

"Unusually," she answers, raising one eyebrow.

"If you're so satisfied with Stuart's Ph.D., why are you after bachelor number two?"

"I am not *chasing*," Lisa says indignantly. "It was happenstance."

"Listen, Sense and Sensibility, cut to the chase and tell me how you met this other . . . what's-his-name?"

"Harry."

"Harry? I'm not even going to comment."

"Don't comment."

"I said I wouldn't."

"Well, I met Harry as I was leaving Stuart's office."

"Go on."

Lisa shoots me a dirty look and continues, "So I was leaving Stuart's office under the auspices of discussing my senior essay—"

"You are an econ major *and* it is first semester junior year. Could you be more obvious?"

Dirty look number two.

"*Anyway*, I ran smack into Harry, who was headed in my direction, and I said it would be nice if we walked together, you know, just to catch up. It was completely innocuous."

"Bambi is innocuous. *You* are something entirely different."

Lisa ignores me.

"On our walk, he invited me to attend a Master's Tea given by a visiting professor on moderate deontology and just-war theory that was taking place that evening. I thought it sounded interesting, so I went."

"And?"

"And it was interesting. So interesting, in fact, that we decided to have dinner."

"Where did you go on campus that would accept food stamps?"

"Shut up. Dinner turned into dessert, and dessert turned into more conversation, and more conversation turned into—"

"Schtupping on his Goodwill couch?" I volunteer.

"Well . . ." Lisa hesitates.

I look at her pointedly.

"Yes," she says.

"You had sex with two professors in one day, both of whom work in the same department."

"I'm in moral purgatory!" she wails, and puts her head down on the sticky dining hall table.

Two football players sitting a few seats away look over at us. One mouths "Purgatory?" The other shrugs his shoulders and they both resume scouring their hamburger-filled plates. I can't even imagine the calorie count on those.

"Lisa! Calm down," I hiss. "Let's think through this rationally," I reason, returning to my normal tone.

"Okay," she replies, sniveling.

Actually, inside her five-foot-two frame, Lisa carries a heart of gold. We met September of freshman year, almost exactly two years ago. I had just broken up with my high school boyfriend, Derrick—correction, he had just broken up with me—and was sitting dejectedly in the common room of my suite with several pints of Ben & Jerry's Phish Food ice cream and every teen movie filmed between 1986 and 1989. *Dirty Dancing, Sixteen Candles, Pretty in Pink, Girls Just Want to Have Fun*, and, well, the *Die Hard* series, because there was a little part of me that felt like blowing something up. Suddenly there was a knock on my door and this beautiful Korean girl with thick straight black hair and the most flawless skin I'd ever seen stood in the doorway asking if I had a copy of Plato's *Republic*. She took one look at me and without hesitation diagnosed me with post-breakup-trauma syndrome. She explained that she had fallen victim to the very same ailment only a few weeks earlier and nothing, she insisted, could cure my woes like a bottle of champagne to go along with all of that ice cream. Barely five minutes later, she returned with a case of the worst but bubbliest bubbly I've ever tasted. She also proceeded to tell me several pretty incredible stories about her mildly insane diplomat father and their worldly adventures—elementary school in Bangladesh, seventh grade in Turkey, vacations to Monaco, Brazil, and Fiji, and high school spent in Germany as a punk rocker. She convinced me to run off with her after graduation to become international madams à la Heidi Fleiss, Lisa's personal heroine—something that I insisted would be impossible given my nontrustafarian status (read: one lacking a trust fund). She replied that we could split hers fifty-fifty. We stayed up all night laughing, talking, and drinking, and have been inseparable ever since.

"Chloe!" Lisa says, snapping me back from my thoughts, "are you even listening to me?"

"Yes, yes, yes," I say hastily. "I'm sorry."

"So what should I do?" she asks again, this time almost on the verge of tears.

"Well," I say soothingly, "you've only been seeing these guys for about five and a half minutes. You are not nearly informed enough to make any kind of final decision."

"But, Chloe, you don't understand. I'm carelessly leading the two of them along, preying on their sentiments, their passions. Just as their feelings deepen"—she pauses dramatically—"I discard one. And based on what? That Stuart is a better lover? Or that Harry once gave me a B-plus on a paper?"

"Harry gave you a B-plus?" I ask incredulously. Lisa does not get B-pluses, she gets only As.

"Yes. But that's not the point."

"I know. I'm just a little surprised."

There's a pause. It seems I'm not helping very much.

"Lisa," I say, trying again, "why don't you think about this situation like you do shopping classes?"

"Can you just be serious for once? Please!"

"I am being serious. Listen. For the next two weeks, you are going to be going to class after class, sometimes visiting one more than once, just taking them all for a trial run. So why don't you do the same with Stuart and Harry?"

"Go on," she says.

"What I mean is, why don't you try them both out? You're not being insensitive, you're just checking out the syllabus, you know, trying out some of the reading. How are you going to know what you want to take if you don't shop around?"

"I guess."

"So you see, it follows that you need to be more informed about Stuart and Harry before you make any kind of real decision. You're essentially just checking out your options before fully investing."

"Unlike classes or stocks, Stuart and Harry have emotions," she says with a sigh.

"Well, if we're going to be international madams, you're going to have to start learning how to break some hearts."

Lisa smiles. "I'll try my best."

"On another note," I begin cautiously, "I'm curious. Who is better in the sack, Not-So-Little-Stuart or Happenstance Harry?"

A slow grin spreads over Lisa's previously serious face. "Two orgasms both times."

"You had four orgasms in less than twenty-four hours?"

"Uh-huh. Is that unusual?" she asks, egging me on, fully knowing that that is *very* unusual.

"Well, I really don't know what to tell you. Choose one, don't choose one, you're still going to get laid."

"You don't understand," she says, shaking her head with a laugh.

"You're right, I don't understand because things like this do not happen to me. Sex for me takes place every other full moon—and that's when that Farmer's Almanac book is predicting a good year. Plus, I'm thinking of becoming a born-again virgin."

"You write a sex column," Lisa points out. "You cannot write a sex column if you're born again."

"Who cares if I was born the first time around? I know how to do it, don't I?"

"I don't know. I've never slept with you."

"Well, I'll have you know, I'm very good."

"What about Marcus?"

Like most exceedingly smart people, Lisa is not very good with details.

"Maxwell," I correct her.

"Well?" she pries.

"Well, he didn't call me," I reply, looking down at my half-eaten lunch.

"He didn't call you?"

"No."

"You have a phone, don't you?"

"Are you off your rocker? Are you saying I should call him? I will not . . . I would never . . . I mean, him not calling me is like . . . is like . . . giving the finger to the Dalai Lama! It is completely rude."

I am most impressed with this analogy. Lisa, however, is not.

"Let's not think so highly of ourselves, shall we," she snorts.

This does not deter me.

"He is practically asking to go to hell. He's saying, 'Please, banish me to a social inferno! Allow me to walk over some hot coals! Burn me on a spit! Stone me!' "

I am practically yelling at this point, but Lisa is an eccentric, so she isn't embarrassed. To really drive my statement home, I stand suddenly and prepare to bus my tray.

"Sit down," Lisa says sternly.

I obey.

"Did it ever occur to you, in the depths of that narcissistic, narrow-minded cranium of yours, that Maxwell might be *afraid* to call you?"

"He was not afraid of my vagina. Nothing is scarier than a vagina," I say, trying to mask the embarrassing truth: I am actually hurt, and the last two guys before Maxwell haven't called either.

"You're not exactly a wallflower, you know."

"You're *deflowering* the entire Philosophy Department. What *exactly* is your point?" I shoot back defensively.

"Maybe he's frightened of, oh, I don't know, appearing in one of your columns? Falling victim to that sharp tongue of yours?"

Lisa pauses for effect. "Perhaps," she continues, "he's fearful that he won't be able to perform up to par with you, if you gather what I'm saying."

"Perhaps he's just an asshole," I retort.

"Because he didn't call you? Interesting idea." She pauses purely for effect and then continues evenly, "What are you so worried about anyway? The last time I spoke to you, you told me—and I quote—'he has the IQ of a spoon.' You don't even *like* him."

"It's the principle that counts," I insist.

"So what you're saying is, mediocre or not, you just need that phone call for your ego? Are you really that desperate?"

Before I can respond, Lisa stands up and gathers her mess.

"Well, dear, I bid you farewell," she says, leaving me on my own. "I have another philosophy class to shop."

"Good luck," I say quietly.

And with that, she is off, ready to conquer the rest of her day, or perhaps Yale's remaining single faculty members.

I, on the other hand, am left alone and depressed, still wondering about stupid Maxwell's stupid phone call. It makes no sense to fixate on this one mostly nondescript man, but I do. Just as Lisa feels that she ought to choose one professor before she has had time to fully evaluate how she feels about either, I need the security a phone call from Maxwell will provide. It's as if any other chance with any other eligible bachelor Yale has to offer has disappeared into the recesses of my mind, leaving me to wonder about Less-Than-Spectacular Maxwell.

I am certain that Max is not sitting around his room hoping—no, praying—that I will contact him. Maybe ask him out for a drink. And while Lisa and I just spent sixty minutes of valuable time dissecting every move that Stuart and Harry (barf) and Maxwell have made in the last week, I doubt that any of them have discussed our existence with their numerous male friends, save maybe a casual "Yeah, I scored," followed by a high five, or in Lisa's case, a "She does have quite an extensive knowledge of Rawls." In fact, I highly doubt that our existence has prevented them from talking, flirting, fucking, calling, contacting, kissing, or any number of things with any other girls. Meanwhile, I find myself in a self-imposed male quarantine that I cannot escape.

Herein lies the ultimate collegiate contradiction. As women

prepare to enter college, they are told that they will meet the man they are going to marry. You, the masses tell us, are going to fall in love. You—yes, you! they shout—will have a date to every formal, semiformal, and not-so-formal event in your Yale career! You are going places! In fact, you are going places with a big fat rock on your left hand! He will be dreamy, he will row crew, wear khakis, and sport an adorable old blue baseball cap with a proud Y stitched into it.

LIES, ALL LIES!

Guys, on the other hand, are fed a completely different fantasy. After watching *Girls Gone Wild* for nine straight weeks before arriving at Yale, they are convinced that there will be hordes of girls walking around campus in bikinis, just waiting for a man to come into their view so that they can show off their very perky set of—books. Of course, after merely a week, men understand that this type of behavior is reserved for Saturday-night dance parties at Toad's, and that during the rest of the week, the knockers from the University of Florida will have to suffice (on the small screen in their common rooms, of course).

Yet, despite the fact that some of their hopes are dashed, it seems that they continue to make the rules. They can pursue one, two, three— hell, six women at once. Why can't we do the same? Are we unable? Or are we simply too well trained?

I decide to put my mental rant on a well-deserved pause and skip shopping (the scholarly kind) and spend some real money at the three "luxury boutiques" New Haven has to offer. I am bound to find something that I will regret splurging on later. Plus, it's a gorgeous afternoon; no use spending it studying Homer, Dante, and Virgil (though that would qualify as thinking about three men I haven't dated).

It is an incredible late summer New England day. The sun is strong enough to give everyone a sort of golden glow, and it's still warm enough to wear a skirt (which I am taking advantage of today, since I shaved my legs). I pass Saybrook and Trumbull colleges with their big iron gates and walk up past York Street. Past the Flower

Lady, who turns one syllable into five: "Wooould yoouu liiike to buuuy a flooooweerrrr?" she screeches over the noise of the midday traffic. She is a constant presence on the corner of York and Elm, just outside of the staple Au Bon Pain, often shouting useful tidbits at the students. Like the time I asked her how she was doing, and she told me I needed a new winter coat. A *homeless* woman told me that I needed a new winter coat. Thanks for the heads-up.

As I walk past her, I merit a "Hey giiirrrlfriend!" and a big toothy grin.

I smile at her and look up the street, wondering if I will hit J. Crew or Urban Outfitters first. It's slim pickings, so order is very important.

As I debate the khaki-versus-vintage flavor of my options, I catch sight of Hot Rob and (gasp!) Maxwell, walking in my direction. Well, I guess Hot Rob and Hot Maxwell. I give a little wave. Rob grins while his compadre looks directly at me but makes no indication that he has actually seen me—strange. I push my sunglasses onto my head and stride (with about as much confidence as I can pump into my trembling legs) toward them.

"Hey, guys!" I call out, forcing a smile.

Max turns toward Rob and mumbles something unintelligible. To which Rob replies by turning beet red.

"Hi, Chlo," Rob replies.

Maxwell is silent.

"Hey, Max," I say, employing the cock-my-head-to-the-side stance that worked so well during our hookup.

"Hello, Chloe," he says—rather unenthusiastically, I might add.

"How you *doin*'?" I say in a mock New Jersey Guido accent.

When in doubt, turn to humor, I tell myself encouragingly.

Max stares at me blankly and Rob laughs uncomfortably. This is not going according to plan.

"Been better," he mutters.

I widen my eyes, and feigning all the concern I can possibly muster, I reply, "Why? What happened? Is everything all right?"

"I don't know if I should tell you. I mean, don't you have an article coming out at the end of this week? Wouldn't want *my* uninteresting problems plastered all over the front page."

I look over at Hot Rob for some clue that will help me decipher Max's comment, but he seems to be caught up in examining his size 13 feet.

"Well, no one is interested in your uninteresting problems," I say jokingly. "Everyone tunes in each week to read about the semi-pathetic existence of yours truly."

Self-deprecating humor is my specialty. Thank you, New York! And good night!

Yet I cannot get a smile out of this kid to save my life. Hot Rob is now shaking his head, still seemingly fascinated by his feet.

"Really?" says Maxwell. " 'Cause the next time you want to improve your hand-job skills, try another willing, or should I say unwilling, candidate."

Oh.

Shit.

"Max, I'm . . . really . . . I mean . . . I didn't mean to . . . You know, I just thought you wouldn't think it was a big deal. No one knew who I was writing about, at least," I stutter, glancing at Rob. "I'm sorry."

Hi. My name is Chloe, and I'm a recovering lowlife.

This shopping trip is going to cost me a *lot* more money than I initially thought.

Max laughs sort of mockingly. "At least give me a little more credit next—"

"Heeey!" Rob *finally* pipes up. "Max and I are going to be late for class."

I just glare at him.

"Chloe, we still on for grabbin' a beer tonight?" he adds quickly.

I continue to shoot him the look of death, which translates into a "Why didn't you warn me about this? You are definitely going to hear from me later."

"Yeah. Beer sounds great," I reply halfheartedly, and the two begin walking away.

"Um, Max?" I call out uncertainly.

"Yeah?" he replies.

"I really am sorry."

He smiles, a little less cruelly this time. "Whatever, Chloe. It's over now." And with that, he walks away with Hot Rob trailing close behind him.

Yeah, it's over, but not before he made me feel like a complete idiot (maybe deservedly). Something, I might add, I am quite used to doing all by myself.

I continue my stroll along Broadway with exponentially less confidence than I began it.

Does he really have the right to be mad about all this? What is he afraid of? That people know he got a hand job? Or worse, that people know he hooked up with me? Where do I draw the line between private and public knowledge?

With these questions swimming in my head, I walk into Urban Outfitters and begin perusing the racks absentmindedly, only mildly annoyed by the pseudo-punk teen-angst sound track that makes the Urban Outfitters shopping experience so priceless.

I reach the T-shirt section, which stores dozens of tops meant to look as if they are vintage duds from a hip boutique, but instead are manufactured by the thousand in Bangladesh. They all have clever slogans like "New Jersey; Only the Strong Survive." Or "Redheads Have More Fun." I wish I could go through life with my own clever slogans plastered across my chest, indicating to the world what to do with me. "Just because I'm looking at you does not mean I want to have sex with you." Or "I feel like an asshole right now because I swore I'd never talk about my own hookups in the newspaper, but oops, I did it again."

I move to the jewelry rack, pick out several pairs of earrings that I will wear only once, and make my way over to the register. Nothing pleases me more than pointlessly spending my hard-earned summer dollars on unnecessary items when I clearly need to buy things such as books and, you know, food.

Maybe I should write Max an apology e-mail. Something short and sweet that will indicate that I have come crawling back with my tail between my legs and my foot in my mouth. Or maybe I should just threaten to tell people he shaves his balls if he doesn't smarten up and be nice to me.

Though something tells me approach number two will not be all that effective.

About fifteen minutes later, following a stop at Koffee Too for a skim latte, I rush into Sterling Memorial Library, newly inspired by my idea to redeem myself with Max.

I plop down at one of the computers near the entrance of the majestic-looking building and it navigates me straight to the *Yale Daily News* website.

I quickly scan a few articles regarding Yale labor disputes (which I will never understand and make little attempt to). Before I change over to my e-mail, I switch to the online version of the column I wrote on Friday. I often check the site's message board for constructive criticism and (on good days) praise for my column. Maxwell may not have found my views on post-hookup phone calls exhilarating, but perhaps someone else did.

"One comment on this article!" pops up on the screen. *Oooh!* I think excitedly. Maybe it's something funny.

But it is not.

It is not funny at all.

I would even go so far as to say that it is unfunny.

MESSAGE FROM: YALEMALE05

He didn't call you? Big surprise. After that, neither would I. Although I might dial you up with a you-need-some-advice call (YNSAC)? Maybe next time you could get a guy's opinion on the way hookups and relationships should work. We do have thoughts and opinions, you know—we go to Yale, too. Better luck next time.

I stare at the screen in disbelief. It is biting. To say the least.

My eyes quickly fill up with tears, but I blink them back, because the only thing more embarrassing than crying alone in public is crying alone in the library.

This is Maxwell. Maxwell wrote this. It must be him. How could it not? Who else would do this? (He's a little more clever than I gave him credit for.)

I am panicking.

I am furious.

How could he do this to me?

"Because you did it to him," my mind replies. But I ignore it.

I pull out my cell phone and completely disregarding the library's (in my opinion outdated) cell-phone-free environment policy, I dial Lisa's number. It rings. And rings. And rings. Just before the machine picks up, a breathless Lisa answers.

"What?" she says, irritated.

I hope I didn't interrupt torrid illicit sex.

"Is this a bad time?" I say in a shaky voice.

Detecting that I am in less than stellar spirits, she replies, "No. Well, yes. I was in class. It was rather humiliating."

"You should have put it on vibrate," I snivel.

"I know. What's wrong? Where are you?"

"In the library. I just checked the post board and I think Maxwell wrote a message about my last column."

"Uh-oh," Lisa says, in an unusual moment of not knowing what to say.

"It's mean. He said I needed help and he would never call me."

"At least he's true to his word," Lisa comments.

"Not funny."

"I know, I'm sorry. How do you know it's him? Did he write his name on the post board? That's a pretty bold move."

"No, no name. But who else could it be?"

"Have you made life difficult for any other males lately that you'd like to tell me about?"

"No."

"Chloe, first of all, we don't even know for sure if it really is Maxwell. Second of all, if it is, there is no reason to get upset about this. He is being infantile about the situation—though, granted, he's giving you a little taste of your own medicine. And third, if you sit around all day complaining about it, you're going to beat yourself up and get depressed. So I suggest you either go shopping or eat something delicious."

"I already shopped and I'm not hungry."

"Well, pull yourself together and don't dwell on this. There's nothing that you can do now."

"Fine, fine," I say, tired of Lisa's intense lack of sympathy and the fact that she is absolutely right.

"Don't just say fine. *Do something productive.*"

"Okay!" I reply, irritated.

"Go seduce someone or something," she adds.

At least I am giggling by the time we hang up the phone. Though now every single person within forty feet of me is giving me the evil eye as if I murdered someone in the library and am now tap-dancing on their body instead of merely using my cell phone. I stare haughtily back and gather my belongings to leave.

Once outside on the huge expanse of green they call Cross Campus,

I make the decision to go to the gym and smoke a cigarette (in that order). I reward my gym-going with cigarettes.

I'm still fuming at Max as I put my sneakers on and head to the land of skinny anorexics. Nothing perks me up like a room full of people more fit and less fat than I.

THE YALE DAILY NEWS

SEX AND THE (ELM) CITY
BY CHLOE CARRINGTON

The Touching Diary of a
Recovering Shopaholic

I went to seventeen classes today. It was the most atrocious experience of my entire life (barring, of course, all of freshman year). Welcome to shopping period. No one, it seems, has pity for me, because everyone is going through the exact same thing. "The Creation of the American Politician." "Conservation Biology." "Japan Before 1868." Does it really matter what happened in Japan before 1868? What happened in *this* country before 1868? The list goes on and on.

Shopping period makes me frazzled. More than frazzled. It makes me insane and stressed out. I eat more. I exercise less (and less than nothing is really not that much). I drink more. I smoke more. Shopping period ruins my life for the first two weeks of every semester.

I noticed that it ruins most of my girlfriends' lives as well. A few nights ago, as the madness began, four of us were all sprawled out in a Saybrook College common room. No one said a word. We were hot and sticky and bothered (no, we did not take off all our clothes), as we had just completed two hours of alleged "blue booking" during which we realized that all classes offered at Yale meet at the same time on the same day. For the next forty-five minutes, we were silent, save for the occasional sigh or the odd imploring wail of "Whaaat am I going to dooo?"

My anguish continued all week long. I've been scurrying from class to class, my hands full of syllabi and notebooks. And of course my trusty blue book. As I plopped down to take a shot at my eighth preindustrial, non-Western history of the week, it seemed as if I had reached shopping hell. I looked to my right, and there sat my good friend Steve, calm, cool, and collected, in great spirits (and even a good outfit).

"What's wrong?" he asked, looking concerned.

"What's wrong?" I replied. "Everything is wrong! Shopping is the worst!"

(Whoa. I never thought I would say *worst* and *shopping* together in the same sentence. I implore the gods to grant me forgiveness. Prada, please accept my deepest apologies.)

Steve looked at me strangely and in a mocking tone said, "Dude, shopping period rules. What are you talking about?"

And then it dawned on me. Shopping period is sexist. It's biased. It is created for men, not women. Shopping period epitomizes male dating habits. When was the last time you heard a guy get upset because he was dating two or three or even four girls at once?

Shopping period allows a little taste of everything without committing to anything right away.

Just like tapas—and we wonder why so many Spanish guys are on the prowl.

Women, on the other hand, rarely date more than one

guy at the same time. We are usually slaves to one man and one man only, even if he exhibits weak signs of interest and poor wallet-opening capacity.

A few days ago, I met a good friend of mine during my lunch break. She was faced with the dilemma of the century. She had two guys who were interested in her (yes, life is hard when you're twenty and single). One was a man of many words. A charmer, a lover of the arts and sciences. The other was a looker. Hot like a latte in July. Like working out in a sauna. *Hot.*

She asked what she should do. She said that she needed to choose. She had been on only a couple of dates with each, yet she needed to commit (even if he didn't). She wanted to choose one man and stick to him. Pursue him. Take him to the hoop and slam-dunk him.

Uh. Right.

The girl is business savvy, yet she refuses to diversify her portfolio. I have noticed this pattern everywhere. Women are too considerate. We shrink from the possibility of playing someone or of hurting someone's feelings. Yet by doing so, we don't reach our optimal dating potential.

There is nothing wrong with keeping a roster of men instead of just one designated hitter. Guys do not hesitate to date five girls in consecutive time slots. Yet we get propositions from an athlete and a comedian on the same day, and shit hits the fan. We don't know what to do, so what's the answer? We choose one.

So, to kick off this grand old school year, I am dispensing a little advice. Yes, I rarely do this, but something has to be said. Desperate times call for desperate measures.

Shopping classes is like dating: You need not reach a verdict, the final schedule, until the deadline approaches and you are going to be fined $35. Exercise all of your options; it will be well worth it.

Oh, and since I'm already handing out advice, freshmen, put your IDs in your wallet and your keys on a key chain. The whole around-the-neck phenomenon is très Zach Morris circa 1995.

3

"HEY! HEY!" I SAY, motioning toward Ken the bartender. "Can I get a vodka soda with a lemon and a lime?" I yell over the blaring techno music.

"Comin' right up, Chloe!"

Toad's Place is an institution. It's a staple—like the little black dress, like diamond studs, like Miller High Life (the champagne of beers).

Toad's looks like a barn and smells like a barn. In fact, its mating rituals are similar to those that take place in a barn. But it is hands-down the best Saturday- (or Wednesday-) night party in town. It is an oversize techno-hip-hop version of Cheers. Everyone here knows your name, and taking a lap around the centrally located bar is the social equivalent of the Indy 500. At the bar, each group occupies its own place. Lacrosse players (or *playas*, whichever you prefer) hover on the right side of the bar, near the entrance. If you are lucky (or a lacrosstitute), one of them will order you the Lacrosse Shot, a concoction which is perhaps the most deadly drink ingested by anyone ever. Their bartender is a gem named Ken who is responsible for most of the action that they receive on a given Saturday night (after all, he is the brains behind the Lacrosse Shot). He is also currently pouring far more soda than anything else into my drink.

On the other side, the hockey players reign, with Dave the bartender at their beck and call. The near side of the bar belongs to football, while the dance floor and far side are taken up by basketball players, who do not have a bartender of their own but can collectively break it down better than any other sports team out there.

Toad's is also home of the booty cam and the thong contest, and was voted best college bar by *Playboy* in 2001. So believe me when I say it doesn't get any better than this.

Over the course of this short night, I have already made my sixth lap around the bar looking for Crystal (Chris), my Favorite Gay (FG). We came here together, hoping to lift my spirits after my major Maxwell faux pas. And since the subsequent shopping trip left me with only twenty-three dollars to my name, I accepted his invitation on the condition that he buy me a drink. But of course, only thirty-seven minutes into the night and Crystal is nowhere to be found in the sea of men, half of them sporting tight black T-shirts and the other half sporting khakis and a baseball cap. I challenge you to guess what my FG is wearing.

I don't mind Crystal's constant disappearing act—he always comes back to me. Nothing can come between a girl and her FG (well, nothing other than a man). You see, flaming homosexuals are my favorite people on the planet.

Crystal is my soulmate. In a single breath, he can put down my hairstyle, share in my secret love for Matthew Broderick (pre-*Producers* era), and uphold any major literary criticism of Rushdie's *Satanic Verses*. In fact, that is how we met—sort of.

Well, let me back up. We actually met at the beginning of last year in a class called "Doomed Love in the Western World." Which, if you replace *in the Western World* with *at Yale University*, is pretty much the story of our lives. Crystal and I spent the semester eating cheesecake and Fresca (in a staggering coincidence, our favorite snack) while alternately commiserating about the downfall of the male species and discussing the reasons that *Anna Karenina* is the greatest masterpiece of all time. Crystal is the only person in the entire world who knows if I could sleep with a single individual, dead or alive, it would be Leo Tolstoy. Hands down, no-holds-barred.

Crystal is very trustworthy.

"That'll be four!" Ken yells at me.

"Come on? For a pretty girl like me? Four? Ken, I'm *broken*."

"Broken?"

."Well, I'm broke. I have, like, two dollars to my name."

"Chloe."

"Yes?" I reply sweetly.

"I don't care."

"Some sympathetic bartender you are . . ." I mutter, pulling a five out of my wallet.

It's a routine we've taken to repeating every week since my first visit to Toad's.

I was a lowly freshman, thrilled that my fake ID (that officially made me a twenty-four-year-old Ashley Pixie from Compton, California—I swear) had gotten me in the door. I was dressed to the nines, wearing the most unbelievable pair of black stiletto slingbacks (courtesy of Gucci and my entire summer paycheck) and a simple white tank top paired with the sexiest jeans I owned. Little did I know that Toad's limited one's footwear options to sneakers or flip-flops. Heels, it seems, turn into muddy flats in about three and a half minutes.

Ken took one look at me and said, "You're underage."

"Well, once you're twenty-one, you stop coming here," I shot back.

We've been friends ever since, though that night he charged me a whopping seven dollars a drink as payback for my charming comment. Now two and a half years later, I've finagled him down to regular price.

I begin sipping my drink and scanning the immediate surroundings for a dance partner, when I spot Cara chatting up a naive freshman across the bar. He is wide-eyed and hanging on every word that spills out of her mouth (which is definitely faster than he can take them in). Cara is notorious for employing the "Demi takes Ashton" tactic, most commonly used in Hollywood circles. That is to say, she preys on freshman boys, wholesome and unaware, not to mention much easier to drag into a semi-committed relationship. To her credit, she zips through them like a Chihuahua on Adderall—fast.

I attempt to catch her eye from where I'm sitting, but she doesn't see me, as she is too busy charming the pants off Mr. Right Now. I make my way over to her side of the bar on the off-chance that I will take priority over prospect numero uno. (The night is still young, so I'm banking on the fact that she's still got plenty of time to search, conquer, and destroy.)

Cara is leaning seductively on the bar, her breasts accidentally spilling out of her too tight top (oops!) as she ropes Monsieur Maintenant into buying her a shot.

"Cara!"

She ignores me.

"Cara!"

Ignores me again. Finally I lean over her shoulder and say, "It's eleven o'clock, do you know where your children are?"

"I don't have any children!" she says, laughing nervously and directing her comment toward Freshmania.

He looks frightened.

"Hi," I say, extending my hand. "I'm Patricia. I'm a freshman. What year are you?"

Cara and I play this game occasionally, where we convince fresh-men that we are part of their tribe. Tonight, though, it seems that she's not into charades.

His face breaks into a smile. "Hi! I'm a freshman, too! I'm Peter."

Cara looks at me suspiciously. "You are not a freshman," she says curtly to me and turns toward Peter. "This is my friend Chloe. She's a *junior*," she says with extra emphasis.

"Hey! Yeah! I thought you looked familiar," he says.

Uh-oh. I quickly scan my brain for idiotic things I've done in the last three weeks, which might help indicate why he recognizes me.

"You write that sex column thing!"

I breathe a sigh of relief and smile modestly. No need to worry.

"Why, thank you, I'm glad you enjoy the column. I like this guy," I say, turning to Cara.

She shoots me a look that says, "Okay, now leave."

Peter, overcome with enthusiasm, chimes in, "I gotta go call my girlfriend! She'll be so excited I met you."

"Girlfriend?" Cara repeats, her voice raising about four octaves.

And with that he's bolted toward the door to call his significant other, leaving Cara significantly pissed.

"Look what you've done, genius," she mutters, signaling to Ken that she *needs* another drink (and she's not fucking around).

"Cara, the kid has a girlfriend!"

"He's a freshman, Chlo, he's not going to have her for long. Plus I was just getting him to forget about her," she whines.

"Oh, please."

"I was!" she insists, but already she's got her radar going, search-ing for the next man off the bench.

"Wouldn't you rather spend time with me?" I ask sweetly. Cara is usually quick to forgive.

"Yeah, yeah." She sighs. "Actually," she continues, perking up, "what happened with Maxwell? Aren't I the best fixer-upper *ever*? I mean, you guys would make such a good couple. He's just the cutest. And the nicest. I mean, yeah, he's not that interesting, but those abs, have you seen those abs? Well, of course you've seen them, but—"

"Stop," I interrupt her.

"What?"

"Max and I—not so good."

"What do you mean, not so good?"

"I mean *not so good*. Another word I could use to describe the situation would be bad," I reply sarcastically.

"What happened?" she asks, very interested.

I am tired of repeating this story. And I really don't want to talk about Maxwell. What I really want to do is get drunk and dance and not think about Maxwell or any of my other failings, including my lack of musical talent and my dismal performance in any type of team sport, as well as my inability to truly open up to people.

Then again, who cares about what I want?

"Umm . . ."

"Oh my God. I read this week's column. That was him? He didn't call you, right?"

"Yes, Matlock. Why are you asking me if you know the story already?"

Cara looks at me sheepishly. "Because it's so much better when you tell it. I like the inside scoop. You owe it to me, I set you up."

"Well, in that case, *you* are the one who owes *me*."

"Not true! I made your hookup résumé that much better."

"What?" Cara is a dictionary unto herself. Hookup résumé? Superstar dick? All these terms sound like porn specials on channel 135. I think I've actually *seen* Superstar Dick.

"You are now more desirable because the average hotness of your hookups is raised due to your involvement with Maxwell. It's a simple mathematical concept. You add the hotness of each person you hook up with and divide that figure by the total number of hookups," Cara says matter-of-factly.

Of course! How silly of me. Until now I was unaware that hotness is actually a quantifiable quality.

She is now looking at me expectantly. As if I owe her a big hearty thank-you. Or at least a hug.

"Is that like your GPA?"

"Sort of."

"I think my hotness hookup quotient is higher than my GPA," I say.

"If you can't do it with brains, do it with brawn." Cara shrugs, not minding that she makes absolutely no sense at all.

I thoughtfully take a sip of my vodka soda, mulling over this theory.

"Sooo . . . there's really no inside scoop, then?" Cara pries further, not one to let any tidbit of gossip pass her by.

"Well . . ." I begin cautiously.

"Well what?" she asks excitedly.

Oh, what the hell, she can keep a secret. Right.

"He shaves his balls."

"Shaves his balls?" she repeats too loudly.

"Yup, shaves his balls," I say with finality.

Cara, true to form, does not miss a beat. "I've never had a shaved ball."

"I would hope not."

"I mean, I've never been with a shaved ball."

"They're not that great."

"I imagine it's a little easier to navigate the area."

"I don't think the terrain down there is rough enough to merit navigation aids."

"How did he shave it?"

"Probably with a razor."

"Did you ask him?"

"I didn't know how to insert that question into the conversation."

"Well, you could have said something like, 'So, you shave your balls, huh?' "

"I don't think that would have gone over so well."

"Do you think he did it himself?"

"I don't know who he would ask to do it for him."

"Interesting."

"Yup."

"You know that from now on, every time I see him I'm going to think, *Wow, you have bald balls.*"

"Well, unless the hair grows back."

"But we're probably never going to know if it does."

"Probably not."

Cara, spotting an unoccupied bar stool (and looking somewhat inspired by my revelation), grabs it and sits down.

"Well, this clearly calls for a drink," she says conclusively.

"Should we have one for each ball?"

"Why, yes," she replies, and asks Ken for two shots of Southern Comfort.

Ken pours us our drinks and winks at Cara's breasts. "These are on me, girls."

"I think Ken wants to give you a little Southern Comfort," I whisper to Cara.

"He's too old for me."

"He is out of diapers," I concede.

"Shut up!" she exclaims, laughing. "I have a toast!"

The two of us ceremoniously raise our glasses and I prepare for a patented Cara Classic. She gives great toasts.

"We might not get what we want. We might not get what we need. But in the end, here's hoping we *never* get what we deserve!"

"Amen!" I call out, beginning to feel the buzz. We down our shots. "Do you think I deserved the shaved balls?" I ask.

"Of course not," Cara replies like any good friend would, and the two of us make a beeline for the dance floor.

About three long hours later (most of which have been spent being elbowed by girls in sequined tube tops and black hip-huggers), I have finally roped Crystal in from MatingFest 2003. The two of us are ready to pack it in and call it a night. But no college adventure is ever complete without a high-carb, high-calorie nightcap—hence our trip to Yorkside Pizza. Yorkside does not make good pizza. In fact, I might go so far as to say that Yorkside makes bad pizza, but the truth is that seven vodka tonics at four bucks a pop (that delight your palate much like Drano) can make even household cleaning supplies taste like culinary delicacies.

So, as this Saturday night winds down, Cara has found a young bachelor to hold her attention, while Crystal and I find ourselves at Yorkside at two A.M. shoveling pizza down our throats at a formidable pace between gulps of Diet Coke (as if that's going to cancel out the calories). Amid the bites and the gulps we fit in the postgame wrap-up. Time to go over the evening's plays. Who took a penalty shot? Who traveled? Who drew the foul? You know, the usual girl/gay stuff. To-night I have the unfortunate position of having my back to the door. Crystal and I try to alternate positioning. Last time I was lucky enough to face the entrance and got the first view of Sally Miller's new "skiing accident." And by skiing accident, I mean nose job. Regardless, some-one always has to face the door. How else will you see who walks in with whom and what they are wearing?

"So Ken has a major crush on Cara," I say, popping a piece of pepperoni into my mouth. "Hypothetical: On a sketchiness scale of one to ten, where would you place dating a Toad's bartender?"

"I dunno," Crystal replies. He is being curiously quiet this evening. Customarily he is bursting with a bitchy and sarcastic post-Toad's appraisal.

"So, Ryan is looking kinda chubby these days," I say, trying to perk him up.

Ryan is Crystal's ex-boyfriend. But he's not just *any* ex: He was Crystal's first boyfriend, his one and only. Ryan's looking fat is usually a cause for celebration (and another slice of pizza).

"Yeah." Crystal sighs.

I decide to cut to the chase. "Is this a cheesecake moment?" I ask sympathetically. "My mom just sent me one from Junior's this week. It's sitting in my room just waiting to be devoured," I add seductively.

Junior's is the finest cheesecake the Northeast has to offer. I am able to consume whole pies all on my own (which, I will have you know, is not so simple with a decadent dessert like cheesecake). I am famous in cheesecake-eating circles for this feat. Which is also why my mother's gift came with a note that read SHARE! underlined several times for good measure.

"Sort of," Crystal replies.

"Well, spill it already," I say gently. "What's going on?"

"Something so embarrassing happened to me tonight," he says quietly. "I just can't say it."

"Crystal, it's me you're talking to here. I am queen bee of embarrassing. I am, like, the embarrassing *supernova*."

"Not like this. Nothing like this has ever happened to you."

"How do you know?"

"Trust me."

"I do trust you. And you trust me. So out with it."

"I can't say it out loud."

"Would it help if you drew it?"

"Chlo, this is serious."

"I *was* being serious."

"Well this . . . this thing . . . hasn't happened to me since like seventh grade on the bar mitzvah circuit."

"You kissed a girl?" I ask.

"No. But that hasn't happened to me since the bar mitzvah circuit either. So points for the guess."

"Thanks."

There's a pause. Crystal is biting his thumbnail.

"Okay," he finally says, "I'll tell you. But you have to promise me two things—"

"I promise," I say quickly.

"You haven't even heard the two things," he insists, a little annoyed. Crystal is very into being a good listener.

"Yeah, but I know what you're going to say already. Because I'm a genius."

"Oh, yeah?"

"Yes," I say firmly. "You are going to say that I shouldn't laugh and I shouldn't judge because I am not a gay man and I don't know what it's like to be a gay man."

"Okay, fine. You win."

"So go ahead, gay man, I am a woman and I have no sense of humor."

Crystal smiles broadly. Finally! But as he leans in toward me, his face becomes serious again. "Come here!" he stage-whispers.

I move in a little closer.

"Closer."

I move in even closer. Our noses are practically touching. Crystal, by the way, has the perfect man-nose.

"I was dancing with Sebastian Wise," he whispers.

"Uh-huh."

(Sebastian Wise is a God Among Gays. And as an aside, if you name your son Sebastian Wise, you must know that he is destined to be gay. It's too hot a name to be straight.)

"Well, so we were dancing really close. And it was getting sort of hot and heavy—"

"Score!"

"Yeah. Just wait. So it's that song about shaking your ass and watching yourself or something . . ."

"Uh-huh."

"And then you know . . . *it* happened."

"What happened?"

"I got it."

"Got what?" At this point, I am very confused. I am pretty certain that you cannot contract an STD from dancing, so I really don't know what Crystal is referring to.

"I got an erection," he says and puts his head in his hands. "I ruined it. I ruined it with Sebastian Wise." He pauses dramatically and then adds, "Forever."

"Because you got an erection? On the dance floor? Let me get this straight. You think you ruined things with Sebastian Wise because you got a dance floor erection?"

"Yes!" he hisses. "Could you keep it down?"

"I am keeping it down. *You* are the one who has a problem keeping it down."

"I told you, no jokes!"

"Sorry. Anyway, Crystal, what are you worried about? Everyone gets erections."

"Not everyone."

"Well, yeah. But your half of the population does."

"The gay half?" he asks, sounding offended.

"No, idiot. The *male* half."

"Oh."

"Just because no one ever talks about it is no reason to think that it doesn't happen," I say reassuringly. Just to reinforce my point, I add menacingly, "The dance floor erection. Beware—it could happen to you."

"We should make bumper stickers," Crystal says with a smile.

"Yeah. They could go right below the ones that say 'My Son and My Money Go to Yale.'"

"'My Son, My Money, and His Erection Go to Yale.'"

Crystal and I are in hysterics when all of a sudden he gasps, nearly choking on his pizza.

"Oh my God, oh my God," he says, his eyes widening.

Oooh, this is going to be exciting. Crystal just spotted something wonderful come in the door.

I always face the wrong direction on eventful nights!

"What, what?" I ask eagerly.

"Don't look now . . ."

I do a 180 and stare.

"But," he continues, pausing dramatically, "Maxwell just walked in with UTAG."

"Yoo-Hoo? The chocolate milk?" I say, bewildered.

"No, stupid. UTAG."

"What's UTAG?" I ask.

"Up-the-Ass Girl," he answers matter-of-factly. "You are so clueless sometimes."

Now I am choking. Crystal hands me my Diet Coke and watches as my life passes before my eyes and my face turns from an alarming shade of red to a ghastly blue. Finally I catch my breath.

"Are you finished?"

"Thanks for your concern," I snap.

"Well, that was a little excessive."

"So," I say, trying to act casual, "who is this up-the-ass character?"

"Madison Nelson. Freshman. Takes it in the butt, like a champ," Crystal states.

"First of all, how do you know that? Second of all, may I remind you that *you* take it in the butt all the time."

"I'm gay. I have no other choice."

"Oooh, Crystal's upset," I say mockingly. Admittedly, Crystal is very sensitive about his extracurricular activities. Only recently has he become a member of the UTA club—a high point of gay-dom.

"*You* are the one who's upset. You're mad because Maxwell is with another girl and you're here single and feeling awkward."

Crystal smiles charmingly and crosses his legs, clad in knockoff Prada's latest flat-front pants. The truth is biting.

"You don't even deserve to be my FG," I reply tersely.

"Whatever," he says, turning away.

"Sorry," I say quickly. He was just being honest. I do feel uncomfortable.

Crystal smiles again, this time with at least an ounce of tenderness in his soft brown eyes. Guys love his eyes.

"It's okay, sweetie."

"Thanks."

I look over at Maxwell and UTAG. They are sitting three tables away from us, at an angle that allows Crystal and me to spy on them. They are also within earshot. How convenient.

Straight men are so naive sometimes.

He is staring deeply into her eyes as they smile at each other dreamily. Is this for real? I wonder what he's thinking about. Does he know that she's UTAG? Is he thinking that later he can try out the hypothesis? I want to run over and tap her on the shoulder and ask her if the rumors are true. Did she really? Did it hurt? But most of all, I want to tell her to run. I want to tell her that while she's thinking commitment, he's thinking something drastically different. But then again, I don't even know her, so I think I'm going to let this golden opportunity slide.

I turn away from Maxwell and this UTAG character, feeling very odd. I don't quite understand why. I replay the timeline in my mind—the progression of our pseudo-relationship. We met. I was unimpressed. We hooked up. I was hooked on some type of validation. Which led me to in turn become impressed with him. He didn't validate. I retaliated. He returned the favor.

"Crystal, I forgot to tell you what happened!"

"With Max? You've already told me that story. It's yesterday's news," he says, snapping his fingers diva-like.

"No no. He posted a response to my column this week on the YDN website!"

"He did? The column about him?"

"It was not *explicitly* about him."

"Hate to break it to you, my dear, but it was pretty clearly about him."

"Nuh-uh!"

"Uh-huh."

"Anyway," I say with emphasis, "he wrote that he would *never* date me and that I was a . . ." I almost can't say it. Of all the things he wrote, perhaps this is the most damaging. My life's dream shattered by a bitter hookup.

"A . . ." Crystal says expectantly.

I gulp. "A biased writer. He might as well have said a bad writer."

Maxwell looks over at us, and catching my eye, gives me a small wave of acknowledgment.

I issue what I think might be a smile in his general direction, trying not to meet his eye. Of course it could have also been a grimace. I'm not sure.

"Ouch," Crystal says.

"Ouch is right. Ouch-ilicious. At least he's here with a girl named UTAG. That's sort of embarrassing, right?"

"I have to disagree."

"Why?"

"He might be into that kind of stuff," Crystal replies.

I shudder with disapproval. "I guess I'm just upset," I say dejectedly. "You know what's unfair?"

Crystal looks at me, waiting for me to go on.

"Each week that I write my column, my name is attached to it. I am absolutely responsible for everything I say. You see, at least I endorse what I write. Then here comes high-and-mighty Maxwell, who waltzes in, criticizing and disapproving of me as much as his heart desires, and he doesn't have to take ownership of it. Doesn't that seem unfair to you?"

Crystal mulls over my theory. "It all depends on your definition," he finally says.

"Explain."

"Well, you think it's unfair that he remains anonymous while you make the choice to reveal yourself to the world. And in doing so, you reveal a lot more than yourself."

"What do you mean?"

"You took his anonymity away a few weeks ago. At least some people could guess who it was. Now he's just telling you how he honestly feels."

I think it over, and though I hate to admit it, maybe Crystal is right.

Suddenly Crystal spots Mr. Sebastian Wise ordering pizza. His muscles ripple under his tight black T-shirt as he reaches over the counter to pay. This sends a ripple through Crystal's finely tuned man-o-meter.

Crystal glances at Sebastian over his shoulder and looks back at me for permission to . . . follow that man!

"Go, go," I say reluctantly.

Crystal bounds out of the booth we've been sharing and makes a beeline for Sebastian. "Love to love ya!" he calls over his shoulder. "I'll call you tomorrow!"

And there I am, left alone twice in one week, though this time I am a third wheel on a date I'm not even partaking in.

I take another bite of my pizza, hoping to finish it before Maxwell and the ass-girl leave, which would force them to walk past my table and fake a conversation that I don't want to have.

Alas, I am too late. The two of them get up, and before I can duck my head, they are walking toward me.

I look up and meet Maxwell's eye for the second time this evening. This is not cool at all.

"Hi, Chloe."

"Hi, Max."

He turns to UTAG. "This is Madison. Madison, this is Chloe."

She smiles at me. "Oh, so *you're* Chloe. I see." She pauses, and seems to notice her mistake, so to make up for it, bestows on me an ever-so-graceful "Hi."

Bitch.

"Uh, yeah, I'm Chloe."

Wow, am I ever lucky. What is this, my second absolutely mortifying encounter of the week?

"Nice to meet you," I add, never one to be outwardly rude.

She smiles at me again. "Likewise."

"Are you here with someone?" Maxwell asks.

"Um, yeah," I say at the last minute. Shit, I really meant to say no.

"Who?"

"My friend," I reply. That's not elusive at all.

"Oh, who's your friend?" he asks, seemingly genuinely interested.

"A writer," I say, deciding to stick it to him. "A really good writer."

He looks very confused. "Uh, okay."

"I'd better call *him*," I say emphasizing the word *him*. Just so Maxwell knows that I really do know how to communicate with the opposite sex. "He's running a little late."

"Looks like it."

Madison tugs on Max's sleeve. Isn't that cute? Madison and Maxwell.

Can I stop being so bitter? It's really not that charming.

"We better go," he says in response. "Have fun with your writer friend."

"Thanks," I reply.

And as they walk out of Yorkside I decide to get my head examined.

THE YALE DAILY NEWS

SEX AND THE (ELM) CITY
BY CHLOE CARRINGTON

Is That a Bud in Your Pocket?
Or Are You Just Happy to See Me?

There are some things we are just not supposed to talk about. Warts. Drug habits. Third nipples. Nose picking. Your parents' sex lives. Your sex life (with your parents). These are things that are simply not meant to be discussed.

My mother used to teach me not to say certain things. I always did, of course, like the time I told Mr. Mig that Mrs. Mig boinked the neighbor in the shower while he was at work. I simply loved the reaction I got. This is not something I've outgrown with age. Instead, I crave talking about the things I shouldn't be discussing.

This is precisely why I want to talk about the dance floor erection. That's right, you read correctly. The dance floor erection (DFE). No one talks about it, but everyone knows it's there. It's just like Caltech. Or Canada.

Let me just introduce a little situation in which the DFE might, shall we say, pop up. Lights are turned low. Add a little bass. Maybe a little strobe. Perhaps a booty cam for good measure. Feelin' it? Yeah, you are. And you *really* love this song. You're backing that ass up like it's your job. *Oooh!* And there's cute Bobby. You move sexily toward cute Bobby, who sees you out of the corner of his eye. He smiles. Score. Cute Bobby is really, really cute, and if he doesn't say anything, he's really, really smart, too.

So there you are, and you start dancing with cute Bobby. You throw in the newest little hip swerve you caught in that Britney video. You are the WO-MAN. You back that ass up again, you know, for good measure. Bobby seems to love it: Whoa! What's that?

Yup, that's right, it seems you have backed into, well, Bobby's bobby. Bobby appears to be pitching his tent on your campsite. To put it bluntly, Bobby has a Dance Floor Erection. He's been struck with a DFE.

This situation is not one that is strange or different or weird. In fact it's common. Very common. Every guy I spoke with has had a DFE at least once. And every girl has borne the burden of an erection in the back of her thigh. No one talks about it, though.

We ladies choose to react in one of three ways: continue dancing (this time with a little twinkle in our eyes); walk away annoyed; or pretend that such a thing has never occurred. This is why I'd like to bring the DFE out into the open; perhaps encourage a little roundtable discussion surrounding the—ahem—magnitude of its presence.

Girls were eager to discuss the DFE. Over lunch at Commons, a close friend of mine revealed, "Even though I should be expecting it, it always catches me by surprise." Later, she conceded that her reaction to the DFE depends largely on its owner. If it's a random guy, the DFE can get a little too close for comfort, especially if the aroused party insists on using it as a power tool in your hip bone. "I mean, that *is* his penis!" exclaimed one fragile individual.

I second that motion.

Meanwhile, if the DFE-er is a crush, such as the afore-mentioned cute Bobby, the erection might lead to bigger and better things and can be quite flattering. As I was shrewdly in-formed on my way to history class, "There's a face behind the penis. It's attached to someone, you know?"

Thank you. I was not previously aware of this.

My guy friends were less keen on delving into what lies beneath. In fact, they shied away from it. Some responded to my questions with grunts or strange looks. One guy angrily snapped, "How do you know about that?"

I replied that it's hard *not* to know, though it depends on what you're raising. Are we talking Titanic or Tubby the Tugboat?

Regardless, when I did convince some of my friends to open up, I met with a variety of responses that ranged from DFE shame—"It really sucks. It just sucks"—to DFE pride—"Why be embarrassed? It's part of my game!"

In all my hours of research, I was most interested in dis-covering how exactly the DFE-er reacts to his condition. There are three scenarios that may unfold following the rais-ing of the flag, the salute to the chin, the call to attention.

First, there is the ever-famous and often-used Turn and Tuck. The Turn and Tuck is a series of movements that cul-minate in the masking of the culprit. A turn away from the dancing girl using a Michael Jackson-esque spin, followed by a quick fell swoop of the hand that enacts the tuck-up (into the belt) or the tuck-under (into I don't know what).

The result is a slightly uncomfortable but thoroughly

concealed erection that will eventually simmer down. Even the most chipper of woodies will not survive the tuck-under. This move works best when the dancers begin by facing each other and end in the same position. It should be noted that a certain amount of dance floor dexterity is necessary here.

For the more confident sort, and for those who have received a positive reaction from their fellow dancers, the erection can be used to advantage as a tool of flattery but not of battery. A positive DFE reaction can lead from hip-hop at Toad's to mambo in the bedroom.

Finally, the DFE can cause what I have diagnosed as erecto-mania. Erecto-mania lasts several minutes, which for the stricken can seem like an eternity. The possessor of the DFE flees the dance floor thoroughly embarrassed, muttering excuses to the confused girl of needing a drink, and then claims to his boys that "she had bad breath."

As he stands by the bar, humbled, paranoia sets in. He is certain that everyone in the room knows what just occurred; that everyone in the room is zeroing in on his pants, wondering why they look like that. Erecto-mania may lead to sweaty palms, severe anxiety, jumpiness, and perhaps even a slight tic. These symptoms last only a few minutes and may be easily gotten rid of by several more drinks (preferably shots of Dubra).

In conclusion, I would like to acknowledge the DFE as a reality of today's world. Something that grinding to Jay-Z or Nelly might encourage. I say, do not be afraid to discuss it, even to embrace it. Go to Toad's this Saturday with a new attitude, a new acceptance of the dance floor erection. Do not let Cute Bobby down. Let him stand tall and say, "I am Cute Bobby, and sometimes when I dance, I am aroused."

$\mathcal{M}$ONDAY.

Buzz. Buzzz. Buzzzz.

Much like my mother, I find my alarm clock more annoying every time I come into contact with it. I reach over and try to hit it to shut it up (something I would never do to my mother). My hand lands in the ashtray next to my bed. FUCK. Cigarette butts stuck to my palm. I take yet another swipe at it.

Buzzzzz.

"Why won't you shut up?" I say, looking at it angrily.

"Chloe, your alarm clock—again," Bonnie, my darling antisocial sex-deprived roommate, says, turning over in her bed to face me.

"Sorry," I say meekly.

"This happens every day," she replies sternly. Unusually sternly, I might add, for her.

"Sorry!"

BUZZZZZZ. Is it getting louder?

"Dammit, Chloe! Shut it off! I don't have class for another two hours."

Bonnie Johnson, from a family of six hailing from pleasant

upper-middle-class suburban Maryland, is perfect. Her schedule is perfect. Her GPA is (almost) perfect. She is one of those Yale people who get summer internships in October and find time to run five miles every day while tutoring children from inner-city schools. We have been roommates since freshman year, mostly because we have a grudging adoration for each other, and because each year I tell myself that if I live with Bonnie, she will be a good influence on me. I convince myself that I will somehow magically absorb some of her super-anal-retentiveness. But I don't, obviously. Regardless, I have loved Bonnie ever since she held my hair back as I vomited the entire first week of freshman year. She *used* to be very understanding.

I take one last smack at my alarm clock, channeling all the energy I can muster on three hours of sleep. I make contact and it falls silent.

When I decided to take intensive Italian at 8:30 A.M. every morning this year, I think I was far too focused on the Italian part and far too *un*focused on the 8:30 A.M. part. Italian, I thought, would be so sophisticated. I would go to Europe and fit right in with all the dark-haired sexy people.

Well, it turns out that I am not going to Europe, and I still think that the Italian word for shoes is Prada. Eight-thirty is also the furthest thing from sexy. I snuggle deeper into my warm bed, afraid to look up and meet Bonnie's stony glare. For someone with a sliver of a social life, she is very ungrateful for the entertainment I provide.

Five more minutes, I tell myself . . .

Thirty minutes later, I sit straight up in bed and glance over at my hated alarm clock: "Eight-fifteen," it says smugly. "You should have listened to me the first time around."

Fuck you, alarm clock.

I'm late. I'm late. I am *so* fucking late! Oh, and as an added bonus, I forgot to wipe my hands off after dipping them into that bowlful of ashes, so my bed, my sheets, my face—everything is striped black and smells like the inside of Toad's.

Eau de Toad's is not a fragrance anyone is lining up to buy at Barneys. Trust me.

I leap out of bed and make a beeline for the shower. I am one of the few students on this campus who cannot go anywhere without showering. My friends don't understand this alleged madness of mine, but most of them have significant others. When I have a boyfriend, I won't shower either. But for right now, what if the love of my life is walking down College Street and I whiz by him on my way to class, unshowered, leaving a sour trail of BO? That would be horrifying, to say the least. Instead, I should saunter by him gracefully on my way to class, emanating the sweet yet subtle smell of Marc Jacobs for Women (my signature scent). Now *that* is how one captures the attention of a potential love-of-one's-life-to-be.

I grab the towel off the hook on my door, hastily wrapping it around my "I need to lose five pounds, okay, maybe ten" body, and scoot down the hall to the bathroom.

Maybe this day will start to get better, I think to myself. But apparently I think a little too much. Both showers are taken (hardly shocking when eighteen people share two showers), and the bathroom has the distinct smell of a freshly dropped morning number two. Sharing a restroom with those of the opposite sex can yield disgusting results. Today this is demonstrated by both the lovely fragrance wafting out of stall numero uno and the pile of hair in the sink, formerly part of someone's beard (and I'm guessing it's not that weird Natalia girl who also lives on our hall, though it might well be).

"Can you hurry up in there?" I yell over the noise of the shower.

"Chill out, Chlo!" comes the answer from within the stall. It's Hot Rob.

At least I will experience one pleasant sight this morning.

"Come on, come on, come on. I'm late!"

"Are you ever *not* late?"

"I'm from New York. I will have you know that late is totally fashionable!"

He turns off the shower and steps out, completely naked and dripping wet with, I might add, quite the erection.

"Um, Rob, that's something you're supposed to take care of *in* the shower," I say, motioning toward his morning wood. Although, quite frankly, I don't know what masturbation etiquette is for public restrooms.

"I thought you could take care of it for me," he says, smiling.

"I'm in a rush."

"So am I."

"Get out of here," I mutter, blushing.

"No problem." He grins and struts out of the bathroom, looking very pleased with himself and his rock-hard body. I have to admit that though I do enjoy the spectacle, I have seen Hot Rob naked more times than nightly *Seinfeld* reruns.

The first time occurred move-in day of freshman year, perhaps the most stressful twenty-four hours of anyone's life.

Once my parents had cleared out (and by cleared out, I mean I dragged them kicking and screaming to their car) and Bonnie and I got acquainted, the two of us began wandering the hallways looking for new friends. We drifted into Hot Rob and Activist Adam's room, and not seeing anyone right away, pushed open the bedroom door. There was Rob completely naked, hanging an Anna Kournikova poster above his bed. Activist Adam had yet to arrive because he was working on an organic farm in Tuscany for the summer and his first-class flight was delayed. Bonnie almost started crying as Rob extended his hand to introduce himself, but she got over it, and these days his naked state hardly seems odd at all.

I jump in the shower and switch on the waterproof radio that our floor's computing assistant, Alfred, installed after I promised that I would write a column entitled "Computing Assistants Make Better Lovers." As far as I'm concerned, computing assistants need all the help they can get, so I'm glad to be of service.

I turn the radio to 107.3. I find that morning talk radio can be a good source of information, and this morning is no different than usual.

Apparently, according to always reliable 107.3, a woman had been stopped a few days before at a New York airport for possessing suspicious baggage. Her suitcase, she was told, had been vibrating, and this was clearly a security concern. Slightly ashamed, she tried to tell the security guard that the culprit hidden inside her suitcase was, ahem, a vibrator.

He, taking no chances, insisted on opening up the suitcase and checking the contents out for himself. He did indeed find some good vibrations behind a few T-shirts and a pair of shoes. The woman, mortified and troubled, decided that the only appropriate course of action was to sue the airline for emotional distress.

As I put the finishing touches on my makeup, I am still weighing the merits of the vibrator versus the obvious hardship of a court case. The jury is still out on that one. Unfortunately I have no time to reach any solid conclusions because the clock is looking up at me and saying, "Eight thirty-two. You're late, you're late, for a very important date."

When I finally slip into Italian class in Harkness Hall after a good sprint across campus about seven minutes and twelve seconds later, making me officially nine minutes late, I am greeted by my professor, Professore Raquella, and my second icy stare of the day.

I sit down in the only empty seat, right next to Jordan, the guy that no one wants to sit next to. He's not a bad kid; it's just that he has remarkably bad breath. He also has the tendency to lean over really close in order to ask questions. I'm constantly offering him Tic Tacs, which he constantly declines because he's diabetic.

He smiles at me.

I smile back.

Professore Raquella is still seething. I am late for every Italian class, which, incidentally, meets every weekday.

"Chloe," she says in a booming voice.

"Uh, yes? I mean, sì?"

"Siete in ritardo!"

"Sì," I reply, nodding my head vigorously, hoping that I look apologetic.

"Ancora," she says stonily.

"Sì," I say again, handing her my homework.

At least I can redeem myself in some way. I am very meticulous about my work. Sure, it gets done at four in morning, but it always gets done.

"Grazie," she says, taking it from me, scanning it quickly and then giving me an approving nod.

"Don't worry," Jordan whispers, leaning toward me.

"Thanks," I squeeze out, trying to hold my breath.

What did the kid eat this morning? Fish food?

My friend (and on-again-off-again partner in crime) Veronica grins at me from across the round table, sensing my discomfort.

Jordan thinks she is class-flirting with him and winks.

Who winks at chicks anymore? I feel as if that's very fifties *Rebel Without a Cause*. Jordan is more eighties *Revenge of the Nerds*.

"Do you think she likes me?" he asks.

"Tic Tac?" I reply hopefully.

"No, the diabetes thing. I told you!" he answers angrily.

"Sorry." When are they going to find a damn cure for diabetes?

We spend the rest of the class period conjugating verbs and answering Professore Raquella's questions about our weekends in broken Italian.

After what seems like an eternity, the clock strikes 10:30 A.M.

I bolt out of my seat and head for the door as Professore Raquelle shouts tomorrow's assignment after us.

Every day after Italian class, Veronica and I head to Atticus (which we refer to as Atticooos because that sounds more Italian), a book-store/café that serves the best bread this side of Paris (or at least New York). We spend the remainder of our mornings refueling on coffee and brooding over Italian homework or any assignments that seem to be plaguing us that week. Atticooos is also my first lunch of the day (when you have an 8:3o A.M. class, you need two lunches), and the two of us devour the impeccable house salad with Dijon dressing and two full baskets of that very bread generously dipped in the vinaigrette.

Veronica is the kind of girl who oozes sex. She is not particularly beautiful or thin, but she is certainly sexy. She has a throaty laugh. She always wears red lipstick (even with sweatpants), and it is always glossy. When she asks a question, she arches one perfectly plucked eyebrow and looks at you with an inquisitive glance. When she feels like acting innocent, she widens her eyes and stares up at you from beneath thick, dark lashes. But everyone knows that there is not one ounce of innocence hidden beneath her black lace Wonderbra.

Men worship her. They woo her. She walks into a bar and sex spills out of her like lava out of a volcano. She knows about sex. She knows about vibrators.

She must.

So I figured I might as well ask her the big bad vibrator question.

"So, ummm, do you own one?" I inquire tentatively with my mouth stuffed full of bread.

"Of course, darling." (Oh, yeah, Veronica refers to everyone as darling. It's really annoying.)

"You do?" I ask incredulously.

I figured she got enough bone to supply the Western Hemi-sphere. Why in the world would she need one?

"Uh-huh," she answers. She's losing interest already as she eyes our waiter, Sam (who, for the record, she has slept with, which is why our salads are free every Friday). "You don't?" she asks, raising an eyebrow.

"Um. Nooo," I answer.

"Whatareyoudoingafterbrunch?" she says so quickly that it sounds like one word.

Oh, crap, she's going to want to go buy me one. I really don't know if I'm ready for this step in my life. I mean, this seems like a big deal. I think. Maybe I just have to remember not to pack it when I go abroad.

"Well—" I begin to answer.

"Because, darling, we need to get you one."

Big surprise.

Two loaves of bread, four cigarettes, and twenty-six minutes later, Veronica and I find ourselves standing below an oversized red sign that reads NU HAVEN BOOK AND VIDEO. Why does it have to be red? That's conspicuous: Hi, we sell pornography. And your name is?

Veronica smashes her cigarette on the side of the building and looks over at me. "Ready?" she asks.

I nod. Of course I'm ready, I tell myself. This is my ticket out of boring singlehood, the kind where I go home and lie in bed with a slice of pizza and a bowl of ice cream. I will become sexually adventurous, wise and experienced like Veronica. I will own a vibrator. I will use my vibrator. So what if I don't have a boyfriend. I have a vibrator and that says a lot.

What exactly it says, I'm not sure.

Veronica swings the door open and waltzes in, swaying her booty side to side with attitude borrowed from Beyoncé Knowles.

I wonder if Beyoncé owns a vibrator.

As we enter the store, we walk past rack after rack of *Ass Bangers* (the full collection—I'm talking DVDs 1 through 8) as well as the re-makes of every Tom Hanks movie, from *Forrest Hump* to *Sleepless Sluts in Seattle*. To be honest, I was unaware that those types of things went on in Seattle. People always say the West Coast is different, but this . . .

There are photos of people on those "films" doing things that you are not even supposed to do in the privacy of your own home. Not even if you, a midget, and five other people are the *only* people left on the planet.

Veronica peeks over her shoulder at me and winks.

Finally we arrive at the sex toys aisle. In front of me hang more fake penises than I have ever seen in my life. Not that I have seen that many fake penises, but you get my drift. There are all kinds of vibrators: big ones, small ones, skinny ones, fat ones . . . fatter ones. I scan the wall, trying to decipher which one would be right for me. Veronica looks as if she's in heaven and begins grabbing various models off the shelves and waving them in my direction.

"How about this one?" she asks.

I shake my head. It's called the Waterproof Pleasure Pal and it's ten inches long and covered in purple glitter. I will never be able to take my vibrator experience seriously if it looks like it belongs to Rock Star Barbie.

"Are you sure?" Veronica nudges me. "I have it in pink; it's really . . . wonderful," she says breathily.

"Yeah, I don't think it's quite my, um, you know, style," I stammer.

"Ok," she says, shrugging her shoulders indifferently, already scanning the walls for her next recommendation.

I walk a little way away from Veronica, feeling slightly intimidated by her expertise. I think I might be more successful if I choose a pleasure pal on my own terms.

My First Vibe looks interesting. It's designed for first-timers, and the *i*'s in its title are dotted with flowers. It's also about two inches long, which leads me to believe that some first vibers are about fifteen years old.

I walk further down the aisle past the Glow in the Dark Vibe as

well as *Rhapsody—The Gelatin Rubber Story* (how literary!). I also forgo
the Vibrating Pen (too casual) and the Mach X20 Probe (too Arnold
Schwarzenegger action movie).

All of a sudden, Veronica comes bounding toward me.

"I found it!" she exclaims. "It's perfect!" she says, handing it to
me excitedly. Her lips curve into a perfect glossy smile.

I take a look, a bit grudgingly. It's a basic model from the Classic
Chic Collection. An elegant off-white, it goes well with my room's dé-
cor, and as an added bonus, there are no pictures of naked women
skinnier than me or with nicer breasts on the packaging. It's also
moderately priced at a cool $10.99.

I'm sold.

I think.

"So, Chlo? What do you think?"

"It's . . . you know . . . it seems . . . pleasurable." This is not like
buying a skirt. What am I supposed to say? "Yeah, I think it's going to
look great with my new pink top." Or "I'm sure I'll get lots of attention
when I wear this."

"I think my clitoris is really going to dig it," I say.

Veronica looks at me, slightly perturbed.

"You are so weird."

I blush.

We make our way to the register, and the fat clerk rings up my
purchase and *winks* at me. GROSS. I'm feeling a little nauseous.

(But also a little dangerous.)

I am ready to tackle the world. Who needs a boyfriend when you
have a vibrator from the Classic Chic Collection?

Don't answer that.

As I walk home after saying good-bye to Veronica, I begin to feel
a little more nervous. I will just have to get over my fear by taking the
thing for a test drive. The only thing we have to fear is fear itself . . .
right?

I walk up the stairs to our third-floor suite and check that the hallways are clear. I don't want anyone barging in on me in my moment of glory (or whatever). I am certain that Bonnie is doing something good for humanity this afternoon, so I have our box of a room to myself. I unlock the door and shut it firmly behind me, removing the hanger we use to keep it propped open so visitors don't need to knock. That will not be necessary today.

May the experimentation commence!

I take out my brand-new vibrator. The Classic Chic Collection, which felt so right at Nu Haven Book and Video, now suddenly seems foreign and not at all funny. I put it on my desk and sit on my bed facing it.

"Hello, vibrator," I say.

It just stands there. How am I supposed to be intimate with this inanimate piece of plastic with a battery? At least it vibrates at 60 rpm per minute, something I'm certain a penis could never do.

One point for Mr. V.

"How are you, Mr. V?" I ask. That doesn't sound right. You don't hook up with people you address formally.

"How are you, V?" At least that sounds a little less formal. But this conversation is not going anywhere. At least Max answered my questions. V is just sort of standing there, looking at me with his non-eyes.

I try to think of a Plan B.

Okay, if I am going to do this, I am going to do it right. I am going to use my vibrator in style. Or, as I learned in Italian, with *abondannza di stile*.

I slip into my one and only nightgown. A blue satin slip with light green trim, it is seductive without being trashy. I turn off the lamp and light some scented candles. All right, the mood is looking a little better.

I scoop up my vibrator and lie down on my bed. I turn it over in my hands and examine it. I am not attracted to this object, but I can try.

I close my eyes and switch it on. BZZZZZ. It sounds like my alarm clock, and it's quite powerful. In fact, my whole body is shaking due to the intense vibrations, and I'm still just holding it. I adjust the speed. Now it is lightly buzzing.

Psst. Psst. Psst.

Now it's talking *more* than most guys I've ever been intimate with. Unfortunately this one doesn't have a pulse, or anything else real, for that matter.

All of a sudden I feel panicky. My heart is beating quickly and I am sweating a little bit. But not a sexy sweat. Sort of a test-taking sweat, like when it gets really hot in your armpits and you feel like you're going to fail. I think that I am going to fail at this vibrator thing.

Maybe if I start slowly, this will work. Obviously, with a vibrator I'm skipping the whole foreplay part, so I'll just get used to holding it.

I put it against my thigh.

And I burst out laughing. My vibrator is tickling me. Who knew this would be so funny?

I do it again, this time trying to maintain a straight face.

But it tickles! A lot.

My laugh can probably be heard all the way down the hallway. I am rolling on my bed laughing hysterically—partially out of embarrassment and partially because I have not been tickled in at least six years.

I put the vibrator against the back of my neck. Hmm, nice. Good massage technique. This is a real stress reliever. Maybe I can just forget the whole sexual thing and use it before midterms to ease my aching joints, in pain from being hunched over the computer. This $10.99 investment was not for nothing. I make a mental note to hook my mother up with one of these for Hanukkah.

Wait, stop, I tell myself. A sex columnist unable to use a vibrator? That's like a lawyer unable to lie. A chef unable to chop. I am a fallacy. A charlatan!

I've got to try again. I'm gonna go. And I'm gonna go big. I turn the vibrator on to the highest level, and with what I imagine is a look of determination, I slip it under my slip.

All of a sudden, I hear the key in the lock and the door to my room swings open before I have time to react (much less turn my Classic Chic off). Bonnie and Gina, the seven-year-old girl she tutors every Monday, are standing in the doorway. *Fuck!*

"And this is my room . . ." she says as her voice trails off and they both stare at me.

I jump about two hundred feet in the air.

Make that two thousand.

Make that I want to die.

"Hello, Chloe," she says with as much composure as she can muster.

Gina just looks at me. My face turns beet red. Maybe even purple.

"Why are you wearing that fancy dress in the dark?" Gina asks.

Bonnie looks at me expectantly as if to say, *I'm not going to answer that.*

"I'm in a play," I lie. What kind of a lie is that?

"You are?"

"Yes," I say more confidently.

"Why are you in the dark?"

"Because plays take place in the dark," I reply (duh).

"Oh."

Good. Gina seems satisfied. Bonnie seems very unsatisfied with me.

The right word might be *furious*.

What was I thinking? I should not be using a vibrator in the day-time anyway. I should be doing something like reading. Or writing the twenty-page paper I have due in Homer, Dante, and Virgil next week.

"What's that toy?" Gina suddenly asks.

"Oh, this?" I say, holding up the vibrator. It is still on. I quickly switch it off.

"Yeah," Bonnie adds, "what *is* that toy?" For all I know, Bonnie probably doesn't even know what it is.

"It's a noise-maker."

"Show me," Gina says.

"Um." I turn it on again. It shakes and buzzes.

"That doesn't look like a very fun toy."

"It's not," I reply, stuffing Mr. V under the covers.

Before Gina can ask another question, Bonnie comes to the rescue (finally!).

"We're going to leave now. And maybe we should have a talk when I get back," she mutters at me.

Okay, Mom. Whenever Bonnie begins using her maternal you're-in-trouble voice, I'm in deep shit. She is the oldest of four children, so she's been using it for years.

I just nod my head sheepishly.

"I'm going to drop Gina off at home. Don't go anywhere," she adds menacingly.

About twenty minutes later, Bonnie strides into our room. I have changed into my sweatpants and am sitting on my bed, waiting to be reprimanded.

"You are *insane.*"

I am very embarrassed.

"I'm *not,*" I reply indignantly.

"First of all, it's three o'clock in the afternoon, you are wearing a teddy and using a vibrat—"

"I didn't actually use it," I say, interrupting her.

"What were you doing? Talking to it?"

I don't want to tell her yes, so I remain silent.

"When did you purchase that thing?"

"Today. With Veronica."

"Obviously," Bonnie snorts.

Bonnie is not a big fan of Veronica. She thinks that Veronica is a little too over the top and superficial to be sincere. She might be right.

"What's that supposed to mean?"

"Chloe, you could have at least put a Please Knock sign on the door. What if Gina and I had come in five minutes later? And she had seen you using it? What was I supposed to tell her? Even worse, what would I have told her parents?"

"I, uh . . . I . . ." I stammer.

"I can't believe you. I really can't," she says, shaking her head.

"What do you want me to say?" I reply. "I'm sorry. I don't know what else to tell you. And how in the hell was I supposed to know that you were going to bring Gina back here? Don't you think you should have warned me first?"

"No, you're the one who should have warned me."

"Well, you should have known to knock, since the door was locked."

"On the door of my own bedroom?"

"Yes."

"You are being ridiculous," she says, shaking her head. She's so embarrassed that she can't even look me in the face. I'm glad, because this is no walk in the park for me either. She walks over to her bed and begins unfolding and refolding clothes.

I just look at her. I hate it when she gets so uptight. Yes, it sucks that she and Gina walked in, but I wish she'd be more understanding. Besides, I was trying to use a vibrator. Isn't that embarrassing enough without the post-failed-masturbation lecture?

"Listen, I have to go," Bonnie says, taking a quick glance at her watch. She begins stuffing books into her bag and still refusing to look at me.

"All right," I say, relieved that she's leaving. "I'm sorry," I say quietly. Right or wrong, I hate it when anyone is angry with me. Especially Bonnie.

She ignores me, still not ready to forgive.

"Fine. Well, bye," I say filling the silence.

"Bye," she says, slinging her bookbag over her shoulder and walking out of the room. She lets the door slam behind her, leaving me alone with my thoughts and my vibrator.

I walk over to my bookshelf filled with books that I have accumulated over the years, some of which I have never touched but written long papers about. I pull out my worn copy of *Anna Karenina* and turn it over in my hands, opening it up and reading a few pages. Some people peruse the Bible, choosing passages from it, hoping to make sense of life. I, on the other hand, turn to random pages of *Anna Karenina* to seek wisdom. If only I could write like Tolstoy, or perhaps understand the world like him. Things might be a little different.

Today I come across " 'Stepan Arkadyevitch was a truthful man in his relations with himself.' "

Well, what kind of a man was he in his relations with others?

I put Anna back on the shelf, turning this line over in my mind, peering under it as if it is a rock hiding something waiting to be uncovered. How am I in my relations with others? Probably very much unlike Stepan in his relations with himself; probably an absolute liar.

I pick up Virgil's *Aeneid* and throw it in my backpack. It weighs a million pounds. I add a couple of binders, a laptop, and my class notes to the pile, and throw the bag over my shoulder, determined to accomplish something today (since masturbation went awry).

It is difficult not to fall in love with Yale in the fall. The campus looks like a scene from a movie. Trees turn unimaginable colors, and students read in the grass wearing J.Crew wool Shetland sweaters and occasionally throwing Frisbees around. (Actually, I have been afraid of Frisbees ever since I was hit in the head and nearly knocked out by one in my first week of freshman year.)

I push open the doors of Sterling Memorial Library and step in-side. College libraries are often ugly, but this one in particular is absolutely beautiful. Its ceiling is arched so it looks like Noah's Ark turned upside down. The front desk and book drop-off sit humbly in front of an ornate painting of epic proportions with a long hallway extending off to the right, bordered on either side by stained glass.

I want to get married in this library. And if it didn't look so much like a church (like everything else at Yale), my mother just might let me.

I sit down in the main reading room, and as soon as my butt hits the chair, my mind begins wandering. So much for motivation.

Okay, I'll start studying in ten minutes. Four-thirty on the dot. I swear. I'll just get a soda first. And then I'll check my e-mail. And maybe read a bit of *The New York Times* online. And peruse eluxury.com, and then I'll study. Yes. That sounds like a good plan.

Why am I inexplicably struck with ADD the moment I enter this library?

It's now four-fifty and I have yet to do any work. But I have bought a sweater online. So I guess that counts for something. I click on the *Yale Daily News* website to see this week's column (and of course to see if Maxwell has written anything). Sure enough, there is a message from YaleMale05.

This cannot be good news. But my curiosity gets the best of me, and I'm forced to check out the situation.

> **Chloe, Chloe, Chloe. What have you done this week? Your dance floor erection earns you a dance floor ejection. So why don't you say we go dancing and I show you how it's done?**

Maxwell has some nerve.

Things are certainly not always as they appear.

All this ambiguity in relationships, sexual or nonsexual, has got me thinking. Why don't people mean what they say and say what they mean? After all, I do.

Don't I?

THE YALE DAILY NEWS

SEX AND THE (ELM) CITY
BY CHLOE CARRINGTON

Ambiguity: It Might Screw You Over, It Might Not

My freshman year, I lived on a floor below a group of senior boys. To my untrained freshman eye, they seemed perfect. They were decently handsome, decently smart, and decently funny, and my suite worshiped them. Early in the year, one in particular caught my attention.

He was cuddly like a teddy bear, and we got along fabulously. Often I would venture up to his room to study or just to hang out and watch movies, as his collection far surpassed that of anyone I knew.

His name was Jim. He was from Arkansas and had a penchant for chewing tobacco. It was like nothing I'd ever seen before. He would stuff a huge chunk of it in his mouth and work it around until his jaw was sore. Then he would spit the juice bit by bit into a pot across the room, until there was nothing left stored in his cheek. I was at once fascinated and revolted by his habit. Dipping was sort of sexy and rugged, but at the same time it made me want to vomit—mostly because of the dip residue that would fill various receptacles around the room and the little bits of brown stuff that would make their way to the corners of his mouth.

One evening, during a late viewing of *High Fidelity*, Jim laid his cards on the table.

In his charming Southern drawl, he remarked, "Ya know what I want?" Spit, spit. "I want a girl who dips." And with one final spit, he concluded, "Yup, I want a nice girl who'll dip with me all day long."

I looked at him in disgust. A girl who dipped would be like a guy who knits sweaters for dogs—grossly unattractive.

"That," I said, "is the most absurd thing I have ever heard."

"Well," he replied, "I guess we can never hook up then."

And we never did.

At the time I thought that Jim was a jerk. Who would say something like that?

Now, though, I recognize what a favor he was doing me. He was completely unambiguous. Totally up-front. He knew what he wanted. He laid out his parameters. That was the first and the last time that ever happened to me in college. Why are dating and relationships so inherently ambiguous? Jim's comment was so shocking to me because freshman year was *completely* ambiguous.

Don't get me wrong. When you first meet someone, ambiguity can be a good thing. As a freshman, you go to Naples on a Thursday night. You meet someone there, someone nice and funny. You talk to that someone for an hour even while your friend is violently vomiting in the bathroom. You keep talking through meatheads spilling beer on you and pizza crusts whizzing past your head. You even get past the "What college are you in?" and "Who are your roommates?" conversations.

When you arrive home, you tell your suitemates about this guy. Together, you all face book him and then sigh about how cute he is. You spend the rest of the weekend building him up in your mind. He has become a world-class athlete, a master chef who can do wonders with a rice cooker, and an endearing basket weaver who recites poetry in Spanish—the whole nine yards. He becomes your Chandler on *Friends,* your Dylan on *90210*—whatever tugs your chain.

Fast-forward to junior year.

Now you go to BAR on a Thursday night. You know everyone except for five people, and two of those go to Quinnipiac, and one of them is the bartender. You end up talking to one of the remaining (two) wild cards. He seems nice and funny and smart. You've even taken the same political science seminar.

When you arrive home, you tell your suitemates about this guy, and the floodgates of gossip open up. All of them know who he is and at least one of them has hooked up with him. He has this weird friend he's always with. His armpits smell—a lot. He has a single testicle and, like, six hairs on his chest, but only on his nipples.

All ambiguity flies out the window. There is no mystery. He went from today's hit to yesterday's favorite faster than a New Kids album.

When there is ambiguity surrounding someone, a mystique, a little something that you don't know—that is the good kind of ambiguity. But like lubricants, there is the good, the bad, and the cherry-flavored.

Ambiguity in relationships, on the other hand, can be maddening. As one friend of mine remarked, "Relationships? At Yale? I don't know if I've ever had one." The worst part is that girls and guys are ambiguous at completely different times. The big turning point is always the ill-fated hookup.

It may be true that women know within the first five minutes of meeting a man whether they are going to hook up with him or not. But the trick is never to let the guy in on her little secret. Female ambiguity is the pre-hookup chase, O.J.-style. She may be driving a white Bronco, and yes, maybe she's speeding a little, and you have the entire LAPD behind her, sirens and all, but you still don't know whether you're going to get to handcuff her later.

Women don't want the guy to know he'll be hooking up until he's actually doing it. But soon enough, the power dynamic—and the source of ambiguity—are flipped.

Post-hookup is when guys tend to get ambiguous. It's their payback.

Do they want to hook up again? Dunno.

Do they want to date? Dunno.

Are they straight? Dunno.

Name? Dunno.

They really don't know very much. AT ALL.

In both of these cases, both parties are protecting themselves. Ambiguity, I have discovered, is not inherently bad, nor is it inherently hurtful—though sometimes it has this effect. What ambiguity does do is successfully avoid a committed relationship that would leave one vulnerable. Vulnerability is scary. And scared is not something Yale students like to be. If we are more honest about what we want, someone gets hurt. No one wants to be on the injured list. So how much is too much ambiguity? There are almost no limits, because vulnerability is out of our control. Ambiguity is a factor of our own fear.

But at the same time in some ways, it's good. After all, if everyone was totally up-front, where would the mystery be? The what-ifs? The maybes, maybe-nots? The unknown?

Perhaps if Jim had never told me what he wanted, I would have voluntarily dipped and we would have fallen in love.

Okay, that's a lie.

But the truth is, a little ambiguity can go a long way.

𝓡 5 𝓮

𝓜ELVIN IS LATE. AGAIN.

I check my watch for the twelfth time since I got to the *Daily News* building.

It's really a beautiful building—something I often forget as I rush in and out of it on editing trips. Made of beige stone, it looks like a shrunken fairy-tale castle that should be filled with dwarfs and princesses and peas.

My mind is racing a million miles a minute, crammed with lists and things that *must* get done. This always happens to me during exam time. Testing season is the perennial end of me. For two weeks, my mind recites the things that I have to do again and again, without repose. Study for midterm in "Cold War"; twelve-page paper for "African-American Literature"; buy beer for Harvard Yale; somehow pass midterm in "Financial Markets" (taken only at the *strong* encouragement of my father—and by strong encouragement he meant, I'm paying for that damn education of yours so you may as well put something useful in your brain); eight hundred pages of reading for Homer, Dante, and Virgil; buy beer for Harvard Yale; midterm, midterm, paper, reading, paper, beer . . .

The work is seemingly endless this time of year and MELVIN IS LATE!

I should, of course, explain who Melvin is before I continue my rant.

Melvin is my editor at the paper.

He is also the herpes of friendship. I don't mean that in a cruel way, he just is. Everyone has a Melvin. You picked him up at some random party, gave him your phone number when you were drunk, and now you can't get rid of him. You say things like, "Oh, I have Melvin tonight." You have to warn people about your Melvin. Just like herpes.

He's annoying. He's obnoxious. He thinks he is smarter than you, and he lets you know it.

We have known each other since we were in ninth grade in my very first class at Bronson High School. It was math—my worst subject and Melvin's best. We were learning trigonometry (sine, cosine . . . you know) when a skinny boy with a mass of dark curls strode into the room twenty minutes late. Something I would come to know as typical Melvin behavior. He plopped down in the seat next to me, introduced himself, and without warning reached over me and grabbed the extra pencil I kept on the edge of my desk in high school (when I was still diligent and cared about getting into college). From that day forward, I have not been able to get rid of him, and he has continued to borrow pencils and many other things without warning. Senior year of high school, we both applied to Yale early—and got in. As one of life's little jokes, he also ended up being my editor at the newspaper.

Leave it to Melvin to disappear off to never-never land when we are supposed to meet. I swear this is his weekly payback for all the adamant nos I've given to his various romantic proposals.

The newspaper is buzzing with activity, as it is every Thursday night. The *Scene* editors are running around trying to fill pages with mediocre CD reviews and yet another article about the use of alcohol on college campuses (conclusion: PREVALENT) or the obligatory article about what it's like to be a full-time student and a part-time stripper. (They interview the same girl every time they run the article, changing only her pseudonym—very sneaky.)

Thursday nights here are more fun than any other, as first and second drafts are accompanied by the alcoholic kind—beers galore. Shouts of "Where's my beer?" and "Who's writing the story about Levin's dog?" bounce off the building's stone walls.

I figure that while I wait for Mr. Herpes himself, I may as well go upstairs to the Two Room. This is where all the *real* stuff happens at the paper. Late-night editorial meetings, barking, frustrated managing editors, the layout staff . . . they're all here.

Brian, the hardest-working student I know and the best editor in chief the *Daily* has ever seen (and a brief sophomore-year fling of mine), is sitting at his computer. He spends so much time here that he has his calls forwarded to the paper.

"Hey, Brian!"

No answer.

It usually takes him a while to respond, a source of severe angst during our three-week foray. The upside to which was an illicit encounter atop the big table in the YDN conference room. It's about twenty feet long and made of cherrywood. It's the table equivalent of Everest. I felt like Sir Edmund Hillary (adventurer!).

That is, until Brian prematurely ejaculated on my leg.

Evidently his responses are either delayed or a little too prompt:

"Brian!"

"Hmmm."

"Brian Greene, look at me this instant," I say in a mock bossy tone. He looks up and grins.

"Sorry, Chlo, it's just that some fuckin' freshman doesn't quite understand the definition of fact-checking. You know, as in 'to check facts.' It's not that hard."

Uh-oh. The permanent stick up Brian's ass is wedged just a shade higher tonight. Not a good sign.

"It's all right. How are things?"

"Well, one of our photographers lost five thousand dollars' worth of equipment, the head of the Political Science Department is threatening us with a defamation lawsuit, and the *Harvard Crimson* just won a journalism award, leaving us in the dust for the third year in a row. But other than that, life is just brilliant."

Told you so.

"So . . . that probably means that you don't know where Melvin is," I say, being aware that he probably knows exactly where Melvin is.

Brian knows everything that goes on at *his* paper. It's part of what makes him so good at his job. He will probably do something fabulous with his life like edit *The New York Times* while I beg him to hire me to fill some measly unglamorous position that he will have to give me because (1) we slept together, and (2) after we slept together I promised not to tell anyone that he is the premature ejaculation sensation. Something he claims has happened only once. It also happened to be with the sex columnist. Kid's got shitty luck.

"Melvin went to go get pizza. Why don't you just wait around and keep me company until he gets back?" he says optimistically.

"Sorry, darlin', your current girlfriend plays rugby and I'm a writer. The odds are very much stacked against me. Plus," I say, checking my watch, "she's due in for her nightly visit in seven minutes and thirty-six seconds."

Brian's current love brings him cookies every night at the paper at 9:00 P.M. on the dot.

Smart girl.

"Okay," he says, having already lost interest in me and eyeing his e-mail inbox, which is feverishly flashing with twenty-two unread messages.

"Don't get an ulcer," I remind him, beginning to make my way back downstairs, but not before grabbing the last Pabst Blue Ribbon off his desk.

Who ever said the *Yale Daily News* doesn't do it in style?

He laughs. "Okay, okay. Don't get an STD."

I blush what I'm sure is a deep, unflattering shade of red, choosing to ignore his comment.

I scamper back down to Melvin's station, annoyed as ever at his absence, ready to go home and not deal with the world. Dealing with it requires far too much energy.

I sit down on his swivel chair and begin spinning myself around, still preoccupied by the long night of studying I have ahead of me and hoping to spin myself right into Thanksgiving break and right out of my responsibilities.

Just as I'm starting to get dizzy, I see Melvin rushing toward me, balancing a pizza on one hand and pushing his glasses up with the other. His brown curls are bouncing all over his forehead. He's got his cell phone wedged between his shoulder and his ear and is practically yelling into the mouthpiece.

"Okay, Mom, okay. I promise. I'll call Grandma *tomorrow*. *Okay*, Mom!"

"You're late," I say sternly when he bids his overbearing mother farewell (until she calls back ten minutes later).

"You're beautiful."

"I hate you."

"I love you."

"Melvin," I say menacingly.

"Chloe," he replies lovingly.

He is *infuriating*. But still, I can't help but have a soft spot for the wanker. He is, after all, one of my oldest friends.

"Melvin, I have a million and a half tests to take and papers to write this week. I don't have time for your bullshit, so just tell me why you brought me here tonight."

"Calm down, Chloe. So, how are you?"

"What?"

"How are you? I like my writers to be relaxed. I just want to know how life is treating you. What's making you happy these days?"

"Don't patronize me," I reply sardonically.

"Okay, okay," Melvin concedes, finally cluing in to my impatience. "I wanted to talk about the big Harvard/Yale issue."

Harvard versus Yale or "The Game" is the annual football game that takes place every year, a week before Thanksgiving. It is one of the most exhilarating times of the year, as all-out debauchery replaces midterms. It's also a mediocre display of college football.

"What about the issue?" I ask, curious as to what Melvin has in mind. Irritating or not, the kid is usually brimming with brilliant ideas.

"Well, I was thinking about what *Scene* was going to look like this week, and I want it to really blow everyone's mind. I want your column to be *hilarious*. I'm talking laugh-out-loud, piss-your-pants, stomp-on-the-floor-and-clap-your-hands hilarious."

Wow. So no pressure at all.

"Can you do that?" he asks impatiently.

"I mean . . . I can try. I always try . . ." My voice trails off.

Suddenly I am feeling a little paranoid. And very nervous.

"Have I not been funny lately? Are my columns not up to par? What's wrong?" My voice is rising an octave a second. I'm in no mood for criticism.

Especially not from Melvin.

"Well . . ." he begins, again pushing his glasses up onto the bridge of his nose and pausing thoughtfully.

"Melvin," I say threateningly, "cut to the chase. I have a ton of work and I want to get out of here."

"I just think your columns could use a little kick. You know? Something with a little more . . . edge."

Is this for real? The King of Uncool is telling me that I need a little more edge?

"What do you mean by *edge*?"

"You know, Chloe, edge. You need to be a little more on the forefront. Try and push people's buttons. Test their limits. Be crazy! Be more sexually free," he adds.

More sexually free? Melvin can't have sex when they're giving it away for free.

"Ummm. Well, what am I supposed to do?" I stammer.

"Chloe," he says very seriously, "trust me. You can do it. Just believe in yourself. You're a talented writer. Show me what you can do."

"Those are not good instructions," I say. "In fact those are not instructions at all. You are my *editor*. If you want something, go ahead and tell me what it is."

"Okay, Chloe," he says evenly, "I want a column that'll blow my socks off. And that will top anything Harvard puts in the paper," he adds quickly.

Ahhh, so the real reason for this inconvenient meeting is revealed: Melvin wants to beat Harvard using his sneaky newspaperman wiles.

"So this is all about Harvard, isn't it? Did Brian put you up to this?" I ask, ready to storm back upstairs and give the premature ejaculation sensation a piece of my mind. But the rugby girlfriend is visiting, so I calm myself.

"No, no. Nothing like that," Melvin says reassuringly. "I just want to do something *great* with this issue. You're my only hope. I need you to be great." He is resorting to flattery. As if that will work on me.

(It does.)

"Fine," I snort, "I'll give you edge. I'll give you so much edge you'll cut yourself on it."

"Great!" Melvin exclaims. He continues, a little more quietly, "Thanks, Chlo. I knew I could count on you."

"Yeah, yeah," I say hurriedly. I don't want Melvin to get senti-
mental on me and try to hug me or anything crazy like that.

"Seriously," he says softly, "you're the best."

"Okay, okay." Before he can get much more out, I sling my bag
onto my shoulder and stomp out of the building.

The night is cool and crisp, and I breathe it in quickly before I
coop myself up in the library for the night. I run across campus,
through piles and piles of leaves, hoping not to trip, over to SML, where
Lisa is waiting to help me with studying for "Financial Markets" (the
test is *tomorrow!*), for which I have yet to pick up a book. And now, of
course, I'm late because of Melvin's delay.

He's always screwing everything up, I say to myself, but with a
touch of tenderness. Despite our faux love-hate relationship, he is
the person I cried to when the SATs got too hard, when college appli-
cations began piling up, and when trigonometry made no sense. He,
on the other hand, called me to write "Sex and the (Elm) City," beg-
ging me to give it a shot because, as he asserted, he knew almost no
one else who could write like I could, nor did he know anyone as
funny as I can be.

When I arrive at the library, I head straight for machine city and
purchase the six Diet Cokes, two bags of chips (sour cream and
onion), three bags of Skittles, and one bag of M&Ms that will help
catapult me through this night. For those interested, this feast weighs
in at 1,500 calories and 67 grams of fat.

I feel around inside my coat pockets for Marlboro Lights. Check.

Lovely. Now that I have guaranteed myself an extra seven
pounds, acne, and lung cancer, let's get this studying business on
the road.

When I finally show up in the main reading room of SML, I scan
the hundreds of stressed-out midterm-absorbed students, shoulders
hunched over books and laptops, empty soda cans littering nearby
areas. Several poor souls are asleep on their notebooks, strings of

drool obscuring what could be the most important notes they've taken all semester.

Finally, my eyes land on Lisa. She is wearing a slinky mauve slip-dress, huge fur-lined boots, and a pink cardigan. Eclectic, to say the least. I shamefully look down at my own Yale sweatshirt and ratty gray sweatpants. This is what studying gear is *supposed* to look like. Lisa is also filing her nails and alternatively taking bites of a giant ice cream sundae perched in front of her atop *The Wonderful World of Finance* textbook.

The girl weighs no more than a hundred and ten pounds but eats like a linebacker. She chalks it up to an overactive thyroid. Incredible metabolism irks the hell out of me.

She looks up at me and shakes her head, furrowing her brow. "Tardy again!" she says in a loud whisper.

"Sorry," I shoot back, "it's all Melvin's fault."

"Do you blame him for everything?" she asks, irritated.

"No! Really, we had a meeting at the paper and he showed up a century late—as usual."

"Okay, okay. Let's get started. I'm meeting Harry in a few hours to discuss Hume's naturalism. I'm writing my seminar paper about it."

Seeing my look of bewilderment, she adds, "It's really fascinating."

I think of asking what exactly Hume's naturalism is, but I decide against it, fearing a long-winded explanation that will have nothing to do with financial markets. Instead, I decide to ask about the present state of Lisa's love triangle. At least that's geometry.

"Wait, so you decided on Harry?"

"Well . . ." she begins sheepishly.

I look at her expectantly.

"I had dinner with Stuart earlier," she admits with a sly smile. "I still don't think I'm equipped with ample information to make my final decision."

"Of course not," I say, nodding enthusiastically.

"Mind you," she concedes quickly, "I'm not really breaking hearts, just having some fun. Your advice was actually rather good. I may just owe you a thank-you."

I laugh.

"SHHHH!" comes a chorus of voices around us.

We look at each other sheepishly and open our books.

For the next three hours, without a single break, Lisa and I discuss options, futures and forwards, stocks and bonds, mutual funds and mortgages.

She patiently explains each concept to me again and again, never once getting frustrated as to why I can't wrap my uneconomic mind around the mathematical explanation for the CAP-M model—or any other model that isn't wearing designer clothes, for that matter.

The way I see it, is that CAP is a type of hat and M is the size between small (S) and large (L). I really don't understand how either of these things can begin to explain stock market fluctuations.

Lisa finally gives up as she describes the Modigliani and Miller model, which I mistake as a joke about an Italian guy and a British guy that walk into a bar . . .

"You're hopeless!" she declares, frustrated, and gathers her things to leave in order to go over naturalism with Harry (and then of course to show him her own definition).

I am feeling dizzy and nauseated by the two hundred Skittles I've ingested.

"Please don't go!" I plead.

Lisa looks at me sympathetically. "Calm down, you still have a lot of studying to accomplish."

I am perfectly aware of that. And that's precisely why Lisa can't leave. Without her, my textbook will become a pillow rather than an instrument of scholarship.

I give her my best "Look at me, I'm a friend in distress" face.

She, not one to take a challenge lying down, shoots back her best "Look at me, I'm a friend about to get laid" expression. She dashes out of the library, leaving me to contend with all of those around me, who are ready to take me down à la Jean-Claude Van Damme.

Fearing for my life, I look around apologetically, not meeting a single compassionate face. I duck my head sheepishly and continue my studying.

Four hours later a crackling voice comes over the library's ancient PA system. "Attention, patrons," it says, "the library will be closing in *fifteen* minutes."

The announcement jolts me out of a very sound and rather enjoyable sleep.

Sleep?

Shit.

Oh, my God. Please don't let this be true, I think as I blink at my watch groggily. My contacts are cemented to my dry eyes, and my mouth tastes much like Hot Rob's protective cup must following a four-hour soccer practice—in the rain.

You get the idea.

Panic is beginning to set in, in a major way. My test is less than twelve hours away and . . .

I have been sleeping for the last four hours.

I am going to fail.

I will be forced to drop out of school.

My parents will disown me.

No, really, they will.

I will have to peddle fruit from a cart in Queens and donate blood on the side for extra cash.

I begin hyperventilating and packing up my stuff to leave the library so that I can head back to my room and burn the midnight oil. It's more like the five A.M. oil at this point, but who's counting?

I stuff all of my (unread) class notes, textbook, pens, pencils, into my bag. Okay, where's my calculator?

Where is my fucking *calculator*? I rummage furiously through piles and piles of paper. I am also making a giant scene as I mutter profanities under my breath.

Oh. There it is.

I wouldn't want to lose the bane of my existence.

I leave the library and decide to smoke a cigarette to calm my nerves on my way home. With trembling hands I fumble through my pockets and pull out a lighter and a single cigarette from my close-to-empty pack.

I put it in my mouth and light it as I scurry through the streets of New Haven as quickly as possible so as not to be harassed by the city's exuberant homeless population.

My mind is whirring again, thinking about everything I have to do and the four lost hours I spent snoring away in the library. I am cursing myself for the umpteenth time when I feel my flip-flop get caught somewhere.

(It's too damn cold to be wearing flip-flops, but I insist on displaying my pedicure until it snows. No point in paying twenty-seven dollars to look at your own toes.)

My book bag goes one way, my foot another, and the rest of my body a third.

I land on the cold, hard pavement directly on my knees, and once I realize that I have not severely damaged any part of my body, I check around to see if anyone of significance has seen me fall.

I spot a twosome sauntering casually toward me, arm in arm. I squint in the dark to get a closer look, and I realize that it's Crystal and Sebastian Wise. Dance floor erections are apparently the newest pickup trend sweeping the nation.

Some people have all the luck.

I also realize that I have face-planted in the company of two of the most well-manicured individuals on the planet. How can God hate one person this much?

I attempt to hide my face with my hair so as not to be detected by the Heavenly Homos. Mind you, it's only because I love Crystal. No one wants to be best friends with the girl with smudged mascara sprawled on the ground like Robert Downey Jr. outside of the Viper Room.

Yet, my luck, it seems, has run out. A distant voice calls, "Chloe? Honey? Is that you?"

I look up and come face-to-face with Crystal and God Among Gays.

"Yes," I reply meekly, trying to suppress my tears.

"This is Sebastian," Crystal says uncertainly.

"Hi."

"Are you all right?" Sebastian asks. He looks like an angel staring down at me, his blond hair forming a halo around his perfectly chiseled features.

"Why are you gay?" I want to ask, but instead, I simply say yes, making no attempt to laugh off my miserable existence.

The two of them help me to my feet. Together we silently pick up my belongings and place them back into my bag.

Crystal wraps his skinny arms around me. "I'm going to make a lot of fun of you later," he says with a grin, "but for now, go eat a tub of ice cream or something."

"I have a midterm tomorrow," I wail helplessly, more to myself than to him.

"All the more reason," he says, and Sebastian nods vigorously.

"Harvard/Yale is like five minutes away. You're gonna get through this. And then we can drink excessively," Crystal adds cheerfully.

"You're right, you're right," I say, futilely attempting to convince myself that he does indeed have a point.

"Where are you off to?" I ask, trying to divert attention away from my world title of Loser at Life.

"Oh, just on a walk back to my place," Crystal replies nonchalantly.

He is most definitely trembling inside.

"Have fun," I say with a devilish grin. Crystal hasn't been this excited about a man since Ryan. Perhaps Sebastian Wise is the one that will take him over the hump.

Get your mind out of the gutter! Not *that* kind of hump (although I'm sure he'll do that, too)—the hump that follows every breakup. I am a firm believer in the idea that no one is fully over an ex until the next fling comes striding into his or her life. I'd take Sebastian Wise as my next fling any day. Although I'm pretty certain I'm not equipped to be his.

I slowly make my way back to my room. When I've finally climbed the three flights of stairs, I am feeling even less optimistic. The probability that I'll pass this test is growing less by the minute, and it's already two-thirty. My literal trip home cut a big chunk of time out of my schedule.

I fling the door to my room open and deposit my heavy bag on the common-room couch. A flicker of light is coming from the bedroom. Bonnie must be awake. Odd, she's usually a lights-out-at-midnight kind of girl. I open the door a crack and there she is huddled over her computer, banging on her keyboard as if she is an angry Lars Ulrich.

"Hi, Bons," I say brightly.

She glances stonily at me. Bonnie is still mad about the vibrator incident.

"Bon Bon," I say hopefully. It's a nickname that I coined for her freshman year, and it usually brings out Bonnie's softer side. Especially when she's angry with me, which usually never lasts too long.

"*What*, Chloe." She says it more like a statement than a question.

"What are you doing?"

"Writing a paper," she replies plainly.

"Oooh, good. We can study together!" I exclaim, mustering all the enthusiasm that is left in me.

"I'm about to go to bed."

"I hope you don't mind if I keep the light on for a while," I say tentatively.

"Whatever, Chloe."

Deciding to give her a few minutes to cool down, I sit down at my computer and check my e-mail. Nothing too interesting.

I decide to see if YaleMale05 has thrown me a nugget of charm this week.

Did I fail to mention that I'm a masochist?

I am also hoping that perhaps he will reveal his identity, even though it is *clearly* Maxwell.

I think.

I log on to the *Yale Daily News* web page for the millionth time this week, and wait until my column pops up so that I can click onto the message board.

Sure enough, just as predicted, YaleMale05 has indeed taken time out of his busy schedule to pay me a little attention.

I scroll down the screen and see only one simple sentence under his pseudonym:

Is this column about me?

YaleMale05 thinks quite highly of himself. Of course, the truth is that his cagey identity helped provide me with fodder for last week's column. How on earth, though, did he manage to figure it out? I haven't even *seen* Maxwell all week.

Perhaps he's a little more perceptive than I initially thought.

As I ponder this thought and prepare to log off to *really* begin studying, I notice that there happen to be several other messages posted this week.

DEVILGRRRRRRRL88
> Chloe, whomever you are, you cannot write. I am an English major and you can barely string three sentences together.

NATHALIE S.
> Some women like to be treated like human beings, not like puppets. Don't make the rest of us look foolish. I pity you.

I stare at the screen blankly. I have no biting response, not a sarcastic comeback in my usually plentiful annals. I feel like a failure, empty and even . . . hated.

Can no one appreciate the humor and irony behind my columns? Simple observations about the way we act when we are trying to mate. It's as if the painstaking thought I pour into my column each week is wiped out by these faceless critics.

Without warning, tears well up in my eyes and begin falling onto my keyboard. I hate crying. Not only is it bad for your complexion, but crying is like turning yourself inside out. I cannot control the tears. My disastrous night starts pouring from my eyes, slowly at first and then in gouts.

How can people that I don't even know hurt me so much? How can my writing, a great source of pride, also be my most public catastrophe?

I gasp for air and turn around blindly, groping at the box of tissues on my nightstand. Suddenly I feel exhausted. All I want is to lie down fully clothed atop my covers and go to sleep, hoping to wake up somewhere else. With someone else. Or perhaps wake up two days from now, at Harvard, forgetting about all of this.

Bonnie looks over at me, and her face softens. She grabs the tissues that I have been unsuccessfully reaching for and walks toward me, extending one out to me kindly. I grab it and wipe my nose, reaching out for another, which she graciously places in my hand.

She lets me cry for a while. Bonnie is endowed with the innate knowledge of when to do that kind of thing. She knows a lot more than I give her credit for.

After several minutes, when my blubbering has finally dwindled into sniffles, she asks, "What's wrong? What happened?"

I look up at her. "Nothing," I reply softly.

"So we have been sitting here as you cried for the last ten minutes because of nothing? Well, that's a relief. I should get to bed then," she says, her voice dripping with sarcasm.

I look at her, silently willing her to go to sleep, but she stares back, patiently waiting for a response. Bonnie will go to sleep at midnight every night of the week, but if I shed a single tear, she'll console me until the sun rises. She has much more patience than I do.

Finally I give in, and the story comes pouring out of me in fragments. Melvin doesn't like what I'm doing with the column. At least I don't think so. And I am going to fail my test. And I tripped. And then the comments. *The comments.*

"Nothing is going right," I conclude quietly.

Bonnie listens thoughtfully.

"Let me see these postings," she says. "Who are these people without an ounce of humor coursing through their veins?" she adds.

She walks over to my computer and pauses silently for a couple of seconds as she reads. "Did you see this one?" she asks.

"Bonnie!" I exclaim angrily, "are you trying to send me over the edge? I really don't need to read about all the other thousands of people out there that hate me."

Okay, so I'm exaggerating a bit.

"Whoa, Nelly. Just come over here."

I lean over her shoulder to read the comment she's pointing at, and there are four little words on the screen.

BR02

You make me laugh.

"You see!" Bonnie exclaims brightly, "people like you!"

"Yeah, for every three people that think I have the literary ability of Paula Abdul, one lone gunman thinks I'm funny. How uplifting."

"Chloe," Bonnie says, looking me dead in the eye, "shut up."

I look sheepishly at my feet.

"Do you remember," she continues, "at the beginning of sophomore year, when I was running that tutoring program?"

"Uh-huh." I nod my head, uncertain as to where this is all going.

"And there were some people in the group that disagreed with the way I was running it. They thought I was making some administrative mistakes and so on."

"Yes."

"Do you remember what you said to me?"

I look at her blankly. I have no recollection as to what I said to her.

"You told me, and I quote, 'If you don't piss some people off, you're not doing a good job. In fact, you're not worth knowing. You're boring.'"

I smile. "I did say that. I'm so wise."

"No, you're not." She pauses. "Chloe, do you think you are going to write a sex column and be everyone's best friend? You write about things that push people's buttons. It's okay if some people don't like what you say."

"But why do they have to say that they don't like *me*? That one girl said she pitied me!" I wail.

"And you don't pity her for taking time out of her schedule and her life to write about you on a college newspaper online *post board*?" Bonnie says this with so much disgust in her voice, I almost believe her. But the harsh words are still cemented in my mind.

"I guess so," I reply, only slightly convinced.

Bonnie checks her watch and gasps. "Holy shit! Three-thirty already?"

"You said shit."

"I know. You have to study," she says, reading my mind.

"That is true."

"Now give me a hug so I can go to bed."

I fall into her arms, thankful for her patience.

"Okay, okay. Get off me. I have to sleep. I need to go on a run to-morrow morning. And if your alarm clock goes off . . ." she says menacingly.

"Don't worry. It won't. Doesn't look like I'm sleeping tonight."

She looks at me sympathetically. "How about a celebratory lunch tomorrow when you're finally done?"

"I can't," I say apologetically, "I still have to finish my paper for Af-Am lit."

"Ooooh, I'm sorry."

"Yeah. Me too."

Bonnie never has a ton of work during midterms. Mostly because she likes to get an early start on things. Mrs. Johnson has indoctri-nated her children with the mantra "The early bird catches the worm." Procrastination is like the Antichrist to Bonnie.

I am the Antichrist to Mrs. Johnson. So it all works out.

I SIT UP in my chair and look around to save myself from falling asleep (for the third time in the last fifteen minutes). Everyone around me is writing furiously and punching numbers into their calculators with even more vigor, if that is indeed possible.

Assholes.

I look down at my paper perplexedly.

Answer 5 of the following 10 short answer questions.

I have answered two of these, and am having trouble identifying another three for which I might be able to come up with a legitimate guess.

3. What is a Bermuda Option and how does it work?

"All-inclusive four-star hotel" is the only answer I can muster, so I write it down. Maybe I'll get points in the humor category. Clearly I did not cover the chapter that dealt with the tropics in *The Wonderful World of Finance*.

I check my watch: forty-five minutes left.

I turn the test over.

Answer 2 of the following 4 mathematical questions.
Show all of your work.

Ugh. This section coming from the man who wrote *Irrational Exuberance*. A condition I am not struck by today.

As the minutes tick by, I struggle through the test, answering a total of four questions.

So much for attempting to put something useful in my head.

I have already resigned myself to the fact that all signs point to failure. Which at Yale, given the grading curve, will probably translate into a B-minus.

Fitting, as I am currently scoring a B-minus in life.

The hours after I hand in my test are spent in a crazed state of madness as I rush to pack and write a paper analyzing the theme of religion in Alice Walker's *The Color Purple,* something that I can actually posit interesting ideas about. Of course in typical fashion, I manage to forget to buy beer—the only Harvard/Yale task assigned to me by Cara, the chief organizer of our Harvard/Yale endeavor. She happens to take her job *very* seriously. She's from Texas, and they treat their football (and their guns) with great reverence. With such reverence, in fact, that Cara came up with the brilliant idea to rent an RV for the occasion.

"It's our last Harvard/Yale *at Harvard,*" she insisted as I questioned why exactly we are each paying $200 to make the three-hour trip from New Haven to Cambridge. Though admittedly I do like the idea of an onboard bathroom and a built-in kegerator. Not to mention the fact that I am the only person in the history of my entire family ever to ride in an RV.

Our plan is to park rogue-style in Harvard Yard for the next two days, hoping—nay, praying—not to get arrested and have our rented RV towed. Which would inevitably result in walking to Southie to retrieve it for some ghastly price from a man named Vinnie with an eye patch and four teeth.

Okay, fine, that's my own personal nightmare.

It is this scene that I am replaying in my mind to my great amusement as I run to Old Campus to meet my friends outside of Phelps Gate and finally get on the road (a traditional half hour behind schedule).

I arrive, breathless and exhausted. Thankfully I am a New York City kid and hence carry a Metrocard in lieu of a driver's license; thus I will not be charged with the task of navigating this monstrosity of a vehicle through the madness of rush-hour traffic. I instead will be sure to spend my RV experience funneling beers with Hot Rob and Activist Adam (in the most ladylike way possible), and perhaps catching up on sleep before the famous Harvard pub crawl that will take place tonight.

"Hi, guys!" I exclaim, brimming with excitement. Harvard/Yale is my favorite time of year. It's a giant reunion and a great relief from midterm madness.

Cara is standing in front of the RV, her hands planted firmly on her hips, squinting in the sun. She is wearing a T-shirt that reads:

THE Y GAME:
HARVARD SUCKS
AND
PRINCETON DOESN'T MATTER

She looks at me sternly. "Number one, you are late. Number two, where is your assignment?"

I feign a lack of knowledge. "What do you mean?" I ask, opening my eyes wide à la Veronica. I think I'm doing a very good job.

"You know what I'm talking about," she growls at me, pulling two thirty-packs of Natural Light from the RV. "I knew you'd forget, so I got some myself."

Natural Light—neither natural nor very light; discuss amongst yourselves.

"Thanks, Cara," I say, genuinely grateful. It ain't Harvard/Yale without copious amounts of cheap beer.

The whole eclectic gang has gathered. Bonnie, the designated driver, is currently studying a map, trying to figure out the easiest and *safest* way of getting to Cambridge. Activist Adam and Hot Rob have gotten hold of Harvard's face book and are scanning it for girls to target this weekend while heckling Bonnie into figuring out the *fastest* route possible. Veronica is hunched over the football program hoping to hook up with (in weight) one thousand pounds of man this weekend. That would amount to about 4.62 football players.

Ambitious but doable.

Crystal is leaning against the van wearing a great pair of distressed Diesel jeans and closely studying this week's *New Yorker*. He is currently engrossed in the issue's fiction piece. He is forever submitting short stories to this magazine, only to be rejected, week in and week out. Luckily, when it comes to his writing, he has nerves of steel.

"Is it any good this week?" I call to him.

"Not as good as the one I sent in," he says, shaking his head and returning to the story.

Cara, the party Nazi, is on board the RV, equipped with a checklist sorted into sections: food, drink, maps . . . the whole nine yards. Once she is satisfied that everyone and everything is present, she lets out a howl. "This is going to rock!" she exclaims.

Toad's Freshman Peter, looking thrilled to be alive, grins widely. He broke up with his girlfriend last week and Cara snapped him up faster than Manolos on the clearance rack.

"Hold your horses there, Football Barbie," I remark dryly.

Peter laughs as if it's the funniest thing he's ever heard.

Cara shoots him the look of death and he chokes off the laughter.

Well trained after only a week—you gotta hand it to her.

Lisa, wearing dramatic eye makeup and smoking a cigarette, is pacing and talking absentmindedly on her cell phone. She tosses her long dark hair over her shoulder and sips on a Zima hidden in a paper bag.

Zima? Lisa is so confusing sometimes.

"I'll miss you, too, darling," she whispers into the phone and then rolls her eyes.

"Who's that?" I ask.

"Stuart," she mouths back.

"Ah, yes."

"All right, people!" Cara calls out, clapping her hands together. "Let's get in this RV and get going!"

"Shhh!" Lisa hisses. "I'm on the phone with Harry."

Harry? I thought she was on the phone with Stuart.

We all pile into the RV, excited to get the weekend off to a boisterous start.

As Bonnie pulls onto the highway, with her hands on the wheel at ten and two, I am overcome with a warm, fuzzy feeling. It feels as if it's the first time I've sat still all week, not plagued by a single responsibility and surrounded by the people I love. As clichéd as it sounds, few things are better in life than to be among good friends. And one of those few things is to be among good friends about to head into three days of self-induced oblivion.

"So y'all will never guess what I heard," Cara announces to the group, jolting me out of my thoughts.

"Beer?" Hot Rob asks, directing the question at no one in particular as he opens the on-deck fridge.

"What would you do if you knew that that beer was bottled in Colombian sweatshops employing people who work fourteen-hour days with no bathroom breaks, and hardly any pay, only to profit heartless imperialists and multinational corporations? And that's not to mention the pollution generated by those plants." Activist Adam's voice trails off.

Hot Rob looks at him, annoyed. "Do you want a beer?" he asks again.

"Yeah, I'll take one," Adam replies, reaching out.

Bonnie hears the two of them crack their beers and glances at them menacingly in the rearview mirror. "If you are even *thinking* of drinking those in here, I will pull this car over and let you out right here, on the side of the highway."

Veronica looks up from the mirror she is holding, her lipstick midway to her lips. "Humph," she snorts unappreciatively. "Are you always such a loser, darling?"

Bonnie, looking very displeased, doesn't answer, but mutters something barely audible under her breath.

Adam and Rob burst out laughing.

In retaliation, Bonnie pulls onto the shoulder of the road and brings the RV to a screeching halt.

She crosses her arms over her chest smugly and turns to look at the two of them. Bonnie means business.

Cara, annoyed that no one is paying attention to her and that her plans of arriving at Harvard at 8:05 P.M. on the dot may be foiled by her one and only designated driver, pipes up.

"Bonnie, get back on the road," she says sternly, quickly adding, "open containers of alcohol are allowed in RVs."

Bonnie eyes her suspiciously.

"I looked it up," Cara says, lying through her teeth.

"Fine," Bonnie replies grudgingly.

"Now," Cara says, satisfied that she's had her way and the caravan is moving again, "y'all will *never* guess what I heard."

"What, honey?" Freshman Peter replies hopefully, playing with a dark curl that rests on her bronzed shoulder.

Cara is a fan of the fake-and-bake technique. She is always either beach-babe bronze or a funny color of orange, depending on when her last session was.

She looks at Freshman Peter as if he's transparent.

"What did you hear?" I ask, happy to amuse her.

"Y'all will *not* believe who is a *lesbian*." She enunciates the word *lesbian* with so much emphasis it sounds like *lays-be-an*.

"Who?" I reply.

"You say lesbian as if it's a disease," Lisa remarks.

"Well, I didn't mean it in a bad way. It's just shocking."

"Spit it out already," Veronica butts in.

"Julie Cooper," Cara announces dramatically.

"Who is Julie Cooper?" Freshman Peter asks.

"You don't know her," Cara says, brushing him off and looking at the rest of us expectantly.

"Awesome!" Hot Rob exclaims.

I look at him oddly.

"I hooked up with her freshman year," he explains, "and sophomore year, for that matter. I can check that one off my list," he says in Adam's direction.

"Check what off your list?" I ask.

"Hooked up with a lesbian."

"What list is this?"

"The 'things that might be fun to do before I graduate from college' list," he answers matter-of-factly.

"Hook up with a lesbian is an item on that list?"

"Sure, why the hell not."

"Cara," I say, turning toward her, "Julie Cooper is not a lesbian."

"Yeah, she is. She's a *lipstick* lesbian."

"How did you find this out?"

"Yes," Lisa says, nodding, "where did you procure this information?"

"Well, remember how she used to date Billy Dunne?"

"Uh-huh," we all say in unison (except Freshman Peter).

"So I'm taking that class 'Popularity' with him."

"Wait," I say, interrupting her, "you're taking a class called 'Popularity'?"

"Yes," Cara says, "*everyone's* taking it. It's very interesting. It's about what qualities make people popular."

"Uh, okay," I reply doubtfully.

"Well, Billy and I sit next to each other, so we talk. On Tuesday, Billy came to class looking very distraught, and I was trying to console him."

"Of course," Lisa says, nodding emphatically.

"He told me that Julie is a lesbian! She had just come out to him the week before. He's upset because he thinks it's his fault."

"Billy didn't make Julie a lesbian. That is just stupid," I say. "How can he possibly think that?"

"Well, he *did* break up with her. It makes sense that he feels bad."

"Breaking up with someone can't make them a lesbian," I reply.

"Maybe the sex was bad," Veronica pipes up, "so she thought it might be better with a woman."

"I personally think Billy would be very good in bed," Cara says.

Freshman Peter gives her a dirty look and scoots over to the corner to sulk.

"Who cares?" Veronica pipes up. "So Julie's a lesbian, that's just less competition for us."

"I care," Bonnie calls from the front seat. "I think Julie is really cool. And good for her for having the guts to come out."

"Good for her?" Crystal asks. "*Everyone* at Yale is gay."

"Everyone *you* know at Yale is gay," I remind him.

"Not true!" he shoots back. "You know what they say: 'One in four, maybe more; one in two, it might be you!' "

"Or Julie Cooper," I reply with a laugh.

"*Anyways*," Cara says, "I just thought it was good gossip."

"Can we change the subject?" Lisa remarks.

Adam, who has remained relatively quiet the entire time (very unlike him), quickly agrees. "Yes! This is frivolous. Does anyone want to go to an environmental rally when we get to Harvard?"

No one answers.

Lisa reaches into the large Dior weekend bag sitting at her feet and rummages around. When she sits back up, she has pulled out some weed and rolling papers and begins assembling a joint on the table in front of her.

I pray that Bonnie doesn't turn around and see her, because she will freak out. Pot-smoking is *definitely* not legal inside *or* outside an RV.

Lisa, reading my mind, says mischievously, "That's what the bathroom is for."

Adam scoots over to sit next to her to ask if he too can join in the festivities. He is in love with Lisa—has been since freshman year. Lisa, for her part, thinks that Activist Adam is—and I quote—"pretentious as fuck."

She might not be wrong, but the kid has a good heart and is not a member of the faculty. For any other girl that would work in his favor, but with Lisa, things aren't quite so simple.

"So, Lisa," he begins nervously, "I was reading John Rawls's *A Theory of Justice*, and I thought it would be interesting to get your thoughts on it."

"You read?" Lisa asks.

Adam looks at her, not quite knowing what to say. Being as suave as he is, he decides on "Well, yes, of course."

"That's nice," she answers politely.

"I know how much you love philosophy," he begins.

Lisa glances up at me and shoots me a look that says, "If he knows about Harry and Stuart, I will *crucify* you."

I shake my head no, indicating that I kept my word and my mouth shut.

"So anyway," Adam goes on, oblivious to our exchange, "I was wondering what you thought about that whole thing he's got going on about the veil of ignorance. I think it's rad."

"Rad? *You* are a veil of ignorance," Lisa replies, turning away from him. "Now let me go smoke my pot."

"Pot? Pot?" Bonnie shrieks from the front seat. "There will be none of that in this RV. None!"

"Okay, okay. I'm sorry," Lisa says quickly, kicking herself for having blown her own cover.

Luckily, unlike Veronica, she genuinely appreciates Bonnie. "I need to make a phone call," she declares. She grabs her cell phone, slips the joint in her bra, and turns to me. "Chloe, come help me dial the numbers."

"Okay," I say eagerly, and the two of us cram ourselves into the minuscule bathroom and rekindle a long-standing Harvard/Yale tradition.

"Remember freshman year?" Lisa asks as she puts the joint in her mouth and lights it.

"Oh my God, it's a miracle that I do remember it."

"Behind the Beta Theta Pi tailgate, we had to pee so badly . . ." She dissolves into giggles.

"We were so drunk," I add, shaking my head. "All I wanted to do was eat a hamburger."

"Yes! Yes!" she exclaims. "It was barely noon!"

"And of course, all you wanted to do was smoke pot."

"There you were, squatted on the ground with a joint in your mouth, pants around your ankles, practically in plain view of the entire crowd, while I had a hot dog in one hand and a Bloody Mary in the other . . ."

"Because we never did find that hamburger, huh?"

"Nope. Shameful, too. For a tailgate, there should have been plenty! But of course, by noon they were all gone."

"And we had lost *everyone.*"

"But it was so funny."

"Especially," Lisa says, gasping for air between laughs and puffs, "when Josh caught the two of us, practically peeing on the Beta U-Haul."

"Oh, Jesus. He was so mad."

"That's the first time you two met, right?"

"Yup. I think I fell in love with him right then and there," I say wistfully.

Lisa nods and eyes me, gauging my reaction.

"You never pulled your pants up from then on, huh?" she jokes.

"Shut up!"

"Good times," she says, laughing.

All of a sudden Cara pulls the door open and a puff of smoke billows out of the bathroom. "How *dare* the two of you have fun without us?" she asks.

"This is anything but fun," Lisa says seriously.

I nod in agreement. "Not fun," I say, "not fun at all."

Bonnie, smelling what Mrs. Johnson would call reefer, yells back to us, "Put that out right now! I am going to *kill* all of you!"

"She is going to panic if we don't," I whisper to the two of them.

"Fine, fine," Lisa says, and dumps the joint in the sink.

Cara, Lisa, and I move up to the front, where Bon Jovi's "Livin' on a Prayer" is blaring from the speakers. Even Bonnie begins singing along.

I WAKE UP at 8:3o a.m. the next morning with Cara standing over me.

"Up. Wake up. Tailgate time. Now."

I rub my eyes groggily.

"Are we arrested yet?"

"Nope," she replies happily. "One criminal-record-free night spent in an RV in Harvard Yard down. One to go."

"Wonderful," I reply, with genuine joy in my voice. "I need a shower."

"This is a tailgate. No time for showers."

"But all the cute recent alums are going to be there. I want to be pretty," I whine.

"They will be drunk. You don't need to be pretty."

"You're so pretty, babe," Freshman Peter says adoringly from across the van.

Cara looks up at him and smiles sweetly. "This is not going to work out," she says.

"What?" The poor kid looks like he was just nailed by a linebacker, and not in the way in which Veronica wants to be nailed by a linebacker.

"You and me," she says sternly, "not working."

"Huh?"

"Are you deaf? I'm breaking up with you."

"With who?"

"With *you*."

"Why?" he asks innocently.

"You're much too nice. I just can't deal with it," she replies.

The last time a boy was too nice to me was definitely in the first grade. Carl Borinksi. He gave me half of his graham cracker during snack time and let me into the boys' fort at recess. I got tired of him and left him for a big man on campus—Ricky Stevens, who never gave me any cookies, but did give me lice.

I hope Cara doesn't get lice.

"Too nice?" the poor kid asks, definitely confused.

"Yes," Cara hisses. Hit with a fleeting moment of guilt, she adds, "You can stay with us for the rest of the weekend, but then it's over. I'm just warning you."

Freshman Peter looks like he's going to cry. The mere sight of him breaks my heart.

I sit up in my makeshift bed and look around.

Lisa is on her cell phone again, while Bonnie has just returned from a morning run.

Crystal is filing his nails.

Hot Rob and Activist Adam are nowhere to be found, as they definitely got lucky last night.

Humph, I want to get lucky. A pox on both their houses!

Suddenly the RV door swings open.

I lie back down, convinced it is law enforcement officials. Maybe they won't see me.

Alas, it is Veronica, dressed to the nines from the night before. Magically, her mascara is not even smudged.

I make a mental note to ask her about that later.

She rips her four-inch black pumps off her feet and hurls them at the wall, narrowly missing both Bonnie and Cara, who duck to avoid her wrath.

"I am *done* with men!" she exclaims, tossing her hair over her shoulder. "DONE!"

She looks at us all expectantly, waiting to be pumped for further details.

"Whoa. Hold up there, Sister Sledge," I say, annoyed. I wanted to get a little more sleep before the debauchery begins. Besides, the mere suggestion that Veronica is actually done with men is laughable.

Bonnie and Cara roll their eyes at each other. Bonnie has a limited tolerance for Veronica's antics, and Cara believes that the spotlight belongs to her alone. It's called the Cara Show, and it's on every channel 24/7.

Veronica shoots the two of them the look of death and waits for me to respond.

"So," I say expectantly, "what happened?"

"So I'm fucking this Harvard guy, right?"

"Could you *be* any more crass?" Bonnie asks.

"Soooo . . ." Veronica continues, ignoring her. "I met what I thought was Mr. Right last night. Also known as Ziad," she adds.

"Ziad?"

"Uh-huh. He just saunters up to me at John Harvard's, you know that bar on Duncester Street?"

I rub my eyes, trying to think. "Oh, yeah, I had my eighth and ninth beers there last night."

No wonder I suddenly feel a little under the weather.

"That's nice," Veronica says without interest. "So I was trying to order a drink, and he was standing next to me, staring down my shirt the entire time," she continues.

"Lovely."

"And then he motions to the bartender and says, 'Get this lady whatever she wants, on me.' "

"And you said?"

"Well, I had no idea what he wanted from me," she says innocently.

"No idea, huh?"

"Well maybe a smidgen of an idea," she concedes. "I decided to ignore him, take my drink, and be on my way. He really wasn't that cute."

"Okay."

"And I was sticking to that plan, when he said the absolute funniest thing I'd *ever* heard. He just looked at me and said, 'Fat penguin.'"

"That is not funny."

"And I said, 'What?' And he repeated himself. So I asked what he meant again."

"Okay," I say, beginning to tire of the story.

"And he said, 'I just wanted to say something to break the ice.'"

We look at her blankly.

"Get it?" she says excitedly. "Fat penguin. Break the ice."

No one laughs.

"You slept with this dude?" I ask her.

"I thought it was funny," she replies indignantly.

Bonnie snorts loudly. "You sleep with everything that's funny?"

"What's wrong with that?" Veronica replies angrily. "At least *I* get laid," she says, looking Bonnie up and down.

"So then what happened?" I interject yet again.

"Anyway, so I decided I was going to use the bathroom at John Harvard's before the next stop on the pub crawl. Ziad said he would walk me and wait for me."

"That's nice of him," I say encouragingly. I have a sneaking suspicion I know where this story is going.

"So we get to right outside the women's restroom, and all of a sudden he grabs my wrist, just as I'm about to go inside. And then he throws me against the wall, with my hand over my head, and kisses me."

"In the middle of the bar?" Bonnie asks, horrified.

"That's hot," Cara concedes.

"Isn't it, though." Veronica sighs.

"Then what?" I ask, intrigued. This is getting good.

"Well, then I did the most obvious thing to do."

"Which is what?"

"I fucked him in the bathroom."

Bonnie chokes on her orange juice. Her eyes nearly pop out of her head.

"So why is it you hate men now?" I ask, confused.

"It was the worst lay I've ever had," she replies stonily.

"Well, technically it wasn't a lay," Cara interjects, "as there was more standing up than lying down."

"When did I say that?" Veronica replies smartly.

Gross.

"Wait, that's what you said about the last four guys you've been with," I say.

"I *know*," she replies, "the male species is doomed. I mean, how hard is it to get someone off? Really. Let's be honest here."

"Women are harder than men," I begin slowly.

"I don't fucking care who's harder than whom, if he's going to make a big show of buying me a drink and then pressing me up against the wall, he should know what he's doing."

"The first time with someone is never that good," I say.

"Well, if the first time isn't good, why would there ever *be* a next time?" Veronica asks pointedly.

I have no answer.

"So what did you do?" Bonnie asks, looking like someone who has driven past a car accident. She wants to look but knows that it's wrong.

"I faked it."

I stare at Veronica, shocked. She fakes a lot of things—nails, boobs, purses—but orgasms? This is a first.

"I know," she says, meeting my gaze, "I couldn't believe it either, but I just did it. It was as if I lost control of my body."

"You?" I ask, shocked. "You are the no-fake queen. The valid vixen. The honest ho."

"I know!" she exclaims. "But I got so fed up. So angry, I just couldn't take it anymore. And I felt bad for him. He was working so hard and had this oddly hopeful look on his face, so I just did it."

"In the bathroom, huh?"

"Yup."

"Were you loud?"

"Loud enough."

"What does that mean?"

"Well, loud enough to attract the second guy I faked it with last night."

"Okay, that's enough," Bonnie exclaims. "I can't take it anymore. We have a tailgate to go to, and I might be nauseous if I hear any more of this story."

"I'm kind of intrigued," I admit.

Now it's Bonnie's turn to kick me.

OTHER THAN THE fact that it is cold enough to freeze the devil's balls, it's a gorgeous day for Harvard/Yale.

Lisa and I, as tradition dictates, are making our way through the tailgates, greeting old friends and lovers.

We began about three hours ago, when it was really freezing, but at this point, we have ingested enough coffee and Frangelico to enable us not to feel anything at all.

The two of us are standing in the middle of a huge field outside of Harvard Stadium fenced in by U-Hauls filled with kegs, cheap vodka, and scrawny boys, proclaiming their various allegiances: TD. Silliman. Saybrook. Trumbull. SAE. Sig Ep. Beta. This list goes on and on. On top of every U-Haul, in typical tailgate fashion, sit the drunkest kids of the castle shouting to their friends down below to come on up. The last time

I attempted to climb a U-Haul was last year's Harvard/Yale. It's safe to say that the result was not pretty. But then again, if you must know the details, I slipped on spilt beer halfway up and slid all the way down the hood of the U-Haul, dragging along with me the poor (and very cute) boy who was trying to hoist me up. We landed in a pile of mud, which drew a crowd that began rousing chants of "Mud wrestling!" I narrowly escaped the madness, managed to ruin a great blow (dry) job and a pair of jeans, and spilled beer down the front of my shirt.

I look up ahead to the Beta tailgate and squint in the blinding sun. A rousing game of beer pong is taking place. Two teams face off on opposite sides of the table, aiming to sink their ping-pong ball into the opposing team's cups filled with beer. Pledges versus brothers. The brothers are kicking ass. They have about eighteen years of combined drinking experience over the poor freshmen, one of whom is having an inordinate amount of trouble standing upright.

I make a mental note to stop by later in the day. I will have you know that I have quite the aim when it comes to beer pong.

Lisa is next to me smoking a cigarette and taking sips of her seventh coffee/Frangelico combo.

She is looking oddly in place in an oversized Yale sweatshirt and her fur-lined boots.

"I need to pee," she comments.

"The Porta Potties are that way," I say, pointing to the massive lines that have formed about fifty feet ahead of us.

Nothing gives the bladder a good workout like three liters of beer on an empty stomach.

Which reminds me, I'm hungry.

"I will not use those," Lisa says adamantly. "They are perhaps the most disgusting invention in the history of the world."

"Worse than nipple clamps?" I ask, teasing her.

"What?"

"Nothing."

She looks at me strangely.

"Hold it, then. I am not peeing behind a tailgate again. It was mortifying enough the first time around."

"How about on that Jag," she says, pointing to some alumni's ridiculously expensive car. The license plate reads YALE 92. In other words, "Hello, I made a truckload of money during the Internet boom. And I have hair plugs that cost $3,000 a pop. What's your name?"

"How about not?" I reply.

"Chloe," she says, looking at me very seriously, "have I taught you nothing?"

"What?"

"If you are going to urinate, do it in style, my dear."

"Shut up."

At that moment Cara runs by the two of us with Freshman Peter in tow.

"This schmuck keeps following me," she hisses at us.

Lisa sticks her foot out and poor Peter trips while Cara takes off.

Are we in middle school? I help the kid to his feet, knowing the feeling all too well. "Are you all right?" I ask him.

"I don't feel so good," he replies.

Oh, shit. Little Peter here looks like he's got a big date with the porcelain goddess.

"I think I'm going to puke," he continues, his face turning a ghastly shade of white.

"Not on these boots, you aren't," Lisa says unsympathetically.

"Come on," I say, leading him to a somewhat empty area and handing him a bottle of water from my purse.

On my third year of this momentous drink-all-day day, I have learned that even more key than alcohol is a healthy supply of H_2O.

Lisa tugs on my sleeve, taking my attention away from Peter. "I want to do a keg stand."

"What?"

"I want to do a keg stand," she repeats loudly.

"Why?"

"Because they look fun."

"I agree," I say. "Drinking upside down looks fun."

"Let's go!" she says, running ahead.

I follow her. I don't think I'm in any shape to be running.

I check over my shoulder to make sure Peter is all right. He's tasting his breakfast (and lunch) all over again.

Ugh.

We continue through the crowd, not wanting to abandon our mission.

"Oooh!" I exclaim, "there's Lucy Telman" (heiress to the Aunt Jemima fortune, and a major bitch).

"Repulsive," Lisa comments. "And look, she's placing her tits atop Marcus Mosin. We should save him. He is certainly the most gallant gentleman I know."

"I know, he is so cute," I say wistfully.

"She, on the other hand—not so cute."

"Really? You think so? I used to think she was pretty."

"Butter face," Lisa diagnoses.

"Butter face?" I ask.

"Yes, you know. She's got a good body, but her face . . . where have you been, sex columnist?"

"I don't know, but I'm definitely storing that for future reference."

"You should."

We look at each other and burst out laughing.

Finally we come across Hot Rob and Activist Adam pumping overflowing cups of beer at the TD tailgate.

"Hello, friends," Lisa says cordially. "We would like to partake in a keg stand, if you don't mind."

Adam has his arm around a girl who looks as if she hasn't show-
ered since April. At the sight of Lisa, he pulls it away quickly and nods
eagerly.

"Sure," Rob says, "who's first?"

I look at Lisa.

"Fine," she says, "I will be bold. I will be a pioneer."

"Okay, Mayflower," Adam says lovingly, "get over here."

Lisa grabs the sides of the keg, allowing the boy to lift her legs
into the air so that she can put her mouth on the keg's pump.

She drinks beer upside down for a respectable twelve seconds
before shaking her head to indicate that she wants to be let down.
As soon as her feet hit the ground, she stumbles around and lets out a
very un-Lisa-like whoop.

"I'm going to call Starry!" she yells to me.

"Who?"

"Stuart and Harry. Starry."

"Okay! Meet me back here!"

"I will. May the force be with you!" she calls as she lurches away.

"All right, Chlo," Hot Rob says with a wink, "your turn."

"I'm terrible at this," I protest. "I have trouble drinking right side
up. Forget upside down."

"Too late!" he says mischievously while Activist Adam grabs my
hands and puts them behind my back.

I try squirming away, but to no avail. Hot Rob grabs my feet.

"Get up there, honey!" he yells. "There's no turning back!"

"Okay, okay!" I shriek, laughing. "Chill out, I'll do it!"

The two of them lift me up in the air, and like Lisa, I let them
pump beer into my mouth like gas into a '76 Chevy.

I survey the tailgate from a drastically different angle than before. Interesting.

Lucy Telman looks even worse upside down.

I squint in the sun through the crowd. About a hundred feet away, I spot Veronica. She is laughing hard and leaning close to someone, probably hoping for better luck.

That girl doesn't quit. She never ceases to amaze me.

The guy turns toward me and I see the person she's with. It's Josh. Josh.

No.

I begin waving my hands in the air. Beer starts squirting out of my nose.

"Whoa, whoa," Hot Rob says sympathetically, "let's get you down."

He and Activist Adam flip me over and hoist me down from my upside-down position.

"Are you all right?" Rob asks, concerned.

If I so much as open my mouth to answer, I will cry.

Josh is not just anyone. He is the ex. THE EX. The most major ex of my life.

The one that graduated and then got away. Veronica knows that.

Scratch that—the one that ran away kicking and screaming.

I nod in Activist Adam's general direction and begin walking away. I hate Veronica. I hate her, I hate her, I hate her. Of all the guys here, she chooses Josh to seduce.

My Josh.

"Chloe! Chloe!" Rob and Adam call after me, but I continue walking quickly, hoping to lose them. I am headed in the direction of Veronica and Josh, hoping to kill the two of them. Damn, there are *way* too many witnesses around. I'll have to drag them off to a more secluded area if this is going to work.

I hold back the tears that he automatically evokes and try to tell myself to remain calm.

I'm not doing a very good job.

I breathe in and out and take another swig of my Frangelico and realize how drunk I am. Confrontation will not be pretty.

Stay calm, I tell myself. She's probably just talking to him. I'm sure it's innocent. I push through the crowd.

"Chloe! Chloe!" I hear my name being called from atop a U-Haul. No fucking way my ass is getting up there.

I ignore the shouts. I need to find someplace to be alone. That's like finding a nun at a strip club.

All I need is a cigarette. A cigarette will make me feel better. If I just calm down and pollute my lungs, I can think this over. Yes, yes. That's what I'll do.

I see the Living Water (a Christian singing group) tailgate in the distance and head toward it. It's off to the side, and at the moment sparsely populated. No one is interested in hot tea and pamphlets about Jesus today.

I slump down on one side of it and pull out my lighter.

As I concentrate on lighting my cigarette, I hear someone calling my name again.

Fuck, I hope it's not Adam or Rob. I'm in no mood to explain my hysteria to them.

I look up. It's Crystal.

Hallelujah.

"What's wrong, Chlo?" he asks, concerned.

"Josh," I say simply.

"Oh, shit," he says. "What happened? Did you talk to him?"

"No, I don't have the nerve for that. He was talking to Veronica."

"Ugh," Crystal says, disgusted. "She's such a ho. I was wondering what you were doing all the way over here. I thought maybe you had become a Jew for Jesus."

I laugh.

"Veronica's my friend. I shouldn't be so upset."

"And she shouldn't be so proud of being a ho," he jokes.

"I'm sure it was nothing," I say, trying to reassure myself. "I'm sure she's just talking to him—you know, catching up."

"Yeah, that's definitely it." Crystal nods reassuringly.

"Exes," I say quietly.

"Exes," he repeats.

We sit in silence for a moment, each mentally flipping through our scrapbooks of heartbreak. I hand him my cigarette and he takes a drag quietly.

"Wanna go into the game?" he asks. "We're winning four to zero."

"Crystal, it's impossible to score a four in football."

"Really?" he replies.

"Yes."

"Okay, so I made it up."

"I figured."

Crystal is not one to be informed about football. Especially not Yale football. He has an aversion to athletes, which stems from several high school traumas.

"How about we go in and see which team collectively has better asses, Harvard or us?"

"Okay," I concede. "I knew you'd be able to appreciate sports one day."

"Shall we?" Crystal asks, offering me his arm.

"We shall."

"And don't worry about Veronica," he says, whispering in my ear. "She's got nothin' compared to you."

"Shh, bite your tongue. I just overreacted. It's my fault. She's my friend."

"Do you have a penis?"

"No."

"She's not your friend."

Hmm.

We are quiet again as he lets me ponder his snide comment.

"Vanilla Stoli and Diet Coke?" Crystal says, breaking the silence and reaching inside his jacket to hand me a pretty silver flask.

"Sure," I reply, eager to drink Veronica out of my head.

We link arms and join the crowd again, where we round up Lisa and head into Harvard Stadium.

Halftime is over and the crowd is finding their seats again.

I think that this will be the first Harvard/Yale when I actually make it into the game. Point for me.

The line to get back in the stadium is long, and people are pushing. Why push in a line? It reminds me of the assholes that press the elevator button more than once. As if that's going to hurry the process up.

Crystal raises his voice. "Gay man coming through!"

Lisa and I giggle.

"What the hell are you doing?" she says.

"I'm probably the only one!" he says. "I should get special privileges."

"Make way for the 'mo!" he yells louder.

A group of preppy guys (très Harvard-esque) in Nantucket Reds (sooo embarrassing) standing in front of us turn and give us dirty looks.

"Dontcha know any 'mos," Crystal asks obnoxiously.

One of them pipes up. "I know you," he says.

The voice sounds oddly familiar. I look up and meet the speaker's eyes.

Maxwell.

Terrific.

"Hey, Chloe." He smiles sweetly. "Wanna beer?" he asks, reaching into his jacket pocket and pulling out the remnants of a six-pack.

Heineken. Classy.

But I am too off-guard to muster a coherent response.

"You," I say instead.

His friends look at me as if I have a third nipple. On my forehead.

"Finish the sentence. You shave your balls," Lisa whispers in my ear. "Say it!" she encourages, itching for a good laugh.

For the sake of everyone involved, I decide to ignore her. "I mean, hey," I say, regaining composure.

"Enjoying the day?" he asks. "Haven't seen you around in a while. I've been missing you."

"Well, you've been making *your* presence felt," I say, giving him a sly smile. I'm so sneaky.

"I have?" he asks, looking confused.

"Yes," I say, smiling again, "you have. Besides," I continue, "if you miss me so much, you could always give me a call. I am, after all, quite lovable."

"Oh, yeah?" he asks.

"You should know," I say with confidence, pushing past his friends with Crystal and Lisa close behind me.

"Excuse me," I add, "we have a 'mo coming through."

"Well done!" Crystal exclaims when we get out of earshot.

We walk through the long tunnel and into the student section. I for one am feeling pretty damn good about myself. Perhaps this day isn't a total bust.

The crowd is on its feet. It's already the third quarter. We on the Yale side are a sea of blue, facing the crimson-covered opponents.

"Safety school! Safety school!" they yell at us in unison.

Yale quickly scores a touchdown and our crowd goes wild.

Melvin, who happens to be sitting in front of us, turns around. His wool hat is lopsided on his head and his cheeks are rosy from the cold. Wisps of unkempt curls peek out around his ears. I hate to admit it, but he actually looks sort of cute. In a Melvin kind of way.

"This is *awesome!*" he yells, a grin plastered on his face.

"Hi, Melvin," I yell over the noise, slightly comforted to see him. But only slightly.

"Did you think of something for the column?" he asks excitedly.

I think for a moment. "Why, yes, I did," I say. "Thanks for asking."

"What is it?" he asks.

"Faking orgasms!" I yell loudly.

The entire section I am seated in, which has quieted by now, turns and looks at me.

"What?" I ask, laughing. "There isn't a woman here who hasn't!"

"Damn straight!" a girl seated two rows down yells back.

"Sing it, sista!" another calls out.

Melvin, drunk and happy, spreads his arms and wraps them around me so unexpectedly and tightly that I nearly fall down.

"Melvin!" I squeal. "Get off me. Get off me right now!"

He grudgingly lets go. "I love you, Chloe."

Hey, at least someone heterosexual does.

Lisa and Crystal smile at me.

"Another drink is in order . . ." I whisper to them.

"I heard that!" Melvin says, feigning anger.

I stick my tongue out at him and turn my attention back to the game.

THE YALE DAILY NEWS

SEX AND THE (ELM) CITY
BY CHLOE CARRINGTON

More Than You Ever Wanted to Know About Fake Orgasms

We are going to Harvard this weekend. They want to throw the pigskin around with our boys so that they can be embarrassed in front of the masses—again. Imagine for just a moment (really, just a moment) that you are a Harvard fan. Let me set up a little scenario for you:

Your team faces a fourth-and-goal situation, down by 5 with a meager thirty seconds left in the game. The ball is snapped, and you're on your feet. This is going to be *amazing*. You're screaming at the top of your lungs as excitement builds. The quarterback sends a long, smooth pass to the end zone in the direction of your star receiver. He's open, without a single defender on him. The ball is sailing straight toward him; with outstretched arms, he waits in the end zone for his moment of glory. The ball's flight is interrupted as it grazes his fingertips and falls to the ground.

He's missed it. Game over and your team—Harvard—didn't score. You lose. You stop screaming. In fact, you're silent. You feign being a good sport, you smile at your Yale friends, congratulate them on their achievement (again), but deep down, you're disappointed. No matter how loud, how convincingly you cheered, you didn't get yours. This play has been run before, and you know that it has been completed. Others have scored, so why not you? The quarterback, the receiver, the offense, *someone* screwed up, but why today? And most important, why you?

This is exactly what faking an orgasm feels like.

Harvard and Yale are coming together this weekend, and the number of hookups per capita may very well soar as debauchery, tailgating, and DFEs take over campus. The number of orgasms faked this weekend will also soar. Tremendously.

Girls fake it all the time. Fake it in the morning, fake it in the evening, fake it in the afternoon. According to detailed research (me asking all of my friends), women return the punt less than half the times they play. But why? Convincing everyone in the room that you're wearing a diamond when in reality it's a cubic zirconia *is* fun, but it still doesn't beat a good, hard quality—rock. Knockoffs that say Fenbi are cheaper than the genuine, but let's be honest, if someone handed you a *real* baguette, would you turn it down? Settle for a Fucci over a Gucci? Frada over Prada? No, thanks. But some fakes may have to tide you over before the real thing falls into your lap.

Over dinner with my girlfriends a few nights ago, I broached the subject. After much discussion and debate, we reached the consensus that we've all been there, moaning and breathing and screaming à la Meg Ryan in *When Harry Met Sally,* like Elaine on *Seinfeld.* Some do it out of boredom, as fatigue and hunger creep in and he's nowhere near the end zone. Others fake because, let's face it, when the game clock is ticking, who has the time to map out a whole new play? My hallmate confessed, "If it's a random hookup, I don't have the time or the patience to coach these people, so I fake it."

If you have the time, you can fix the problem. That is exactly what preseason is for. Practice. Training. Coaching. Scrimmages. Players have natural talent, but often talent is not enough on its own. It needs to be cultivated. Drills are done over and over again until strength, endurance, and accuracy reach their threshold. I'm talking finger exercises, tongue strengthening, endurance training. Boys, try turning a light switch off and on with your tongue twenty times a day; grab your remote (the other remote) and see if you can press the power button a hundred times in one minute. And for God's sake, ask your girl what works. It's the $64,000 question.

Yet there is simply no time for this kind of hands-on training if the relationship is short-lived (like one night). Therefore, a fake is in order—for the good of the team, of course.

There is also the Good-hearted Fake. This is the sweetest

kind there is—we're talking Dwight Hall here. Sometimes players need to be benched, but their efforts are so valiant, so painstaking, that a charitable fake is necessary to avoid injuries of the ego. "Sometimes they're down there working so hard that it breaks my heart. I just give in and fake the best that I can," said one kindhearted friend of mine. She works at a soup kitchen three times a week and reads to lepers.

Some women find that faking gives them time to sit back, relax, and think a little. You know, ponder life's great questions. I call them the Overly Organized Orgasmers. Their fakes give them time to plan, list, and revise. Between a moan and an oh! Oh! OH!, she can map out her day. She's thinking, *If this ends by nine, I'll have time to write the rest of that paper, pluck my eyebrows, and maybe alphabetize my DVD collection.*

There's also the Materialist, who speculates to herself, *I wonder when those boots will go on sale.* "YES! YES! YES!" *They'll go great with that distressed denim jacket that I just bought from Urban Outfitters!*

There is also the Philosophical Orgasmer. Hint, men, these are the chicks who look mysteriously concerned while they're getting excited. They may even say "Uh-huh" and hesitantly nod their heads. Let me let you in on something: even if you've seen that in porno, it's not for real. They truly *are* baffled. It's hard to keep a smile on your face when you don't know what the hell is going on.

All of this information is probably rather discouraging, even demoralizing for many of my male readers, but fear not, boys, I have discovered something in my research that is unbelievable. It will give you hope to go on, continue to hook up with as much confidence as you once had. It is the so-good-that-I-start-believing-it-myself fake. As its name implies, this is the fake-it-till-you-make-it approach.

"You can psych yourself up for an orgasm; all it takes is a little effort, getting yourself into the right mind-set. The buildup to the big O involves lots of moaning and dirty talk, and then before you know it, you *mean* what you're saying, and the moans are real—and wow, you're on your way," said one lucky lady. By *lady,* I mean, of course, magician. She's literally pulling a bunny out of a damn hat. Even I was surprised at (and admittedly a little jealous of) this discovery.

The fake orgasm was far less popular (to say the least) among guys. During sit-ups at the gym, one studly friend divulged that the fake was his worst nightmare. Appalled that girls would resort to faking, he said, "Don't fake. Please don't. We'll try, try, and try again until we get it right." You gotta love the persistence, that determined look I saw in his eyes. (Call me, I'll give you his number.)

One overconfident dude told me that no one has *ever* faked with him. I inquired as to how he was so sure of this. He replied that he *always* asks the girls he's with if they, you know, had the big O, and the answer was always a firm yes.

Hmm.

Okay, champ, let's do a little critical thinking. If she's already gone to great lengths to fake it, you think that she'll ruin the job by blowing her own cover? Lying to your face is even easier than lying to your penis.

Another, shall I say, less sensitive individual said, "I don't care about *you.* It's a race—whoever gets their cookies first."

Nice. I have a feeling this gentleman has been beating his own eggs for quite a while now, so I want to know, how can you get cookies if no one is doing any baking?

The solutions to the faking problem are few and far between. The truth is, it just takes a little more for girls than it does for guys. Just remember that practice, practice, practice makes perfect. Or, for a quick and easy solution, come to the Game on Saturday. I've been told by numerous sources that you'll *never* have to fake it with the Yale defensive line. The men, the myths, the legends . . .

Go, Bulldogs! (I mean that for real.)

6

GOING HOME FOR THE holidays in college is simultaneously a curse and a blessing. You see, in college you begin to learn that your parents are mostly right about everything they have ever told you. You no longer hate them with the fervor you did in high school. Which is fine, except that now you are wrong more often than ever before. Also, going home for the holidays generally involves several unpleasant conversations about money (you spend too much of it) and boyfriends (you don't have one). Which then leads your parents to believe that you are an expensive lesbian. This is the way my Thanksgiving holiday generally begins.

Let me back up. First, a little background info on my parents. My father's name is Richard (Dick) Carrington. I've always wondered what type of people are named Richard and choose to go by Dick. I've reached the conclusion that it is people like my father.

He is a major Wasp. Tall and blond, square jaw, sweater vests, Jameson on the rocks. He went to Harvard, rowed crew, and is now a successful investment banker in the blah blah blah group at Blah, Blah & Company.

His favorite pastimes include being a Republican, sailing, and furiously guarding his emotions so as to never make a scene in public. Or in private, for that matter. Who can blame him? After all, he is married to my mother.

Channah.

Yes, you read correctly, my mother's name is Channah. And she's Jewish. But not just any kind of Jewish. She's Israeli. Most people don't quite comprehend what this entails because there are about 3 million Israelis on this planet and only they understand one another, but I will try to explain.

Israelis are loud and obnoxious and never stand in lines. They push at airports. They yell, but believe they are speaking at normal volume. They tell you exactly what they think, even if you never asked for their opinion. Deep down inside they are generous, kind, and funny, but I remind you, these qualities are *very* deep.

Channah is also beautiful. She has a head of thick, dark hair, and in her youth starred in low-budget shampoo commercials for her local Israeli hairdresser. She also has wide green eyes, full lips, and smooth olive skin. Since she turned forty (about ten years ago) she has been on a constant unsuccessful mission to shed fifteen pounds. My mother is the kind of woman who goes to the gym for three hours and then eats six bagels with low-fat cream cheese. Additionally, she has an abnormal affection for sequined hats. And Keds.

Don't get me started.

My parents are the oddest couple known to man, or at least to anyone who has ever met them. They themselves met at a New Year's party hosted by a mutual friend (how they ever managed to have a mutual friend is beyond me), where my father fell immediately in love and demonstrated this by ignoring Channah all night. Channah, for her part, asked the hostess loudly "Whaaat eeeees wrrrrrong weet dat men?" as she stuffed baked ziti into her mouth, thanking God for both her youth and her metabolism.

He called her two days later, and four months into the relation-ship, to the horror of their respective families, they were married at New York's City Hall—hands down the sketchiest place on earth to exchange vows.

My mother wore a white-sequined baseball cap.

Since that day, she has regretted marrying a "wesp" (Wasp to those of us who speak English) because my father refuses to duke it out with her. She picks fights and he clams up like Snuggles at a whorehouse.

Dissatisfied with their own marriage, my parents wish only the best for their kin—me. Thus, they are constantly trying to fix me up with guys that they think are "just my type." Apparently my type is se-verely socially retarded. Thanksgiving tends to be a wonderful time for fixing up. My father brings home the ugliest analyst on his floor (sometimes gay), who is always dressed in seersucker pants and named Chip or Trip. My mother, on the other hand, seeks out the nicest Jewish boy in the building, who more often than not goes to Columbia Law. She seats him right next to me at the Thanksgiving table and then encourages me not to eat anything and him to eat everything. Last Thanksgiving his name was Larry and he chewed like a ruminant.

It follows that I never end up with the gems my parents force on me. Instead, to make them both equally unhappy, I lead them to be-lieve that I am an expensive lesbian.

After my thrilling weekend at Harvard/Yale, which, by the way, ended with a near-death experience trying to pull the RV out of Har-vard Yard, I arrived home this morning exhausted and ready for a week of detox. This seems plausible, as I have only two remaining high school friends. The rest have managed to sleep with my ex-boyfriends, are in rehab, or have modified their personalities in col-lege to be less than compatible with my own.

I am greeted at the door of our apartment by my mother. She is suited up in her workout clothes and headed for the gym, her hair tucked under a cap with GYM! written in red sequins on the front, her feet outfitted in red Keds that coordinate perfectly with her red sweatsuit with black stripes.

"Chloeee!" she exclaims happily, wrapping her arms around me.

"Hi, Mom!" I reply, exceedingly glad to be home, and hoping she has cooked something delicious and is ready to give me liberties with her credit card.

"Let me loook et you," she says, holding me at arm's length.

Her face distorts slightly.

"What's wrong?"

"I see you hev a new look," she says, sounding disappointed.

"New look? What are you talking about? I dress the same as I always do."

"I see," she muses. "You er just fet."

"Fet?" I repeat.

"Yes. Fet."

My fifteen-pounds-overweight mother is calling me *fat*. This is not going to be a delicious Thanksgiving. When she gets into these modes, it's soy crackers and low-fat cheese with cucumber slices for all.

Thrilling.

When she finally clears out of the apartment, I breathe a sigh of relief and take my habitual place on our overstuffed leather couch, where I will probably remain immobilized for the next six days. In fact, I find myself in that very position at this moment, watching my fourth hour of MTV/CNN and contemplating why parents are around for the sole purpose of making you feel bad about your life.

Suddenly the sound of my cell phone jolts me out of my vegetative state.

I rush to get it, nearly tripping over my still-unpacked suitcase. I find the culprit at the very bottom of my purse (figures) and I don't recognize the flashing number on the screen.

I contemplate for a split second before deciding to answer. Perhaps it's a long-lost lover . . .

"Hello?"

"Hi, um, Chloe?" asks the deep, familiar male voice.

"Yes?" I say tentatively, unable to identify the speaker as yet.

"Hey! It's Josh."

"Josh?"

"Yeah, kid," he replies with a laugh. "You remember me, don't you? Or have you forgotten already?"

Forgotten? Hardly.

"No, no," I say nervously, "of course I haven't forgotten, how are you?" I add, regaining my composure.

"Mighty fiiine," he answers, with a trace of his southern drawl coming through. "And you, darlin'?"

"I'm just fine, thank you."

"Didn't see you at the game."

"It was a busy weekend," I say quickly.

"Of course. Saw your friend Veronica, though."

"Oh, really?"

"Yup. She's something else."

"You could say that."

"I just did," he replies, and I can almost see his smile through the phone.

"So to what do I owe this pleasure?"

"Getting down to business right away, huh? That's unlike you."

"Well, I've changed a bit since you've known me," I say a little defensively.

"No way."

"Way."

"Well, the reason for my call is that I was hoping to take you out to dinner."

I think I might pee on myself with excitement.

"*Moi?*"

"Yes. *Toi.*"

"Well, you should. Now that you are a rich and successful invest-ment banker, I wouldn't expect anything less."

"Rich and successful, huh?"

"That's what I hear."

"So is that a yes?"

"It's not a no. It all depends, of course, on where you're taking me."

"You always were a snob."

"I am *not* a snob."

"Not even a little?"

"Okay, fine. Maybe a little. But who says that's a bad thing?"

"No comment."

"So where are we going? If I decide to go, that is."

"Biltmore Room."

I pause, impressed, to say the least.

"Does that suit your tastes?"

Does one of the most romantic restaurants in the city suit my tastes? Um, yeah.

"It'll have to do. When?"

"How about tonight?"

Tonight? I can't be ready by tonight. We're talking manicure, pedicure, intense emotional preparation . . . maybe even a facial.

"I have plans."

"That's a lie."

"It is *not* a lie."

"Of course it's a lie. You just want me to think you have plans, but I'll bet if I hadn't called, you'd be plunked on that black leather couch in your parents' living room watching reality television all night."

Besides my parents, Josh has also been endowed with the magical ability to make me feel bad about my life.

"I don't watch reality television."

Another lie.

"How about eight tonight at the Biltmore Room."

"Only if you pay."

"Was that ever in question?"

"So you're not cheap anymore?"

Now it's his turn to be embarrassed. "No. And I never was," he says indignantly.

"Tee-hee."

"I'll see you at eight, then?"

"Yup."

"Don't be late," he warns.

"I will be."

"I know."

"Bye, Josh."

"Bye, Chlo."

When I hang up, I'm trembling. And confused. This phone call from Josh is out of left field. I can't possibly fathom what he wants from me.

The way I figure it, every girl has two types of exes in her life. There is the ex with whom you're still in love and hope that one day you will be reunited with by romantically running into him on a busy street in New York after years of not seeing each other.

In this scenario, you are just breaking up with another dude, only to discover that you and your ex are perfect for each other.

And you're Gwyneth Paltrow.

He's a dreamboat: yacht-owning and Armani-clad. Sweet, wonderful, kind, rich—sigh.

And then there's what I like to call the Funk-Master-Sketch-Ex. Funk Master is that dude in high school—in my case, Damien—who really screwed you over and left you an emotional wreck. Funk Master

Sketch also applies to the dudes (notice the plural) who screw you over in college. Funk Master Sketch has a way of reentering your life, whether it's in person or in the form of a bill from your psychiatrist.

With a name like Damien, I should have known he was destined to be trouble. But as usual, I was blinded by pecs and convenience. Damien happened to (happens to) live in my parents' building, and he is a Funk Master Sketch to the max.

First, he thinks telling you that you need to lose five pounds is a compliment that should be given daily.

It's not.

Second, he has this little back-hair problem (which I *swear* I discovered only after we started dating), and third, he thinks he's a porn star (also discovered after we started dating, which definitely exacerbated the back-hair thing). Debbi and Danni may be good teachers, but my opinion is, if you're not old enough to rent it, you're not old enough to do it.

I was sixteen. Enough said.

But I digress—back to Josh. He is a combination of the dreamboat and the Funk-Master-Sketch—always a little surprising.

I met Josh because I stalked him.

He was a senior when I was a freshman, and he caught my eye at Exotic Erotic. Actually, all of him caught my eye at Exotic Erotic. He was dressed as a computer and his ass was the screen. In short, he was wearing a box with the entire back part cut out of it and with holes for his arms, legs, and (very cute) head.

I, being the impressionable freshman that I was, thought he was hilarious, so I did what any other self-respecting girl would do.

I Googled him.

I found out that Josh played soccer, lived on 18 Elm Street, wore braces throughout high school (attended in Georgia), and had won a county-wide speech-writing contest in the sixth grade with a piece entitled "Fishing with My Grandfather."

I gave him points for being a family man and then made it my business to meet him.

Three months later, I did, as he caught Lisa and me peeing behind the Beta tailgate (the fraternity of which he was president) at Harvard/Yale, something we laughed about for months to come. When we got back from Thanksgiving that year, after a late night at Toad's, I committed the ultimate relationship mistake. We went home together. And then we slept together.

I went home the next day and cried, certain that the glorified relationship I had been having with him in my head was over. After all, I whined to Bonnie, what was he going to think of me?

Well, apparently he thought I was a good lay, because he called.

Again. And again. And again.

I was head over heels.

He took me to Sally's, the best pizza joint in New Haven. Miya's for sake bombing and sushi. We went to Ingall's Rink so I could see a hockey game for the very first time. To my glee, we made out on Old Campus, where my freshman friends walked by, jealous of me and my senior boyfriend. He took me to Rudy's, an exclusively senior hangout and the best dive bar this side of the Mississippi (his words, not mine), for beers and fries.

And three weeks before graduation, he broke up with me.

Post-Toad's.

I look down at my hands. They're still shaking after gripping the phone so tight that my knuckles turned white. I need to get a grip. I also need to figure out what I'm going to wear.

Why is he asking me to dinner? And why, after two years, do I still care so much? Has nothing changed?

FOUR HOURS LATER, I am standing in the middle of my room stark naked, surrounded by piles of clothes.

There are plenty of choices, since the two of us haven't been out to dinner in nearly two years, so no danger of repeating an outfit. But how do I dress to say "I don't care about you, but if you want to get back together, I will in a heartbeat?" I'm going for sexy nonchalance. Hmm. Something black and off the shoulder. I grab a cashmere sweater that's *Flashdance*-esque. This is a good start. Definitely with jeans. Although what jeans? I settle on light denim ones, frayed at the knees. These of course lift my ass so high you could serve a cheese platter on it. Top it off with heels, but not too high—something in the two-inch range.

Pleased with my relatively speedy decision-making, I slip into my thick chenille bathrobe and venture into the kitchen to satisfy the bottomless pit I like to call my stomach.

I stand in front of the fridge with the door open, grabbing a pickle here, fruit there. Oooh, and cheese, yum! My mother walks in.

"Hey, sweetie."

"Hi, Mom."

"Are you home for dinner?"

"Nope," I reply happily.

"Where are you going? You come home and leave. We never see you!" she complains.

"I have a date," I reply happily.

"Wit who?"

"Josh," I say casually.

"Jewish?" my mother asks. This is her first question, always.

"No, Mom. You know Josh. Josh from freshman year."

"Oh."

"Oh, what?"

"Notting."

"Mom!" I exclaim, exacerbated. She's thinking something annoying and it's only a matter of time before she tells me. I prefer sooner than later.

"I don't went to interfere."

"Since when don't you want to interfere?"

"Okay. Fine. I don't tink you should go wid heem."

"Why not?"

"Because he does not like you."

"How do you know that?"

"You don't go wid heem anymore. But you still like heem. To go on a date is not a goot idea."

"It's fine."

"Okay, fine, but don't cry to me."

"I won't."

"Eees he paying?"

"What kind of question is that?"

Like mother, like daughter.

"I want to know."

"I don't know."

"Is he peecking you up?"

"No. We're meeting at the restaurant."

She snorts.

"Mom!"

"He is not gentleman."

"Mom, he's perfectly nice. You liked him when we dated."

"Not Jewish," she says simply.

"Dad's not Jewish."

"Yes. And you see what happens wid heem."

"What?"

"Notting good," she says, smiling. She's happy deep down inside. She just likes to pretend that my father is a schlub, as she says. It makes things interesting.

She takes off her hat and shakes her hair out. It's not as long as it used to be when I was growing up, but it's still as thick and dark. She's famous for bragging that she has not a single white hair. Something that is bound to work in my favor some thirty years from now.

"So how's school?"

"It's good. I'm doing really well in my English classes. We just finished reading *The Color Purple*. I think I wrote a decent paper about it, too. But 'Financial Markets,' on the other hand, is not going so hot. You know—that class Dad wanted me to take to put something useful in my head?" I say, mimicking his booming voice.

"I pay thirty thousand dollars for you not to do well? Are you werking hard?"

"Of course I am!" I say, lying through my teeth. I gave up on "Financial Markets" on day two of the class.

"How is Bonnie? Does she hev boyfriend?"

"She's doing well. She's running a marathon in the spring, so she's training like a madwoman. And of course she's doing well at school and all of that. But no boyfriend. I hope she gets one soon. She needs to get laid."

"She needs whet?"

Oops.

"Nothing."

My mother gives me a disapproving look.

"Whet time you going wid Josh?"

"I'm meeting him at eight."

She checks her watch as I grab another pickle from the fridge.

"Come talk to me unteel you have to leave."

"Okay," I say happily. Despite or perhaps because of all her idiosyncrasies, my mother ranks among my favorite people in the world. She is charming and funny, and though our opinions differ on just about everything, I find myself becoming more and more like her every day. A secret I like to keep to myself. It would please her far too much to know that's the case.

I take two Diet Cokes out of the fridge and we make our way back into the living room, where I reclaim my spot on the black leather couch.

Another thing I forgot to mention is that my parents sort of don't know that I write "Sex and the (Elm) City." And by sort of I mean not at all. It's not such an easy thing to tell a parent. "Hi, Mom, not only do I have sex, but I also write about it. Aren't you glad that expensive Ivy League education is coming in handy?"

I think Channah would have a heart attack. Funny enough, despite her rabid boldness in every other area, my mother is a bit of a prude when it comes to sex. She tells me that you shouldn't even kiss people you aren't in love with.

Regardless, I've been dreading telling them the nasty truth for months now, but I feel as if I can't hide it anymore. Sometimes you just have to face the music and tell it like it is.

I look over at my mom. She has cracked the Diet Coke and is holding it in her lap, her head leaning back on the couch, probably thinking of all the things she has to do for Waspy Thanksgiving—which will certainly involve calling a caterer and possibly taking a Valium.

Conversing with Grandma Beppy (her mother-in-law) is a task attempted by few and conquered by fewer.

And I don't think my mother even knows what a candied yam is.

She looks so peaceful. I know the news I'm about to give her will certainly snap her out of her calm state. I'm reluctant to say anything, but then of course realize there are much more disastrous things I could reveal. Like that I'm a lesbian and have a tongue ring. Or at least one of the two.

I think of Julie Cooper's mom and wonder how she took the news.

I clear my throat. "So, uhhh, Mom," I begin.

She opens one eye and looks at me. "Yes?"

"I have something to tell you."

She sits up, sensing the gravity of the situation at hand. "Yes?"

"So . . . it's funny, see, I've been getting involved with a lot of different things at school. Like the newspaper, for one thing."

"Good. You hev to starrrt tinking of your career."

"Right. Of course. So anyway, I write a column for the paper."

"Why you don't geeve me to read eet?" she asks excitedly.

"Well, actually, because it's about, you know . . . sex."

There's a pause. I search her face hesitantly for a clue. Like "run for your life."

"Like . . . about STDs?" she asks.

"Umm. Well, no."

"About what?"

"About dating and sex in college."

"What you know about dis? You don't hev boyfriend and you don't hev sex."

"Well . . ."

"You hev boyfriend?" she asks excitedly.

"No."

"You hev sex?" she continues darkly.

"Um . . ."

"Oy vavoy," she says, grabbing her heart and nearly spilling her Diet Coke. My mother, like me, is a bit of a drama queen.

"Mom," I begin.

"So you say you know more about sex den me?"

"What? No, I'm not saying that. It's funny. It's a funny column. People like it."

At least I *thought* people liked it. Now I'm not quite sure. But I don't want to further confuse the discussion by bringing up Yale-Male05.

"My daughterrr, twenty-one yirs old, knows too much about sex. Dis what happens when you raise keeeds in America. Dey become all fucked up."

"Mom!" I exclaim, appalled at her language.

"I can't believe dis," she adds.

"It's not that bad," I plead. "You would like some of them. They're funny. They'd make you laugh."

"Hmph," she snorts, "I lef a lot widout dis."

"Well . . ." I say helplessly, "Julie Cooper is a lesbian."

"Are you a lesbian?"

"No."

"Den what do I care about Julie Cooper?"

Suddenly my father is standing in the middle of the living room with us. We must not have heard him come in.

"Hi, Daddy," I say, standing up to greet him.

"Hi, honey! Welcome home!" he says, enveloping me in a stiff hug.

"You know what your daughter does at school?" my mother asks him, interrupting the moment.

"What?"

"Tell heem," she orders me.

"Ummm . . . well." I hesitate again.

There's no predicting how he's going to handle this.

"What, honey?" he calls, going over to the hallway to hang up his coat.

My mother, too impatient, butts in, "She writes about sex."

She says *sex* as if it's a terrible disease.

My father's back stiffens. He turns around. "What?"

"Well, I write a dating and relationship column for the *Yale Daily News*," I say hopefully.

"Politics?" he asks, trying to ignore the elephant in the room. As usual.

"Yes. Politics," I answer.

"That's great!" my father replies in typical manner. "I used to write about politics for the *Crimson*. Apple doesn't fall far from the old tree," he says with a chuckle and makes a beeline for the bar.

My mother looks appalled. "She is your daughter."

He gives her a dirty look. She is interrupting his denial, something one should *never* do to Dick Carrington.

"Well, guys," I say, interrupting the silence, "it's been fun, but I have to go."

I make a mad dash for my room, leaving the two of them in a staring contest, which my father is destined to win. He is about as animated as Michelangelo's *David*.

I LOOK UP at the dazzling chandeliers at the Biltmore Room and breathe in deeply. I will stay calm. I will not throw myself at Josh. I will not go home with him under any circumstances.

I will not go home with him unless he is unbelievably nice to me and promises to take me out again while I'm in the city.

"May I help you?" The voice, coming from the leggy blonde dressed in black at the reservation booth, snaps me out of my thoughts.

"Yes. Umm . . . I'm here to meet Joshua Miller."

"Of course," she says, smiling condescendingly. "Right this way."

She turns to lead me in the direction of his table, and I notice that she has legs up to my armpits. Two of my scurries equal one of her phenomenally long strides. I make a face and try to follow as close behind her as possible.

I spot Josh far before we reach his table. He is wearing a black suit, white shirt, and yellowish gold tie. Très banker-esque.

He looks so grown up. And handsome. He's drinking his usual— Jim Beam on the rocks.

I'm suddenly hit with flashbacks of long nights of playing Quarters and laughing hysterically. My aim was so terrible that he used Jim Beam while I opted for significantly milder Miller Light. I lick my lips and can almost taste his whiskey-tinged ones.

His dark hair is cut short to disguise his impending baldness. He looks up and his blue eyes meet mine. I smile widely and wave.

He smiles back.

When Legs finally leads me through the maze of tables, he is standing, ready to greet me. Josh gives her an appreciative glance before she saunters away, and then turns his attention to me.

I am ready to give him a polite hello when he grabs me and lifts me off the ground in a huge hug.

"Chlo!" he exclaims.

To my delight, this is getting off to an unusually touchy start. Other diners are staring at us.

"Put me down," I hiss at him, feigning embarrassment.

"What's happened to your sense of humor?" he asks, releasing me from his grasp.

I clear my throat. "Nothing. I will have you know that we are in a very respectable place, and you should act accordingly."

He gives me a look as if to say, "Are you for real?"

"Yes, I'm for real," I answer before he even opens his mouth.

He laughs. "You look good, Chlo, you really do."

"Wish I could say the same for you," I reply quickly.

"Look at the big brain on Brad," he says quoting his favorite movie, *Pulp Fiction*.

"Two years later and you still haven't come up with any new material, huh?" I say, teasing him.

"Whoa, whoa, slow down there, champ. You're lobbing 'em far quicker than I can return 'em."

"Old age slowing you down?" I ask with a smile.

"Maybe a little."

I lean back in my seat, feeling comfortable again, and take him in with my eyes. There's something about Josh that makes people want to be around him. The party always follows him. And Lord knows, for about a year, so did I.

The waiter comes over. "Can I get you a drink, ma'am?"

"Sure. I'll have a Grey Goose and soda with three olives and a lemon."

Josh mouths the words along with me. I'm surprised he remembers. But then again, he always made fun of me for my offbeat taste in inebriation.

"Right away," the waiter says with a nod. "I'll be back with your menus shortly."

"No need to rush," Josh speaks up, "we're waiting for one more."

One more?

"One more?" I ask Josh when the waiter has left.

"Yup. There's someone I want you to meet," he says mysteriously.

"I'm not having a threesome with you. I know how your mind works and there is just no way," I say, laughing. I figure it's really some friend he works with or something like that.

"Crushing my dreams so soon, are you?"

"Yes."

"Wait 'til I get some of that Grey Goose in you. I know what happens to you after about three of those."

"Shut up."

Josh's eyes move somewhere above my head. His face breaks into a giant smile and he stands, nearly spilling his drink. He raises his hand above his head and waves enthusiastically.

I turn to see who has made him nearly burst with excitement. I'm assuming it's our guest of honor.

Coming toward us is a tall, well-dressed woman. She is wearing a smart black suit. A sharply tailored jacket shows off her toned upper body, a lacy camisole peeking sexily out from underneath, her skirt wrapping itself tightly around her (very) round bottom. She screams Dolce & Gabbana (and possibly boob job). Her legs are complemented by *amazing* knee-high Jimmy Choo boots.

"Hi, sweetie!" she exclaims in Josh's direction, showing off two rows of unusually white teeth.

Sweetie?

"So sorry I'm late, I got caught up in a meeting. My boss has been busting my chops."

She sweeps dark curly hair over her shoulder, green eyes sparkling with excitement, her cheeks flushed from the cold.

Josh gives her a sweet peck on the cheek.

I want to give her a swift kick in the ass. Who *is* this chick and why does it seem like she is about to ruin my life?

"It's all right. We were just catching up."

He turns toward me, his eyes still glued on bachelorette number two.

He clears his throat ceremoniously. "Chlo, I'd like you to meet my fiancée Tiffany."

I can't breathe.

"I've heard so much about you," she gushes, extending a hand toward me.

I think I shake it, but I could be mistaken.

Just then the waiter returns with my drink. I grab it and begin sucking it down at a pace that rivals P. Diddy running the city.

"Ah. Your entire party is here," the waiter says, oblivious, along with the rest of my party, as to how much I'd like to hang myself on one of the Biltmore's glowing chandeliers. That would make for some stellar headlines. "I'll get your menus."

"Great!" Josh says. "I hear this place is fantastic," he tells the two of us.

Tiffany beams.

I am still unable to speak, so I just nod and swallow what feels like a huge chunk of my pride.

In the game of seeing the ex over Thanksgiving, Josh has done something totally unprecedented. I came here to face off with my ex, knowing it would be time to battle it out. Who looks better. Who's involved again. Who's fatter. Who's happier. I knew it would be time to bring on the pain big-time. I was going to let him have it, paste on a smile and lie like it was going out of style. But Josh beat me to the punch. Nothing I can say can rival this announcement. He has scored off the charts—a touchdown and then a two-point conversion.

Who gets engaged before the age of thirty-five these days anyway? I certainly wasn't planning on it. Great, now Josh has gone and changed my entire life plan in an instant.

And who in their right mind names their child Tiffany?

The two of them are sitting across the table smiling at me. I grimace back.

"So, Chlo, what's new with you?" Josh asks.

I need to come up with something. And fast.

"So much!"

"Really?"

"Oh, yes, things are just going so well!"

"That's wonderful," Josh replies.

"Yeah! I write the sex column at school! Isn't that funny? And great? I just love it! It's so much fun!"

I am on the highway to hell and I'm going to have foie gras at the first rest stop. And since he's paying for dinner, probably lobster, too. And don't even think for a second that I'm not ordering dessert. Although our friend Tiffany here hasn't had dessert since 1997.

"Well, I did teach you everything you know, so the column must be great," Josh says with a laugh.

Tiffany joins him.

Slut. I smile through the pain and order another vodka soda.

I HAVE WALKED a record forty-seven blocks home in my heels, the pain shooting up my legs dulled by the dinner scenes I am replaying in my mind. I am also replaying possible ways that Josh proposed to Tiffany. I see Central Park in the fall. The Plaza. Vacation in Hawaii. Perhaps in bed on a Sunday morning? I can't decide which is more painful, my fantasies or the reality, which I was too afraid to ask about at dinner, for fear of upchucking the eight-pound lobster I ate right onto the table.

I walk into my building and take the elevator up to the thirty-fourth floor. It's been a long, long day. I unlock the door to our apartment and am relieved to hear the welcome silence. There's one thing I have to be thankful for this Thanksgiving.

I quietly take off my shoes and make my way into my bedroom. The last time it was decorated, I was nine years old. My mother told me to pick out linens suitable for a big girl. I chose pink and purple flowers on a mint green background and ruffled curtains. Despite its utter hideousness, a lot has happened in this bedroom over the years—both good and bad memories.

I'll cry to my mother about Josh tomorrow. She's crazy, but she, like everyone's mother, has had her heart broken a few times. Maybe she'll even give up on the soy crackers and let me eat cheesecake. The entire thing.

I crawl into my twin bed and reach into my bookshelf for my home copy of *Anna Karenina*. Rule number one: Have Anna at the ready in any and all places of residence.

"Now he experienced a feeling akin to that of a man who, while calmly crossing a precipice by a bridge, should suddenly discover that the bridge is broken, and that there is a chasm below. That chasm was life itself, the bridge that artificial life in which Alexei Alexandrovitch had lived. For the first time the question presented itself to him of the possibility of his wife's loving someone else, and he was horrified at it."

The words jump off the page as if they are written specifically for me. Josh loving someone else is a thought that is almost too much to bear. Yet Alexei found himself in an even more calamitous situation than mine. Thinking about him, and of course about myself, sends me into a frenzy of hysterical tears. I put my head in my pillow and smell home. Things really smell wonderful when laundry gets done once a week.

Through my tears I hear the phone ring. I reach over to my night-stand and grab the receiver to answer.

"Hello?" I snivel into the phone.

"Hey, Chlo, Melvin here. How ya doin'?"

Who says a girl can't have everything?

"Melvin," I sniffle, "this really isn't a good time to talk."

"What's wrong?" he asks, with genuine concern. "Great column in the Harvard/Yale issue, by the way. Loved it."

"Thanks," I say quietly, desperately wanting to fake static and hang up.

"Whaddaya say I take you out? A night of you and me is bound to make you feel better."

"No."

"Come on, Chloe. Give a guy something to be thankful for this year."

How can I say no to that? Besides, it might be good to get my mind off Josh. Plus, Melvin is entertaining some ten percent of the time.

"Well . . ." I hesitate.

"Great! How's Friday night? Coffee Shop?"

Friday being less than optimal, as it gives me the entire week to dread the date.

"Umm."

"Fantastic! See you then."

He hangs up.

I fall asleep with the phone in my hand, using *Anna* as my pillow. Pathetic.

MY DATE WITH Melvin was a certifiable disaster. Well, technically it's not over, as I am currently standing outside of Coffee Shop seething with anger and filling my lungs with smoke.

Perhaps I should start from the beginning.

Coffee Shop is a Union Square restaurant that serves overpriced lettuce and hamburgers adorned with guacamole and Brie.

It is also apparently a prerequisite of employment at Coffee Shop that one be (a) an aspiring model; (b) an aspiring actress; (c) a 110-pound waif; or (d) a student at NYU who thinks he's been a New York resident since birth (read: the entire campus population). I'm a heavyweight at a whopping 120. They sat me in a special booth with metal railings.

The date started out on the wrong foot. I showed up fifteen minutes late, which is customary for me. This occurs for several reasons. First, I'm under the impression that it takes only four minutes to get anywhere in New York using public transportation. This is not true at all. Second, I do not enjoy being the person who has to wait for the other person. When I am that person, I feel as if I need to overcompensate for being alone by engaging in extremely unhealthy habits like chain-smoking, having four drinks (if there is a bar), or attempting to pick up strangers in between compulsively checking my watch. Thus, when I am early, by the time my friend shows up, I smell, am drunk, and have made friends with a twenty-eight-year-old student at Borough of Manhattan Community College who is also an avid sperm donor.

Shockingly enough, Melvin was later than me. So there I was, impatiently waiting while my busty blond waitress batted her eyelashes at the guy at the bar I was trying to hit on.

She got his number. I got a vodka soda for fifteen bucks.

When Melvin finally decided to grace me with his presence exactly twenty-seven minutes late, he walked in *talking on his cell phone*. That is rude. I didn't even know Melvin *had* other people's phone numbers.

The waitress came over to give us our menus, and as she breezed by in a flurry of Chanel perfume and clinking heels, Melvin's eyes bored holes in her ass.

We ordered our food and began to talk. Melvin has never been an adept conversationalist, but I have certainly never had a problem talking with him. Apparently, though, Dating Melvin and Herpes Melvin are two different people. Dating Melvin kept on talking about some guy who he found amazing, smart, funny, and talented—that is to say, himself. He spoke as if he were an IPO and he was offering *me* a share of his stock. Needless to say, I was not investing.

I could also barely get a word in—unusual, as he's normally a great listener.

Our food finally arrived, and I busied myself with determining a suitable ketchup-to-fry ratio. I settled on "dip, dip, bite, dip, dip" as I listened to Melvin talk about his second favorite topic: sex.

I was surprised that Melvin had convinced someone to sleep with him. But according to him, he had (once). My second surprise came when Melvin arrived with a *list* (I kid you not) of sex questions to ask me. It's true, I am a sex columnist, but lo and behold, I do have other interests. Melvin of all people should know this, as I have tolerated him since the ninth grade. Melvin's questions were handwritten very neatly on the pad of paper he had stolen from his summer of slavery at Goldman. Numbered and everything.

1. What is the average penis size you have ever been with?

Straight-faced, I replied, "More or less the length of the tabletop."

2. How do you feel about flavored lubricants? Handcuffs?
3. Where is the weirdest place you've ever done it?

I excused myself to go to the bathroom and wondered where the weirdest place I'd ever commit murder would be. I composed myself, determined to pay the check and run—I mean, leave.

When I returned, Melvin was all geared up for round two. When he started talking about how he really stole the show at his brother's bar mitzvah, I decided I'd had enough. I stood up, threw down a twenty, muttered that I needed a cigarette (more than I'd ever needed a cigarette), and bolted out of the restaurant.

As I shiver in the cold, I'm having trouble wrapping my head around why Melvin is acting this way. It's so unlike him. Usually he's nerdy and annoying, but this level of arrogance and obnoxiousness is completely out of character. It just doesn't fit.

I look in the window of the restaurant to check on him, trying to get some clue that would help explain what has gone wrong. The place is dimly lit and bustling with customers and the wait staff. In the middle of it all, pseudo-Melvin is sitting at the booth we shared with his head in his hands. He's taken his glasses off, and they're sitting sort of dejectedly next to him. His eyes are actually a really nice shade of green without the frames. He slowly gets up and sees me looking at him through the glass. I give him a dirty look, turn around and take another drag of my cigarette. If he thinks he can treat me this way, he's got another think coming.

The door of the restaurant swings open and he comes outside, his coat halfway on, one arm in and the other partway into the left sleeve.

"What the hell *was* that in there?" I ask him angrily. I flick my cigarette onto the sidewalk and light up another one.

"I, I, well . . . the thing is . . ." he stammers.

"Seriously, Melvin. Who was that in there? Because I know you, and that was not you."

He looks down at his feet. They are clad in black socks and white sneakers. Ugh.

"Answer me, Melvin. What the fuck? Are you a mute now? Because you had oh so much to say in there."

"I just thought that you wanted that," he says quietly. "I thought you wanted a guy who had confidence. Who did whatever he wanted with whomever he wanted. Like Maxwell. Or Josh. They're always talking about chicks they bagged at Toad's and that kind of stuff."

"I have news for you, Maxwell and Josh aren't like that." My eyes fill with tears for the third time this week. "I thought we were friends, but you just treated me like all I am is a sex columnist, without a single other thought squirming around in my pretty little head. You know I'm not like that."

"*Were* friends? What do you mean, *were* friends? Chloe, please, let me explain . . ." he says, his voice trailing off. I think I see him blinking back tears as well.

"No, Melvin, let *me* explain. From now on, our relationship is purely professional. You got that? The paper and that's it. I'm leaving. And don't . . . *do not* follow me."

He looks crushed. Not just regular crushed, crushed like a guy freshly run over by a Mack truck. "Chloe, wait, please?" he asks, his voice cracking.

"No! Why should I wait?"

"Let me explain, please!" he begins, running after me.

"No!"

"Chloe! Wait, I . . . I . . ."

I start walking away as quickly as I can. I'm more confused than I've been all year. Which, for the record, is *very* confused.

It seems that the art of dating has eluded most of the men in my life. Perhaps Yale should start offering "First Date 101."

THE YALE DAILY NEWS

SEX AND THE (ELM) CITY
BY CHLOE CARRINGTON

First Date 101: It's All About Assets

"I have a huge single unit."

"What?"

"My room," Trevor repeated, "it's a *huge* unit."

Many moons ago, during my freshman year when I was merely a novice at the *Yale Daily News,* I went on a date with a wonderful guy—let's call him Trevor. Trevor also worked at the paper with me, and the truth is that he and I had been eyeing one another for quite some time now. In the dark, lonely world of journalism, it's hard to find a friend. Trevor was that friend. We checked each other out on Thursday evenings during edit. We understood each other. I was certain that this date was going to be the birth of something beautiful.

The location of this late-night tryst (okay, fine, it was five-thirty in the evening) was Istanbul Café. How exotic.

The hostess seated us in a prime-time location. We were VIPs because we are famous columnists known in elite Turkish writing circles.

That's a lie. We were the only people at the restaurant.

"Why did you bring me here?" I asked Trevor, thinking that as a New Haven native, he knew something of the area's Mediterranean delights.

He gazed at me passionately from across the table. "You make me crazy . . . crazy like a headless turkey."

Oh, Trevor!

What a romantic! He even pulled out lines from his Rico Suave annals—just for me!

Sigh.

First dates follow a sequence. They are formulated much like a car show. You, of course, being the car. In a perfect world, you would stand on a rotating podium, all oiled up, wearing a flattering color (black), while an announcer rattled off all the wonderful things about you. Unfortunately, this is not a perfect world. There are no announcers, and there is no one to oil you up before first dates.

How do you showcase all of your best features like a brand-new Chevy?

You revert to the Go-To. The Go-To is that part of you reserved for kickoff situations with a soon-to-be-significant-or-insignificant other. Everyone has their own particular Go-To formula.

For most, there is the Go-To first-date outfit. Mine, for example, is black knee-high boots (sexy) worn with jeans (casual) and a black sweater (cosmopolitan) with an understated accessory (classy). Trevor's Go-To outfit consisted of a forest green shirt unbuttoned to the middle of his chest (gangsta) and swanky brown shoes shined to meet the standards of any army general (military). If you ask me, a rather paradoxical combination.

The Go-To, of course, does not end with the outfit. It extends far beyond that. Each person has the Go-To Conversation. The GTC consists of two main parts. First, it is necessary that one direct the conversation toward one's own interests. This is complicated, as it must be done in a way that creates the illusion you care about the other person, only to revert back to the best things about yourself. You have to show the other person that you are funny. That you are intelligent. That you are spicy (like Turkish food). Second, the GTC encompasses the Go-To anecdotes. There are a few Go-To anecdotes that stand out in my mind as most important. They are the following:

1. The Go-To High School Story. Once you finish college, this reverts to the Go-To College Story. Either way, this story encompasses who you were in high school—jock,

drama queen, artsy-fartsy—while describing your battle with teenage angst.

2. The Go-To Drunk Story. This is used to indicate to the other person that you are a fun and cool kid to be around. It starts with something exotic, like "One time I was so *wasted* in Guadalajara when—" and it goes on to talk about how you met peasants in the jungle and you all hung out and played the travel version of Yahtzee.

3. The Go-To Ex. This is quite possibly the most important Go-To story. It is also the one that needs to be handled with the most care. You cannot have the other person think that either you or your ex is particularly crazy (which you both are). You discuss your ex rationally and make it seem as if you had a healthy relationship that just "somehow" went wrong.

If these three Go-Tos prove successful, you will be lucky enough to slip in that Go-To CD back at your place. It's the album that always helps you score. Like the *Braveheart* soundtrack. Or LL Cool J.

Trevor and I never got to the CD. We did, though, have a delightful dinner filled with fascinating Go-Tos. We also topped it off with a round of Turkish coffee.

Turkish coffee is particularly potent and particularly bitter. It is served in a miniature cup like espresso, but when you finish the coffee, there is a sludge that remains on the bottom. Legend has it that if you turn the cup upside down, the sludge on the bottom forms various shapes indicative of your future.

In my cup, right there, when I glanced inside, was none other than a huge unit. And not the kind you might find on the fourth floor of entryway C in Pierson College.

We're talking the kind you find on a guy with size 16

feet and a mean jump shot—just like Trevor. For the record, he and I never went on a second date. Though we were both charming and listened intently to each other's GTC, we figured we'd be better off as friends. After all, you shouldn't *really* rely on Turkish coffee to predict the future.

7

*I*T'S SAID THAT DIAMONDS are a girl's best friend, and in another life (or ten years from now), that may well be true for me. But these days, wings are a girl's best friend. Wings from TK's, that is.

TK's is New Haven's sports bar to end all sports bars. It's slimy, grungy, and manly, floors slick with beer and boot prints. TK's is also the site of the monthly poker game that has become quite the tradition among my guy friends and me.

Dick (or Dad, whichever you prefer) taught me how to play poker. The summer after eleventh grade, I finally gathered the balls to tell him that I was destined to be a writer and not an investment banker. Needless to say, he was devastated. After a three-day binge of Jameson on the rocks and massive denial, which catapulted my mother into a severe rage and a costly shopping spree, he came around and accepted my fate—and the fact that he would be supporting me for most if not all of my adult life. He then called me into the living room for a heart-to-heart. For the record, I believe, the only heart-to-heart my father and I have ever had.

"Sit," he commanded, perched in his leather chair.

I sat. It was the least I could do after almost breaking his heart.

"Since you have decided not to make money . . . ever," he began.

"Not ever, Daddy," I replied innocently, "just for the meantime."

"Meantime, schmeantime," he said, borrowing a line from my mother, "you don't want to make a living the honest way, like your father here."

"Honest way?" I asked.

"Okay, fine. The legal way," he conceded. "Regardless, it seems that the time has come that I teach you a little game called poker."

I was excited at the prospect. Poker was down and dirty and glamorous. I had seen *Casino* for the first time that year and I for one was dying to lose my virginity. Poker was going to be my ticket to sexual freedom and tits like Sharon Stone's.

I was in high school and was mildly delusional.

I listened attentively as my father whipped out a deck of cards and dealt them. It was a long afternoon of Texas Hold 'Em, but eventually I caught on. And by eventually, I mean about two years later.

Luckily, I caught on just in time for college. Within the first three weeks of school, I had become a legend among the freshman boys in my college. Thus began our monthly Monday-night poker game at TK's. Besides being the manliest place on earth, TK's is also where I gather some of my most interesting and column-worthy information. TK's brings out the worst in men, and incidentally the best in me. The more rowdy and drunk they get, the funnier I become. Or at least the harder they laugh. They're also easier to rob blind, which I see as sufficient payback for the trauma their sex unleashes on my own.

This week I decide to bring Bonnie and Crystal along for the fun. Bonnie because she had become my emotional crutch since Thanksgiving, the engagement holiday, and Crystal because, let's be honest, if things got boring, there is nothing more entertaining than a gay guy at a sports bar.

Our poker-playing group is generally composed of more or less the same people, with an occasional special guest. There are Hot Rob and Activist Adam, both seasoned poker players whose major weakness is overconfidence. Along with those two is Drew, a sarcastic physics major from Oklahoma who wears his lucky cowboy boots to every game; Jorge, a wealthy Argentine who calls me *bonita*, which tickles my fancy; Brandon, a laid-back Californian who finds *Big Lebowski* quotes appropriate for nearly every situation; and Eric, a handsome math major with a competitive spirit who hails from the Bronx. I've had a crush on Eric since freshman year, but nothing has ever come of it. It's a combination of the cardinal rule of our poker playing group—no inter-poker hookups (established on my behalf because, truthfully, if money and friendship shouldn't mix, then money and sex are a deadly combination). In addition, he has had a serious girlfriend for as long as I've known him.

Then again, there's Veronica's favorite mantra: "A girlfriend is an obstacle, not a wall." Followers of such a mantra are never girlfriends, and are in fact most often detested by them. Case in point—Veronica.

Tonight the originals in our group have gathered along with my two special guests. Let me note that another major TK's bonus is that there is a television at *every single booth*. If that isn't genius, I don't know what is. Hot Rob and Crystal are having a major channel-changing showdown. Rob is hooked on the Knicks game, and as this does not involve the type of balls Crystal is used to handling, he is rooting for the *Trading Spaces* marathon currently being shown on TLC.

"It's the $100,000 episode!" Crystal exclaims angrily as Rob asks if he can check the score just one more time.

Rob mutters something inaudible under his breath while Crystal takes a smug drag of his cigarette and a dainty bite of his chicken wing.

The conversation at our poker games revolves around three major topics, for which my advice is sought. First, the hotness, or lack of hotness, of the girls at Yale in comparison to their counterparts at any other given college. The last time this was discussed, Rob proclaimed that comparing the hotness of girls in the Ivy League was much like "ranking Ivy League basketball teams."

The last time an Ivy League basketball player made it into the NBA, Jefferson was in office. As in Thomas.

I took personal offense at this statement.

The two other topics are alternatively masturbation and blow jobs.

I'm praying that we don't talk about either of these things this week, as Bonnie's presence merits better-than-usual behavior.

"Crystal, Bonnie, wanna play?" I ask.

"No, thanks, we'll just watch and cheer you on," Bonnie says supportively.

"There's no cheering in poker," I tell her.

Bonnie laughs.

"No crying in baseball, no cheering in poker," I repeat sternly.

She clams up and Crystal hisses at me. "I'll play," he says in retaliation.

"Pipe down, Minnelli," I reply.

"I wanna play," he insists.

"All right, here we go," announces Rob in his best adult-poker voice as he deals quickly.

The boys get quiet as we each pull out forty dollars and lay it on the table. Rob deals the cards and begins his classic speech.

"Name o' the game is Queen Mariah, gentlemen," Rob says.

"*Ahem.*" I cough loudly.

"And Chloe. Gentlemen and Chloe," he corrects himself quickly. I smile sweetly.

"*Ahem.*" Crystal coughs.

"Gentlemen and Chloe and *Crystal.*"

Crystal smiles happily. This is his first time playing poker and he believes he should be recognized for his bravery. He then turns his attention back to the television. So much for active participation.

"Lowest spade in the hole wins half the pot, deuces wild."

Everyone nods and scoops up their cards.

"I am about to take your money, gentlemen—and Crystal," I say, turning my attention to my cards. In poker and in life, I often have trouble keeping my mouth shut.

"Not so quick, *bonita*," Jorge answers. "Round one is justa beeeginning."

"Say *bonita* again," I demand.

"*Bonita*," he mouths slowly in my direction, raising his eyebrows. Bonnie and I giggle.

The game progresses quickly with little arguing or cheating—rare among our group. You know those Latin Americans.

I'm kidding, I'm kidding.

And Adam, just because he's Adam, is a notorious shit-disturber. Not a round can pass without infuriating commentary.

About two hours later, the cards have been dealt and redealt, and happily I'm holding my own in front of my guests. Nothing can be both more empowering and more damaging than being a female poker player. If you win, every man in the room wants to sleep with you—which is incredible given that you've already proven your sharp bluffing skills. Then again, if you're losing, you're just a chick that can't play poker, like all the other chicks that can't play poker. Brandon, meanwhile, has been dealt hand after hand of a lot of crap.

"I could just be sitting at home with pee stains on my rug," Brandon says, looking at his cards, disappointed, hating life, and as usual quoting *Big Lebowski*.

"You know," I pipe up, hoping to raise Brandon's spirit, "there was a guy who graduated about two years ago. Class of '03, I think. Anyway, he would get wasted when he went out on weekends and was thus pretty indiscriminate about who he went home with."

Brandon looks at me blankly. "Where is this going?"

"Let me finish!" I exclaim.

"Sounds like you, asshole." Adam nods toward Rob with a grin.

"At least mine have the decency to shower," Rob shoots back, barely missing a beat. He turns to the rest of the group. "You can smell the treasures this guy brings home before they even come up the stairs."

Adam has no comeback, mostly because it's true. The dirty, disheveled alterna-look is not the most sanitary of fashion statements.

"Anyway," I say, directing the attention back to me, "he would get so wasted that sometimes the girls would wake up to find him peeing in their rooms, too drunk to get to the bathroom. Could anyone *be* any grosser?"

Crystal giggles. "We used to call him the Urinator."

Bonnie joins him, laughing, while the rest of the boys are suspiciously silent.

"What?" I ask everyone. "What's the big deal?"

"It's, ah . . . it's, ah . . . happened to me a coupla times," Rob stammers.

"Hell," Drew adds in his southern drawl, "where d'y'all think the stains on Brandon's rug come from?"

"That has *never* happened to me," Brandon replies a little too quickly.

Bonnie looks around the table, disgusted, and for once, I have to join her.

"Men," Crystal says, shaking his head.

They all look at their cards sheepishly. Crystal gingerly picks up a wing and bites into it quickly, swiping at his fingers with a Handi Wipe.

"Read 'em and weep!" Brandon howls as Eric puts his head in his hands.

"Fuck you, dude. My balls on a platter, with fuckin' foie gras on the side." Eric is *not* pleased.

"Now that's just ridiculous, dude, no one is going to cut your dick off," Brandon says, citing even more *Big Lebowski* for our listening pleasure.

"With those cards you might."

"I'll enjoy it immensely," Brandon says with a smile, sliding the chips that are left in the middle of the table toward him.

I check the expression on Bonnie's face. I don't think she's been around this much testosterone outside of a bio lab. She's wearing a bewildered half-smile. If I didn't know any better, I would say she was enjoying poker night. Crystal, on the other hand, is not.

"Chloe," he says loudly.

"Yes?"

"This place could use a face-lift."

"So could I."

"Seriously, a couple coats of paint, maybe some new lights. It's gross in here. When I went to the bathroom I couldn't get out for, like, fifteen minutes because my feet were stuck to the floor."

"That's the *beauty*, Crystal. It's not supposed to be neat and clean and lovely. It's supposed to be mean and gross and fit for poker playing."

"Is this what the Belaggio looks like?" he asks pointedly.

"That's a different clientele," I reply patiently.

We look over at Activist Adam, who is trying to pick his nose without anyone noticing, and Jorge, who is making kissy faces at our waitress. Out of the corner of my eye, I notice that Hot Rob is staring at something. I follow his gaze and land right on Bonnie, who is surveying the scene, looking quite amused. Hot Rob is probably confused by her presence tonight.

"See?" I say, turning back to Crystal.

"I guess so," he replies grudgingly, and then slides a little closer to the television. Tile samples are now being discussed on *Trading Spaces*, and Crystal is eager to get back to contemplating the difference between marble and granite.

"You know, I was thinking," Adam begins. As we all look over at him, annoyed, I can't possibly imagine where this is going to go. I suspect downhill.

"What?" Drew asks. "What, pray tell, were you thinking?"

"Well, if you watch the movie *Jaws* backward, it's, like, a totally different film."

"Oh, yeah?" Hot Rob asks, mildly interested.

"Yeah. It's a happy movie. About a really sick shark, who vomits people up and then . . . at the end, everyone has a big party on the beach."

There is a long pause as everyone wonders what to make of this, followed by a wave of laughter.

"I was thinking, too," Drew says.

"You were?" I ask him.

"Yes."

"And?"

"And I had a great idea for a column."

The bane of my life in being a sex columnist is that people tend to do two things. First, they tell me unappetizing things about their sex lives, for which they seek my commentary. Usually I have no advice for them. I don't know what kind of food is best for sexual activity. I don't know what the best brand of handcuffs is. I have never watched any part of *Debbie Does Dallas*, nor have I ever done it in Dallas using a position called the mounted horse. I have no clue what it means when a guy says, "I am in a partially emotionally committed relationship." If I did, I would be both coupled and happy.

The second thing people do is suggest column topics, which are generally sucky. I brace myself for Drew's words of wisdom. "And what is your idea?"

"Do you remember how we met, Chloe?"

"Why of course," I reply.

"How deed you meet?" Jorge asks, curious.

"Well," Drew says, turning toward him, "we were both up late one night studying for a math test."

"Yup," I add, "freshman year, Math 115. I failed that test."

"So did I," Drew says, nodding.

"No you didn't!" I exclaim. "You are a physics major."

"Well, I was quite enraptured by your beauty. You were so distracting I couldn't study."

"Oh, shut up," I say, blushing. All a guy has to do to win my heart is tell me I'm pretty or funny.

"And we were talking about our high school relationships."

"Right, and you told me . . ." I start to laugh.

"That all I wanted in life was a girl that could go down there and give head like a champ."

The rest of our table enjoys this immensely.

"Which I found repulsive," I add.

"So do I," says Bonnie.

"Well," Drew says, "lots has changed since then, but I think that it's still safe to say—"

"That you still want a girl that can go down there . . ." Rob says with a devilish smile.

"Okay, okay, that's enough of that," Bonnie interrupts quickly.

"Bonnie," I say, "this is poker. There are no rules."

"I thought there was no cheering. That's a rule."

"She's got you there," Eric says, nodding.

I narrow my eyes and ignore them. "So, what's the point of your story?" I ask Drew.

"I think you should write a blow-job column."

I smile, pretending that the prospect of this doesn't scare the shit out of me. I can talk the blow-job talk, but can I walk the blow-job walk? I have a sneaking suspicion that talking blow jobs in public might elicit a few reactions I might not be prepared to deal with. Namely from my now-clued-in parents.

"Sure, yeah, I could do that," I say, lying.

"Yeah, you definitely should," Activist Adam says, suddenly back from Planet Rewind.

"Yo, that would be hot," Eric adds.

You're hot, I want to say.

The rest of the boys are nodding. Even Crystal looks at me hopefully.

"Well, what would I say?"

"Spit or swallow is a definite topic," says Drew.

"There are so *many* issues," Crystal says emphatically.

I love it when the worlds of gay and straight come together in peace.

Hot Rob nods in agreement. "You have no idea."

"Well, I think I have some idea," I reply defensively.

"Trust me," Drew says, "you have no idea. Do I have a girlfriend now?"

"No."

"Have I had one since freshman year?"

"No."

"See?"

"Well, well," I say helplessly, "the only thing you're attracted to is those damn cowboy boots. Plus, you have dicked over more girls than Ben Affleck."

"That's bullshit. I just know what I want. I'm very picky, you know."

Rob opens his mouth to say something, but Drew shoots him the look of death. He does a very convincing Indiana Jones in those boots.

"Right. Your standards are sooo high," I tease him.

"Thank you!" Rob exclaims.

As Eric deals the cards again, I entertain the possibility of this column. It has the potential to be funny. But so do a lot of things. Quite frankly, it scares me.

"So whaddaya think, Bonnie?" Hot Rob says. "Should Chloe write this blow-job column or what?"

"I personally would rather be strung from the rafters of the House of Paine [Paine Whitney Gymnasium] while having mad-cow-infected raw beef hurled at me by the entire student body than write anything about blow jobs. But if anyone can do it, Chloe can."

"Thanks for the vote of confidence there, Bons," I comment dryly.

"What's wrong with blow jobs?" Hot Rob asks, chiding her.

"Yeah," I add, trying to psych myself up, "blow jobs can be a little scary. Maybe a funny column would demystify it a little bit."

"Scary?" Hot Rob asks.

Bonnie and I nod solemnly.

"*Nothing* is scarier than a penis."

"Plus," Drew adds, "blow jobs are the hand jobs of your twenties."

"Hey," Adam interrupts, slightly insulted, "I still get hand jobs sometimes."

"Whom are you hooking up with?" Eric asks. "Eighth graders?"

"All right, boys," I interrupt, "let's try and keep it out of the middle school here."

"So, Bonnie," Rob begins, "what's so terrible about Chloe writing the article? Or us discussing, you know, oral sex? Gotta be honest, both totally okay in my book."

I can't wait for Bonnie to respond to this one.

"Umm . . . well, nothing," Bonnie stammers. She looks extremely uncomfortable. "Except, you know, I just, I just, don't want to write about it. Or talk about it."

"What about do it?" Rob asks.

"What about it?" Bonnie shoots back, recovering a little.

"I just want to know for, like, future reference," Rob says, smiling at her.

She blushes a deep shade of red.

Rob reaches over and touches her arm. "I'm only kidding," he says softly. "What would you prefer to talk about? I like second base too."

The whole table laughs.

"Baseball?" Bonnie asks with a smile. She is digging all this attention from Hot Rob.

"Beer?" he asks her kindly.

"Yeah, I'd love one," she replies.

"Um, Bonnie," I interject.

"Yes?" she asks, turning her attention to me, looking slightly annoyed.

"It's a school night."

She laughs as if she's never used the phrase *school night.* For the record, she has, like, numerous times.

"Don't be silly, Chloe! One beer won't hurt me."

Mind you, for Bonnie, this is the equivalent of burning her bra. Additionally, she has the alcohol tolerance of an anorexic sorority girl who's been on a treadmill for the last six days.

"I think Hot Rob is flirting with Bonnie," I whisper in Crystal's ear.

"I know," he whispers back.

"Do you think . . ." My voice trails off.

"Think what?"

"That he, um, *likes* her?"

"Stranger things have happened."

"Not much stranger."

"True," Crystal agrees.

"If Bonnie and Rob get together, I'm predicting the second coming of Christ."

"What are you talking about? Your people don't even believe in the first coming."

"When there's a first coming, there's hardly ever a second," I say.

"Speak for yourself. Clearly you've never met Sebastian."

"Touché."

"So you think maybe?"

"Maybe what?"

"Maybe he *likes* her."

"Rob would flirt with a post if he knew it would go down on him."

"You know," Crystal says slowly, "Bonnie might surprise you."

"I doubt it."

"You never know."

"Whatever," I reply, brushing him off.

"So are you gonna write this column? It could be great. Sebastian and I could help you!"

"I dunno. YaleMale05 would have my head, I'm sure. No pun intended."

"Have you figured out who it is?"

"Nope. But I heard from him after the last column."

"What did he say?"

"He asked if I've ever been on a date and if my method actually worked. He then said he doubted that it did. How interesting could I be? And was I trying to use the word *Turkish* as many times as possible in one column. And *then* he said maybe he'd take me out and show me a good time—but I'd probably never entertain going out with him."

"Weird."

"Yeah. His messages are so odd. Half sound like he hates me, and the other half sound like he thinks I am quite the little minx."

"Well, you are, my dear. You are very minxish."

I bat my eyelashes at him.

"Eww, but not if you do that. Do you still think it's Maxwell?"

"I don't know what I think. He was pretty flirty at Harvard/Yale."

"Agreed."

"But he hasn't made any other moves."

"You said he's shy. Maybe this is his way of getting in."

"By insulting me constantly?"

"It's the fourth-grade tactic. It works on some chicks."

"Not me."

"I dunno, YaleMale05 has sparked your curiosity."

"How could he not? He writes, like, every week."

"You have a fan club."

"Hardly. I have not a single fan among all those posters. Mostly critics. Near his post was someone who asked me what my mother thought of all this, and another person who told me I was loose and would probably burn in hell."

"Which is almost better."

"Almost."

Crystal puts his arm around me. "Write about the blow jobs."

"Crystal, that's way scary. Blow jobs? I would be crucified online."

"What's with all the Jesus references?"

"Nothing, I'm just saying I would be."

"Who cares what other people think? It'll be hilarious. Plus, most Yalies love your column. It's the few and far between who can't take a joke."

"I care about what other people think."

"I know. It's a serious problem."

"Hey, hey," Hot Rob yells from across the table, "I thought we were playing cards here."

"Okay, Poker Nazi!" Crystal yells back.

"Who needs another beer?" I ask. "Next round of pitchers is on me."

"In that case," Eric pipes up, "we all need another round."

"Technically it's on you, as I have done quite the job of robbing you blind."

"What else do you want to do to me blind?"

Bonjour, Eric. It would be so delicious if he is YaleMale05. As I go up to the bar to order two more pitchers of Miller Light, I fantasize for a couple of seconds about the two of us living happily ever after as Vegas poker bandits.

As I walk back to the table, I am concentrating very hard on not spilling the beers. Pitchers are deceptively heavy.

Someone walking past me shoves my arm, causing the beer to slosh over the edges and spill all over my new cashmere poker-night sweater.

I look up, furious, and come face-to-face with Melvin.

Oh, fuck. Fucking Melvin, Lord of the Wrong Place at the Wrong Time.

"Excuse you!" I say, angrily setting the beers down on a nearby table and lunging for some napkins to wipe myself off with.

"Chloe! Hi! Oh, I'm sorry," he replies, stammering.

"You owe me six seventy-five in dry cleaning."

He pulls out his wallet nervously and begins taking out some singles.

"Oh, Melvin. Put your wallet away. I don't want your money. What are you doing here?" I ask him.

"I actually came looking for you," he says, shifting his weight from one foot to the other timidly. I am enjoying this torture, so I just stare at him. He switches to rolling and unrolling his shirtsleeves.

"Why?"

"Because I want to talk to you. About . . . about our date, and what happened."

"I don't want to talk to you," I reply, and try to push past him to get back to poker.

"I know you're still angry about it," he says kindly, "and I came to apologize."

"I'll tell people that you have erectile dysfunction disorder if you don't get out of my way."

"If you tell people that, it means you've seen me naked," he says, raising an eyebrow.

"I'll take my chances," I reply.

The boys at my table have all abandoned poker playing and are staring at us. Bonnie is wincing partially with embarrassment and partially with sympathy. I look up to meet Crystal's eye. He is smiling and snapping his fingers, signaling the gay mantra: "You go, girl."

"I'm really sorry," he says slowly, "for my behavior on our date."

"Let me ask you a question, Melvin," I say. "You have known me for about seven years, is that correct?"

"Yes," he says sheepishly.

"And *what* in that seven years gave you any inkling that it would be at all cool to act like you were on a date with a total idiot? A bimbo?"

"I did not act like you were a bimbo," he protests.

"What about all those sex questions? What's that about? People who *don't* know me think I'm a slut. Look at the website, Melvin! Out there in the big bad world people think I screw for a living. At least this campus grants me the decency I deserve. With one exception—you. This column is funny. Its purpose is to make people laugh. But you, my editor, the person who is supposed to *understand* that, is the first one to treat me like Divine Brown."

"Who's Divine Brown?" he asks, genuinely confused.

"And you call yourself a news junkie," I mutter back.

"Excuse me, miss?" the bartender asks.

"I'm leaving," I hiss at him.

I storm past Melvin over to our table and leave the beers behind.

Hot Rob, not one to let a beer go to waste, runs over and grabs them.

"I'm cashing out," I tell the boys. "Bonnie, are you ready?"

She looks over at Hot Rob longingly.

"Are you ready?" I ask again. I sound like Bobby Knight on a rampage.

"Yes?" she answers, as if it's a question.

"Let's go."

ABOUT TEN MINUTES later, she and I are walking along Elm Street, having dropped Crystal off in his room.

"That was fun," Bonnie says with a smile.

"What?" I ask, still angry.

"The poker."

"Oh, yeah? You liked it?" I say, brightening up.

"Yes. Maybe I'll come with you next week."

"I would like that," I say, squeezing her hand.

"Um, Chlo," she says, clearing her throat.

"Yes, Bons?" I ask.

"What do you think of Rob?"

Ah-ha!

"What do you mean?" I ask, playing it cool.

The key with Bonnie, especially when she likes someone, or potentially likes someone, is to play it cool. Too much excitement scares her off.

"I mean, do you think he's a nice guy?"

"Of course I do. Don't you? We've known him since freshman year."

"Um, Chlo . . ."

"Yes, Bons?"

"Will you teach me how to give a blow job?"

THE YALE DAILY NEWS

SEX AND THE (ELM) CITY
BY CHLOE CARRINGTON

Spit or Swallow? It's All About the Sauce

At the tender age of sixteen, my best friend, Alison, and I decided that the time had come to master the blow job. Yes, young, I know. But we didn't want practical hands-on (or mouth-on) experience; we just wanted to know what to do in case the occasion ever arose when we would have to lose our respective oral innocence and take the plunge. Walk the plank. Head (sorry) into uncharted territory. Technically, we wanted to improve our fellatio IQ. We were certain that someday in the future we would be, uh, tested, if you will.

One humid summer afternoon, slightly embarrassed and rather unsure of ourselves, we snuck into Alison's kitchen and came out armed with produce. Bananas and carrots, we found, fit the bill for our purposes; they were the right shape, and we could tailor the length to our preferences.

Convulsing in laughter, partly because of the hilarity of the situation and partly out of embarrassment, we kneeled at the side of Alison's bed. We laid a very instructive *Cosmopolitan* magazine out in front of us to, uh, direct traffic, and we sucked produce like it was our job. We criticized each other's performance, rating each other on various categories that we had formulated beforehand—endurance, strength, originality, and creative use of body parts. It was like the blow-job Olympics, only it wasn't televised, and we didn't have a live audience yet. But we were certainly working up to that point— slowly and steadily.

Due to a short bout with bulimia, Alison could put almost

a full banana down her throat. Perplexed by the magnitude of her accomplishment, I asked her to help me with my own technique. It was at this moment, surrounded by peels of various sorts, with bananas thrust down our throats, that Alison's mother walked in. Needless to say, she was puzzled at why we were eating on Alison's bedroom floor. We had no answer. She quickly concluded halfheartedly that we probably wouldn't be too hungry for dinner. We weren't.

Years later, when I was no longer on Alison's floor, I realized that although helpful, produce does not prepare one for the crucial blow-job moment. Let's be honest—when was the last time a carrot ejaculated on you at the salad bar?

To spit or not to spit? That is the question. Whether 'tis nobler in the mind to suffer the sour tastes of a thousand sperm or to bring a cup and take arms against a sea of troubles . . .

I am an avid swallow supporter. (Wow. My popularity rating with the male demographic just skyrocketed.) I figure that swallowing is like taking cough syrup. Sure, it's a little painful at first, but eventually the taste will go away.

Surprisingly, I found that eight out of ten Yalies agree with me on this point. Especially males. When asked, most replied that this question should not even be addressed. It was a nonissue. Swallowing, they all said, is clearly where it's at. Some even thought it was an honor to swallow (I swear).

"Our bodies have been working all day long to produce that stuff," a premed student said. "You're getting some really good nutrients; I mean, we're giving you our best and our brightest."

You're right. You have superstar come.

I asked one blow-job aficionado about the calorie question. This has secretly always been a concern of mine. If I'm playing for team salad, I don't want to lose points with my ex-tracurricular activities. Soothing my worries, he asked me to dispel the myth about the extraordinary number of calories per serving. Come is actually surprisingly low calorie as well as chock-full of vitamin E, which just happens to be great for your skin. What a relief!

Despite my personal opinion about the matter, spit is still a choice made by many. Thus, it certainly merits being addressed.

Spitting, I've found, is quite a complicated operation. It adds accessories to foreplay: a cup, a towel, and something to wipe your mouth with. These items comprise what we might call a spit kit. They may be easy to round up beforehand if you know that a little somethin' might be taking place. Yet imagine a situation in which play pops up out of the blue. It is not always easy to procure these items at short notice. I highly doubt that a spit kit of any kind would fit into an evening bag during a night on the town (or at SAE). A purse made ex-pressly for the storage of lipstick, money, cell phone, and keys is not about to accommodate a bath towel and dinnerware—it's hard enough shoving a pack of gum in there.

Aside from arguments about convenience, taste, and fat content, there were two rather interesting issues that were spurted into the spotlight by those who preferred to spit.

First, there was the question of sweet things like care and tenderness. "If he makes you swallow, he really doesn't love or respect you." This is all fine and good, but quite frankly, when was the last time you hooked up with someone who respected you, much less loved you? High school?

A close friend of mine stated, "I spit because whenever I swallow, it goes up my nose. Can you talk about that? I bet I'm not the only one with that problem."

Actually, I hate to break it to you, honey, you are. We are all stupider for having heard that statement, I award you no points, and may God have mercy on your soul.

As this is the last column of the semester, I would just like to wish everyone luck on finals, and a very happy holiday season. Whether you choose to spit or swallow, this holiday season, may your days be merry and bright, and may all your Christmases be—white.

8

"**S**HE'S NOT HERE RIGHT now," I hear Bonnie saying in the other room. "Can I take a message?"

There's a pause as the person on the other end of the line responds.

"No, I will absolutely *not* tell her that. You are a sick, sick person. Do you know that?"

Another pause.

"You don't know that? Well, I'm sooo glad you bestowed me with the honor of telling you . . .

"You need a definition of bestowed? Argh! Do not call here again! Creep!" she exclaims to herself as she slams down the phone and walks back into the common room, where she flops onto the nubby brown Salvation Army couch we bought freshman year. Our common room is furnished completely in Le Collection Salvation. It reeks of grad-school chic circa 1977. So much has changed, but that brown couch has been here through it all. Finals. Vomit. Tears. Sex. If this couch could talk it would say "Wash me."

Bonnie leans her head back, letting her long blond hair fall and hang loosely off the end of the sofa. Her hair is her best feature. Mine is my personality, and according to the last twelve phone calls we've received today, also the fact that I am a "swallow supporter." My words, not theirs.

"Who was that?" I ask gingerly, not wanting to hear the response.

"The devil," she replies, straight-faced.

"Bonnie," I whine, stretching out the syllables in her name as long as I can possibly make them, to emphasize my thorough displeasure.

"I told you not to write that stupid column," she says, glancing at me out of the corner of her eye.

"No, you didn't."

"Yes, I did."

"NO, YOU DIDN'T!" I shout.

"You don't have to yell," she says, "and anyway, remember I said that I would rather have mad-cow germs."

"Yeah, but you didn't say that I *shouldn't* write it."

"Chloe, some things need to be kept private. And that is one of them."

"What is?"

"That."

"What?"

"Blow jobs," she says, almost whispering, as if Mrs. Johnson is going to barge into our room any second and sermonize on the hell-bound certainty of performing oral sex.

"Bonnie, honestly, this is not the time to lecture me."

"I know," she says quietly. "I'm sorry. I just feel bad. With all these people calling . . ."

"I thought the column was funny. A little off-color, but funny still."

"You always think it's funny. That's why you write it."

"Not always. But was it? Funny, I mean."

"Yes, it was."

"Did you laugh? Out loud?"

"Three times," she says, smiling, "and everyone I talked to liked it."

"Yeah, because everyone you know is twenty-one."

"Well, not everyone that's twenty-one quite enjoys you."

"Say more."

"Yale Students for Christ are not big fans. Neither is anyone who works for the *Yale Conservative*."

"Shocking news, Sherlock. What else have you in your massive tomes of secrecy?"

Bonnie just shoots me a glare.

Apparently writing a blow-job column attracts every pervert this side of Harvard. FYI, Yale is *west* of Harvard. There are a lot of people that live *west* of Harvard—everyone from Boston to California—which is why Bonnie has been picking up the phone for the last two weeks straight. We've learned that right-wing Republicans don't like blow jobs. Neither does anyone who is over the age of seventy-seven or anyone who has children. Period.

"Actually," she says, "one other thing."

"Yes?"

"Veronica is telling people that she is more adept in the oral department than you are."

"Can you just say blow jobs? Say it."

"Blow jobs," she repeats grudgingly.

"Trust me, honey, I will let her have that title. No arguments here. In fact, she's probably right."

"She gives those things out like candy," Bonnie mutters in a rare moment of moral weakness.

"Bonnie," I warn.

"That girl's going to hell in a handbasket," she mutters again.

"Now, Mr. Rogers, be nice, that's a neighbor you're talking about. And since we're on the topic, remind me again why you dislike Veronica so much."

"How much time do you have?"

"Seriously, Bons, you're the one always telling *me* that I'm too judgmental."

"Well, you are."

"I'll take that, but what's the deal with Veronica?"

"She's evil. And self-centered and pushy and slutty and unkind and indulgent and—"

"Okay, okay, I get it. Sorry I asked."

The phone rings again.

"Will you get that?" I ask Bonnie, smiling sweetly.

"This is the last time," she says, running into the other room where she left the cordless.

Two seconds later she returns, extending the phone to me. "It's your dad."

"Hi, Daddy!" I exclaim, surprisingly pleased to hear from *mi padre*. But fear not, that feeling is soon dissipated.

"Chloe," he begins sternly, "we need to have a talk."

This is never a good sign. Talks are bad. Talks with boyfriends. Talks with professors. Talks with parents.

In the background I can hear my mother screaming, "Let *me* talk to her!"

"Calm down, Channah," he says.

"You are too calm!" she shrieks back.

When his attention is finally brought back to the telephone, my father tells me that the young analysts in his bank had quite the joke going this week.

"Really, Daddy?"

"Yes, sweetie," he says dryly.

Apparently said analysts had received e-mails from their friends with none other than my illustrious column as an attachment.

Who doesn't love to read a thousand words by their young daughter about illicit sexual acts? Not Richard C. Carrington, that's for damn sure.

"Daaaddddy," I plead with him, but to no avail. He's not listening, and my mother, he says, needed to be caged or at least tied down so that we could have this conversation. He had to confiscate her car keys to keep her and her sequined attire from driving straight to Yale and asking for a refund.

I'm silent as he does his best to reprimand me, in the unemotional, unattached way that he is so used to doing. "I'm disappointed," he finally says, "gravely disappointed."

Disappointed is the most deadly word in a parent's vocabulary. Worse than *I'm angry* and almost worse than *You're cut off. Disappointed* indicates that you have hurt them so much they haven't the energy to yell at you. Which in my family is a rarity.

I finally hang up, citing class as an excuse. As a tip for college-bound freshmen, when parents are paying $3,000 per course, they care a *lot* about whether you attend lectures. Thus, class is a great way to get out of any kind of trouble you find yourself in. This time my excuse is a valid one. It's nearly one-thirty and I am going to be late for "Rereading Faulkner," a class taught by the illustrious Harold Bloom— a god among men here at Yale, and quite possibly the scariest man alive. One of his books is called *Genius and Genius*, a title he would never dream of ascribing to any one of his students.

As I rush over to LC 102, the location of ye sacred class, I can't help but notice the small signs of spring on campus. The air is warmer and smells like fresh mud, which happens to be just about everywhere due to the rapidly melting snow.

When I arrive in class, breathless as usual, I merit but a grim sidelong glance from my TA as I slip into my seat.

Bloom drones on, asking whether the fictions of William Faulkner are the overwritten works of a local colorist who was also an apologist for the New South, or whether they are the high-modernist masterpieces of a troubled humanist. I resign myself to the fact that I don't understand the terms used in his question. I let my mind wander and find myself thinking about my poor parents. And about poor me.

When I began writing this column, I did it solely as a favor to Melvin. And now that my relationship with him has reached its current pleasant state of nonexistence, I wonder why I'm still subjecting myself to criticism and subjects I know too little about. I guess the truth is that at first the column was something wild and fabulous. I wrote about things that genuinely concerned me, plagued my friends, and generally confuse the hell out of most human beings, but somehow I started getting myself confused with "Sex and the (Elm) City." And soon enough, "Sex and the (Elm) City" became who I was instead of what I did. I wish I could be more like Veronica, sexually confident, unafraid, and ready to take a risk at nearly any time. She lives with no regrets. I, on the other hand, live with many. She grabs attention wherever she goes. Men, women, it doesn't matter. There goes the sex columnist, people whisper when I walk into a party—but along with the interest come reviews and judgments. Judgments that, unlike Veronica, I take to heart.

I shake my head as if to rid my mind of the jumble of thoughts stored up there, and spend the next thirty minutes of class writing furiously, in a futile attempt to try and capture the genius of *Genius and Genius*. This week's assignment was to read the first two hundred pages of *The Sound and the Fury* and I'm already behind. I also have a sneaking suspicion that we have a paper due some time soonish. I make a mental note to be disciplined this week and get my work done. Losing myself in books and work is often so much easier than dealing with life. Even if it is Faulkner.

The rest of my afternoon is spent running errands. Pick up dry cleaning. A trip to the post office, where I wince at my astronomical cell phone bill. A stop by the ATM machine, where to my further delight, I notice funds are running dangerously low. This does not bode well for me or my cell phone, given the "conversation" that I had with my parents this morning. I remind myself to ask Activist Adam for advice about quick money-making schemes. In light of his philosophical divorce (his words, not mine) from his parents, he has decided to take on a financial reawakening. In short, he cut himself off from the posh digs that previously decorated his life. Since he's so busy enlightening the world about organically grown crops, the dangers of sweatshop labor, and the legalization of marijuana, he often sells his body to science. The med school, he once told me, is always looking for volunteers to forgo eating for a week or something equally painful, for great sums of money. Activist Adam once made $800 for running on a treadmill for four hours a day for a week. If you ask me, exhaustion is a small price to pay for three pairs of shoes and a bottle of Veuve.

When I get home, I'm exhausted. People say that youth means you need minimal sleep and have a lightning-speed metabolism. I disagree. The life of a college student is really taxing. I wake up at ten in the morning and am thoroughly exhausted by five in the evening.

I flip on the TV and am pleased to find that *Oprah* is still on, followed by an episode of *Martha Stewart Living*. It turns out that deep down I'm actually a forty-two-year-old midwestern housewife. Who knew?

Hot Rob peeks his head into our common room just as I begin to lose myself in Oprah's favorite things.

"Hey, Chlo."

"Hi, hon."

"You seen Bonnie?"

"Nope," I reply nonchalantly.

"What's up?" he says, looking slightly disappointed but stepping inside nonetheless and plopping down on the couch next to me. A brown curl droops down over his left eye, and he pushes it out of the way and looks over at me. "How you holding up?"

"With what?" I ask, pretending not to know what he's talking about.

"With all the column buzz. Bonnie told me about all those assholes online saying shit. And of course the phone calls. Some of them are pretty fuckin' funny, huh?"

"If you're you and not me."

"Yeah," he says quickly, "I'm sorry."

"It's okay. So what's up with you and Bonnie?" I ask, eager to change the subject and genuinely interested in the response.

"You know," he says with a half-smile.

"No, I don't know."

"She's hot," he says, giving me a typical nonanswer.

"Yeah, but that's not what this is about."

"She's cool, too. And really smart. We had this great conversation the other night about Kissinger's writing while he was still at Harvard. We both agree that his best work was done there. I wonder why it's gotten so little exposure . . . I think I'm going to write my senior essay on it." He pauses, blushing. "Don't you guys talk about this stuff?" he adds, grabbing for the remote. Oprah is talking about changing people's lives with cashmere.

Rob is revealing a little more than he bargained for today, and I for one am enjoying it.

"Don't change it! I love her!" I exclaim. "And no, we don't talk about this stuff because getting Bonnie to divulge anything takes a village. I'm only an army of one," I say, prying him for even more info, which I am going to report back to her as soon as she gets home.

"We're going on, like, a date tomorrow," he says, staring at the TV. All of a sudden Oprah is fascinating to the nth degree.

"Where are you taking her?"

"Basketball game. And then . . . you know, dinner."

"Yale basketball? I thought you hated Yale basketball."

"She likes it," he says with a shrug, but he can't help smiling. He digs her, I can tell.

"All right, spit it out. You like her—a lot."

He blushes. "Uh-huh. But don't tell her."

"I won't," I lie.

Rob gets up to go, blowing me a kiss and saying he'll "be back in a bit."

I can't help feeling a pang of jealousy. It's fleeting, but it's there. Bonnie is so clueless ninety percent of the time, but at the end of the day, she just gets it.

I grab a bag of SoyCrisps, chips for us carbophobes who buy into the gospel that *Vogue* preaches, and head toward my computer. I check my e-mail and then navigate, somewhat grudgingly, to the *Yale Daily News* post board. I don't want to face the music, so to speak, and see the treasures that await me, but I'm curious about YaleMale05. He hasn't written a thing yet about this column, and it's sort of surprising. Half of me hopes to find something from him. But only half.

"There have been 362 comments posted on this story! Add your thoughts now!" the web page boasts.

Three hundred and sixty-two? This can't possibly be for real.

I begin to scroll through. Some of them are too disgusting to repeat. Twenty-seven people tell me I have no self-respect. Fourteen agree that I should seek professional help. At least half of those misspell the word "professional." A hundred guys want to date me, and twelve want me to have a one-on-one with their girlfriends to "talk some sense into her." Fifty posts tell the rest of the readers to lighten up and laugh, and at least thirty people have written that they know me personally and not only am I lovely but my column is—and I quote—"genius." Lisa, Bonnie, and Crystal have all used their real names in my defense. Lisa's post exhibits particular outrage at what she calls the "unadulterated cretinism" of some of my readers.

Finally, after about an hour spent violently lurching between laughing and crying, I come across YaleMale05.

YALEMALE05

I have read all of your columns and the writing is excellent. Very funny. I laughed out loud every single time. I have also read the hundreds of comments on your column. They are almost as funny; especially the ones from the prudes, perverts, the self-righteous, the indignant, the horny teens, and the loutish old men who can't wait to IM with you and send you fake pictures of themselves. My particular favorites are from those who assume that because you write about sex, you spend your entire life on your back, your knees, and so on. It's very hard to write in those positions. One last word to your detractors: Learn how to spell. Your message of moral outrage loses a lot when you still can't spell words that you should have learned back in the fourth grade. Chloe, you are wonderful, brilliant, hilarious, and full of energy. Your critics are only proof that you are a success.

I stare at the screen in disbelief. Albeit with far more eloquence than I did, YaleMale05 has captured exactly what I told Melvin at TK's a few weeks back. It's as if somehow this mysterious character has managed, without the slightest hint, to read my mind. What has spurred this sudden change of attitude? I feel oddly overwhelmed with emotion—and an even deeper desire to find out who my anonymous admirer is. I notice beneath the screen name an e-mail address: yalemale05@hotmail.com.

I glance at it quickly. Should I? It's really the only way to find out.

Half an hour later, Bonnie has returned from class and I am still composing my response to Post-Boy. I've decided that it has to be thankful but not too effusive. I need to sound interested, albeit with a hint of aloofness. What I really need to do is find out more about him.

Bonnie walks into the room and peeks over my shoulder. "Whatcha doin'?" she asks in a singsongy voice that is very un-Bonnie-like.

"Writing an e-mail," I reply hurriedly. I'm not sure what Bonnie will think of my detective work.

"Okay," she says casually. Bonnie knows me all too well. If she doesn't probe and pretends not to care, it will take me about thirty seconds to update her on everything.

"Fine. Fine." I turn around in my chair to face her where she is un-dressing to get in the shower. "I'm writing an e-mail to Post-Boy. He wrote the nicest comment online. I was so flattered."

"Are you going to have one of those Internet love affairs?" she asks, wrapping a towel around her svelte figure.

"No," I reply with disgust, "I just want to find out who it is. Maxwell, maybe? Oooh. Or what if it's someone else? Like a secret admirer. So secret that we've never even met, and he's a law student. Who drives a Porsche."

"Could be fun," she says, nodding. "But no one at Yale owns a Porsche."

"Could you just allow me this one fantasy? Just one. Let a girl dream here."

"Just being practical."

"Rob stopped by."

"He did?" she asks, her eyes lighting up.

"Yup." Now it's my turn to play it cool. I, after all, have the infor-mational advantage.

"That's not all you're going to say. You've got to give me a little more to work with here."

"How was class?"

"Chloe . . ." she warns.

"I think the master's office has a package for you from your mom. Maybe it's a brand new stack of Bibles, Bazooka gum, and pretzels like last time," I say, feigning excitement.

"Chloe!" she screeches.

I giggle. "All right." I grin. "I think he's really into you."

"You think so?" she asks. Bonnie hasn't displayed this much excitement since she got an internship with the American Cancer Society—which I told her not to take because they would corrupt her mind with the myth that cigarettes are bad for you. She told me I was insane and accepted anyway.

"Yes, I really think so."

"What did he say?"

"He said you were cool and funny and smart. And hot."

She smiles sheepishly.

"I think you might just be the one to un-whore him."

"Chloe! Don't be rude about my boyfriend." She says the word *boyfriend* as if it's a six-carat diamond—which in some circles it might be.

"Boyfriend? Is that what we're calling him these days?"

"Well, maybe I'm getting a little ahead of myself here, but I would argue that Rob is a stone-cold fox and though perhaps in his earlier days he had some whorish tendencies, I think he's ready for a grown-up relationship."

I laugh at the phrase she borrowed from me (stone-cold fox).

"Yes, indeed, a stone-cold fox. Why do you think I call him Hot Rob?" I ask.

"Because he's a stone-cold fox," she says again, laughing. "That's fun to say. I feel like Pam Grier circa 1972."

She checks her watch. "Darn, I have to hurry."

Darn? Some things never change.

"Where are you going?"

"Well, Rob and I are going to a lecture at Luce Hall on the impact of globalization on the nation-state, and then he's taking me to play beer pong at the frat house."

"Well, aren't you two just ying and yang, meant to be. That

sounds like an eclectic night. You are subjecting yourself to the talons of A-E-Pi so soon? They're a deadly bunch."

"I can hold my own," she says, straightening her back and turning up her nose.

"Talk basketball, that always works, and perhaps humor them with a keg stand."

"Thanks," she says with a smile.

"And then what are you going to do?"

"What do you mean?"

"Spit or swallow?"

"Shut up, Chloe," she says, walking out of the room and slamming the door.

"Remember all my tips!" I call out after her. "Don't overexert yourself the first time!"

I giggle to myself. I can almost see her grimace through the door and all the way down the hall. Maybe Rob will be getting out of the shower and she can get an uncensored preview of what's to come.

I turn my attention back to my witty-sensitive-caring-aloof-laid-back e-mail one more time

MR. POST-MAN,

It seems that you have rung not once, not twice, but several times—and though I have been frequently bothered by your presence, you shocked me quite thoroughly with your most recent addition.

In danger of erring on the side of effusive, I wanted to thank you for your kind words this week. You somehow managed to capture a lot of what I've been feeling these days as I read the comments of some of my harshest critics. The column is indeed meant to be funny, sarcastic, and witty (much like me! . . . I'm kidding), but when it is taken too literally, things seem to go awry.

I'm glad I've succeeded at making you laugh. I hope it continues.

BEST,

~ C

My e-mail sounds slightly formal, but then again, there is nothing wrong with coming off a little intelligent every once in a while. I hope. Before I can second-guess myself, I click on the Send key and wish for the best—or at least a cordial reply.

"THROUGH THE FENCE, between the curling flower spaces, I could see them hitting. They were coming toward where the flag was and I went along the fence."

I am sitting in the softly lit TD library, thinking of anything but *The Sound and the Fury*. The words slip by my eyes as they shut every so often. I glance around to see if anyone has caught me. I am always laden with an immense sense of guilt when I fall asleep in the library. I feel as if some other student is going to catch me, find out I'm a fraud and shouldn't really be here, and then report this directly to the dean of student affairs. From there of course, I will be promptly expelled and all notions of my intelligence thrown out the window. I will have to move to Key West and mop floors for a living while sharing a trailer with a guy named Bubba.

Back to Faulkner.

An hour later, I look up to see that Bonnie and Rob have joined the study party at the table across from me. They are sitting next to each other holding hands and reading—he *Diplomacy* and she *BioChem*. That's really the name of the book: *BioChem*. I can honestly think of nothing more horrifying.

I have been unduly bitter lately seeing Bonnie and Rob all cuddly and lovey-dovey. I hope she doesn't ruin the poor boy, smothering him with boring things like homework and watching hours of chick flicks like *When Harry Met Sally.* Granted, a great film, but not Rob. As soon as this thought runs through my head, I feel guilty and curse myself for being such a major asshole. My mother always tells me that a real friend is one who will be there through the good times, too.

I want to be happy for the two of them, but then jealousy, quite possibly the ugliest and most irritating emotion of all, creeps into my head and takes over. I decide to punish my selfishness by denying myself all study snacks and sticking to bottled water until I pack my books up for the night. Which, by the way, looks like it will be in the near future, as Faulkner is not doing a very good job of keeping me awake or entertained.

I check my watch. "Seven-thirty," it says, looking at me smugly. "You thought it was later, didn't you?" I decide, since my watch is being so mean to me, that it's time for an e-mail break.

I go downstairs to one of the TD Library's many computers and log in to my e-mail. I am pleased to find a response from YaleMale05. It's been only a few hours, so I take this as a good sign.

CHLOE,

It's true, I've rung several times, but I'm sorry to hear that I've bothered you to such an extent. I figured you, of all people, could stand up to the challenge.

I remember that you once wrote that e-mail rules do not apply to phone rules; thus, I made sure to e-mail you back as promptly as possible.

So tell me, there must be more beyond this ultra-sexy columnist exterior of yours.

Favorite movies? Books? What's your major?

New York Times or Washington Post?

Vodka or gin?

Sean Connery or Anthony Hopkins?

Boxers or briefs? I for one prefer boxers.

I hope you don't mind my being straightforward, but I'd like us to be friends. Perhaps someday I'll tell you who I am.

Don't let the critics get to you—they are just fans in jealous disguise.

SEE YOU AROUND,

YALEMALE05

A WEEK LATER, Post-Boy and I have exchanged several more e-mails, and I have decided that I may just be in love. Well, not in love. But in a lot of like. My next quest is to find out the man behind this great mystery, but every time I bring it up, Post-Boy is elusive. He wants to know me before he actually meets me, he says. When I inquire as to whether I know him, he writes: "We'll always have Paris."

What is Paris? Is he referring to something that actually happened or not? I can't quite figure him out. Regardless, the mystery keeps me going, and excited.

It is Friday night, the worst possible Yale going-out night. Wednesdays, Thursdays, and Saturdays often provide entertainment, but Friday is like a big crater of nothingness. It's a choose-your-own-adventure type of night. Tonight, unfortunately, I have resigned myself to staying in. Bonnie and Rob are out doing something couple-ish that could be dinner or a movie or perhaps beer pong at the frat house. Bonnie has garnered quite a fan club among Rob's friends.

While she sows her wild oats (as Mrs. Johnson would surely say), I am sowing my academic ones. Midterm season is once again upon us, and there's no time like the present to begin studying.

I am sitting on our common room couch, books spread all around me. This is the first sign that I will accomplish nothing. I am the champion of taking out all my books at once when I study. A noble effort, but it tends to be a case of overambition, which leads to being overwhelmed by too many books and then turning to online shopping for solace.

I am wearing my most hideous outfit, a large Yale sweatshirt and an atrocious pair of green sweatpants, which do nothing for my thighs. My hair is matted and messy, and I have eaten about fourteen Oreos.

Suddenly the door to the common room swings open and in march Crystal and Cara.

Crystal takes one look at me and scrunches up his face.

"Oh, Lord," he says, turning to Cara, "it's worse than I thought."

"Worse but fixable," she adds, nodding her head. "We'll have to work quickly, though."

"Agreed," Crystal says, nodding seriously.

"Guys, I'm not sure if you're aware of this, but I happen to be sitting right here."

"We know," Crystal says. Both of them fold their arms across their chests and stare at me. The Odd Squad in action.

"Uh, okay. Remind me why you're here."

"We," Cara says in her Texas drawl, "are takin' you out."

"I can't, guys. I have a ton of work. Thank you so much, but I really can't."

"Nonsense," Crystal says, smoothing his blue cashmere sweater. "You will do no such thing. It's Friday night. And *you*, my dear, are lucky enough to have wonderful friends like us who don't want you to sit at home in that monstrosity of an outfit."

"And Post-Man will e-mail you later. Don't become one of those freaky Internet people who sits at home . . ."

"Waiting for Godot," Crystal finishes her sentence in his exuberant literary way.

"Godot? Who's that?" Cara asks.

"It's a play!" Crystal responds, horrified. "You are so Texas."

"Ain't nothin' wrong with that, sister," Cara replies. "Plus, you need something to tell this YaleMale character. Tonight we're shakin' things up."

I look up at both of them and burst out laughing.

"All right, all right," I concede. "What should I wear?"

"Ooh! I get to choose!" Crystal squeals.

"No, me!" Cara shouts, running into my room and flinging open the closet door.

I close up Faulkner for the fourth time this week and promise myself it'll get done—tomorrow.

AN HOUR AND a half later, the three of us are sitting at an old wooden table at Mory's, a veritable Yale dining institution. Mory's has been around for forever and a day. Its walls are lined with old photos of men's crew and football as well as women's field hockey. The tables have been carved on by generation after generation, and the entire place is filled with a soft glow that makes it feel like home, or at least oddly familiar. The old white house on York Street, in which it is located, has played host to thousands of Yale students craving Mory's famous cups—huge trophies hailing from various decades filled with odd alcoholic concoctions, which are passed around the table. When the cup—which holds about a liter, I imagine—is nearing its end, the person who finally finishes it cannot leave a single drop of booze in the container. A song is sung while the last drinker places the cup on his head and spins it around three times. A napkin is put down on the table and the cup is placed top-down on the napkin. If a single drop of the mysterious liquid falls out, that person buys the next round. This is a great old Yale tradition that makes little sense, but for some reason it warms my heart up every time I come here.

At this very moment, Crystal is finishing up the red cup—the best kind—while Cara and I sing at the tops of our lungs with little regard for anyone nearby.

"Sing hallelujah, sing hallelujah, put a nickel on the drum save another drunken bum!"

Crystal turns the cup over on the table and Cara clinks her ring on the side of the cup.

"Turn it over, turn it over!" I sing with glee.

Luckily for Crystal, not a spot remains.

"You see," he proclaims, "that's the luck of the Irish!"

"Whatever," Cara says nonchalantly, signaling the waitress over to order another monstrous cup. It's going to be a long and fabulous night.

"So, Cara," I say, getting her attention once she's flagged down our server.

"Yes?" she replies.

"How goes your HHQ?"

"Hot hookup quotient in full effect. I have my eye on this darlin' football player. Stocky, just like I like 'em."

"How old?" Crystal asks devilishly.

"You'll be happy to know that he's a sophomore," she answers proudly.

"Movin' on up, movin' on out, time to break free, nothin' can stop her!"

"We went on a real date," she says pointedly.

"Where did he take you?" I ask.

"The field house."

"The who?" Crystal asks, confused.

"It's out where the football team practices. You know, near the fields? Hello! Hence the name *field house.*"

"You went on a date to the field house?" I ask in disbelief.

"Did he wear a protective cup?" Crystal asks mischievously.

"Yes and *no.* There was no need for a cup," she says, raising an eyebrow. "Plus, it was very romantic. We had a picnic right in the middle of the Yale Bowl."

"That is cute," I concede. "So when are we getting rid of him? Give us el juice."

"I think," Cara begins slowly, "I might hold on to this one."

"What? No two-week teaser? No fast fling?"

"Not this time around."

Crystal and I look at her approvingly.

"I need to start some kind of program for myself. You're all leaving me in relationship dust!" I exclaim.

"You're not dusty," Crystal says comfortingly. "Maybe just a little . . . rusty?"

"Rusty? What do you mean?"

"Last major relationship: Josh. Last major hookup: hello, honey, six months ago—Maxwell. Wake up and smell the Gold Cup. Girl, you gotta get yourself some action."

"Excuse you," I say, slightly offended, "you can be balls to the wall about things, but can we try and spare a little something called my feelings. And," I add, "I have decided to take a new approach with the Post-Man."

"Which is?" Crystal asks.

"Getting to *know* him before I take my clothes off. In fact," I say in a moment of pure genius, "it's a little something I like to call Operation GLWC^2." Borrowing a page from Cara's book of impossible acronyms.

"Operation GLWC^2?" Crystal asks.

"I've never heard of that one," Cara adds dismissively.

"Which stands for . . ." Crystal asks.

"Get laid with commitment and conversation."

"Expand on that idea, please," Cara says, picking the cup up and gulping it down as if she's just run a marathon.

"Well, it just means that a great relationship is composed of commitment, conversation, and of course great sex. It's genius. Thus far, I have some type of *conversation* going with Post-Man. Our e-mails can be seen as a form of conversation that is enchanting, exciting, and shows we have a lot in common. His *commitment* is exhibited through his frequent posts and e-mails."

"And the getting laid part?" Crystal asks impatiently.

"Takes *time*," I answer. "We all know GL-ing is easy—take Woody Allen, for example. If he can do it, anyone can. But now that I seem to have conquered the WC^2 part, it's smooth sailing from here on out."

"Whatever you say," Cara answers.

As I continue to wax philosophical about the virtues of good conversation and, in my situation, good e-mailing, I look up to see Veronica, confident as ever, strutting toward our table.

Crystal and Cara exchange annoyed looks while I raise my hand to wave. "Veronica!" I call out.

She walks over, and only when she is in closer proximity do I notice someone trailing not too far behind her. That person is none other than Maxwell.

Veronica is wearing a tight black bustier and jeans, her eyelashes heavily coated in mascara. Max looks great as well, dressed in the standard male uniform of khakis and a blue dress shirt. He's clean-shaven, and I wonder if the same is true for the love below, or if he dropped that like the bad habit it was. For a moment, fantasies of discovering that he is Post-Boy dance in my head like sugar plum fairies.

"Where you going, Lady Marmalade?" Crystal asks Veronica disparagingly.

"Hey, hon," I say, slightly bewildered, and then "Hi, Max."

"Hey, Chlo," he says with a smile.

He then turns to Cara and nods hello.

"Oh my God! How are you, Max?" she squeals. "It's been so long. What's going on?"

"Not too much," he answers.

Veronica grabs his hand. "Not too much?" she asks. "Maxwell, tell them what's been going on with you," she gushes.

"Uh. Well. I applied for a Fulbright," he says, looking uncomfortable.

"That's awesome," I reply. "When do you hear?"

"Soon."

"No, silly," Veronica says, hitting him playfully, "Maxwell and I are here celebrating our *one-month anniversary*!"

I look at the two of them in disbelief. Not again! The engagement news was traumatizing enough.

"People who celebrate monthly anniversaries don't last," Crystal mutters under his breath.

"Uh, yeah," Maxwell comments, looking at me apologetically.

Herein lies the difference between men and women: Men cannot stand to be in a room with two women they've dated, whereas a woman can parade around a party full of exes, stringing her new man along like a championship pony. I'm certain Veronica has slept with at least one person at Mory's tonight, and Maxwell happens to be the prizewinning steed of the night.

"That's great, guys," I say, suddenly feeling mobese (morbidly obese) in my chosen attire for the evening. Veronica's breasts are pushed up to her chin. I'm wondering how she can breathe and talk at the same time.

"Chloe," she gushes, "have you figured out who that guy posting all the comments on the *Daily*'s website is yet?"

I curse myself for having told her about that. "Um, no. Actually, we were just discussing that," I say, trying to smile.

"I can't believe you thought it was Maxwell!" she says, laughing.

As soon as the words come out of her mouth, the entire table freezes. Cara is holding the cup up to her lips, motionless. Crystal is staring down at his pants, immobile. Maxwell's eyes are fixed at a spot on the wall somewhere above my head. Only Veronica has the audacity to throw her long hair over her shoulder fearlessly.

"Well, only for, like, a second," I say quietly, "but clearly I was wrong."

"When I told him, we had such a laugh about the whole thing," she adds, making sure to nail my coffin shut. Real tightly, too. Thanks, Veronica.

"Uh. Well, we didn't laugh exactly," Maxwell stammers, "and I am a big fan of your column."

Right.

A look of anger passes over Cara's face. I don't think I've ever seen her so upset. She looks up from the cup at the two of them and pastes on a giant smile.

"Does Maxwell still shave his balls?" she asks Veronica brightly.

Cara, I'm sure, is convinced that she is being helpful, while I try to convince myself that this is all a dream and I'm about to wake up.

Now.

Okay, how about now?

"I'll get back to you on that one," Veronica answers menacingly. "We should go," she adds quickly. "Chlo, call me later, okay? We have to catch up—so glad to see all of you!" she exclaims, and saunters off with Maxwell a few dejected paces behind.

When they are out of earshot, we all sit quietly for a few moments.

"I could kick his ass any day," Crystal says confidently, and then yells after them, "You're a ho!"

"Shhh," I hiss at him, "we're at Mory's."

"And she's a ho."

"Besides, you couldn't kick his ass."

"I'll kick *her* ass," Cara says angrily. "Who does she think she is?"

"She probably didn't think she was doing anything wrong," I reply. I realize that my friends were right about Veronica all along. "She's just really, really selfish."

"I hate her," Cara says.

"Me too," Crystal adds.

They both look at me expectantly.

"You know what, guys? I have to concur."

I RETURN HOME later on to find Bonnie and Rob sitting on the common room couch.

"Are you all right?" Bonnie asks as I walk in. "Crystal called me and gave me a heads-up on what happened."

"I'm fine, I guess," I reply. "Just don't say I told you so."

"Didn't even cross my mind," she answers.

"We'll talk tomorrow. All I want to do is go to sleep."

"Good night," they both call after me sympathetically.

I walk into the bedroom, sit at my computer and begin writing an e-mail to none other than Post-Man. I'm not quite sure why, but it feels good to tell him about it—to write it all down. Somehow I know he'll respond, and somehow I know he'll know just what to say.

Two hours later, I find out that he does.

THE YALE DAILY NEWS

SEX AND THE (ELM) CITY
BY CHLOE CARRINGTON

Sex in the Spring, Ex in the Fall

Spring has arrived. It is finally here in full force, and it seems that spring transforms this campus. All the attractive people begin to emerge. Those people whose pages you dog-eared in the *Rumpus*'s 50 Most Beautiful People issue; those people really do exist.

Alas, they appear only in the spring. All of a sudden everyone is sporting a new wardrobe—tits and ass galore! Tube tops make cameos as miniskirts. Shirtless Adonises stroll calmly down Broadway. People giggle, sections move outside. A warm breeze floats through Cross Campus, just barely rustling the leaves of the trees. Everywhere I turn, it seems that an Abersnobby and Bitch (uhhh, I mean Abercrombie & Fitch) photo shoot is taking place (so we're a little fatter, no biggie). Take a deep breath. Ahh. Do you smell that? Yes, that's right, the trees have begun smelling like semen again.

Mmmm.

Look around, what do you see? Couples. Couples everywhere. When spring turns up, people start mating like bunnies. Everyone does a 180 and goes *National Geographic* on me. Discovery Channel up the wazoo. People frolic in the grass, kissing, loving one another, gazing into each other's eyes. Everyone is so happy. So pretty. So horny. It's enough to make me dizzy.

But I am here to burst your bubble! I encourage you to look beyond spring. Look far beyond, summer is coming—you'll have to break up with your mate. We learned that long-distance relationships don't work, September of freshman year. It's college lesson number one.

What's that? You really like each other? You're going to stay together? Okay, you're a little more optimistic than I thought. Let me turn your attention to December—yes, that's right. Tan—gone. Tits—hidden under a sweater. Ass—huge. So huge, in fact, that you'll be able to see it from the front.

But never fear. Breakups will come if you bikini-wax or if you don't. To prepare you for this, I have compiled a user's guide. A little "Breakup 101," if you will, to dispel a few breakup myths and suggest some key pointers.

Contrary to popular belief, breaking up is *not* hard to do. Instead, it is a mere exercise in both creativity and lying.

Much like any class in English, history, or political science.

When you break up, you are officially prohibited from telling the truth. You cannot tell him that you are not in love with him anymore. That you don't find her attractive. That he farts in his sleep. That the sight of her feet repulses you. That you have been sleeping with everyone in his college. It's not allowed. It's insulting. Plus, who tells the truth to the people they love anyway?

Especially if you want to keep them around for any significant amount of time.

Thus lying is necessary.

The prime breakup lie involves using ourselves as the person to blame—we assume the role of the breakup culprit. This is the classic "it's not you, it's me" cop-out. We all know that we're breaking up with the other people precisely because it *is* them who's the problem. They are the ones who suck, are crazy, or are annoying. If you really liked her, you wouldn't be breaking up. And if it was you and not him, he would be breaking up with you instead of vice versa. The reason that this style is often employed is because it's almost foolproof. The other party needs to be a breakup expert to foil this plan. If she promises to change, it doesn't matter; it's still *you* that's the problem. If he agrees to back off a little, that's fine, but again, he is not the problem, it's you.

Remember that if you have a real psycho on your hands, breaking up in a public place is the best thing to do. That way, she will be deterred from prolonging the process. A large lecture, like an introductory econ class, may be a good place to cut ties. A dining hall might also be ideal, but make sure to have bused your trays—food in close proximity of the breakup scene is a bad plan. If the other person insists on creating a commotion, he will most likely start yelling. When this occurs, make yourself appear to be a sensitive individual and begin crying immediately. Who cares what your ex thinks of you? All that matters is what everyone else thinks, and you'd damn well better look like the victim.

If you are extremely imaginative, a good breakup method might be to employ a few literary techniques—similes, analogies, and metaphors. The basic goal with this approach is to confuse the other person as much as humanly possible so that instead of focusing on the breakup itself, she or he is trying to figure out what exactly it was that you said.

I once dated a boy who employed this technique. When we broke up, he told me that our relationship reminded him of "an eighteen-wheeler barreling down a steep hill, instead of cruising steadily along the highway."

Uh, okay.

This was his opener. Later on he juxtaposed our bond, which he found to be reminiscent of chicken wings (this is apparently bad), as opposed to peanut butter (which is allegedly what a relationship is supposed to be like). At first I blamed his lack of coherence on the fact that he was foreign and in reality didn't speak English very well. I was mistaken. He was just far sneakier than I was, and had learned of the confuse-the-living-crap-out-of-your-mate technique before I had.

Yet another innovative method similar to the one above is to make wildly absurd claims involving your relationship. For example, my best friend in high school, Alison, dated a Funk-Master-Sketch famous in many New York circles. When he cut ties with her, it was extremely traumatic. He was her first . . . everything. It was a beautiful relationship, really it was. On the fateful day of their parting, after he tore her heart out, stomped on it, and spit at it, he asked her the following question: "Are you planning on sleeping with anyone in the next year?"

Through a stream of tears, Alison looked up at him, confused and shaken. She replied that she really didn't think it was any of his business. Then she inquired as to why he was asking. His answer made no sense at all whatsoever. He said, "You know, sex was kind of like our thing. I just think you should hold off in respect of that."

I'm not even going to attempt to mock that response because I think that it does such a good job all on its own.

My favorite type of breakup is the ambiguous breakup. This kind leaves room for continued hooking up and perhaps the possibility of a relationship later on. Really, it's a well-constructed plan to continue getting ass while lowering your level of commitment with said person, all the while waiting for someone better and more attractive to come along. At that point, you can pretend that you had broken up ages ago, and you're not really sure why you kept getting calls. This type of breakup involves using many contradictory statements. Here's an example:

"I like you, but we shouldn't go out anymore. We're dating, but we're not going out. We can hook up with other people, but we can also still hook up with each other. We can sleep together, but only sometimes. We're breaking up, but we're not exactly breaking up. Get it? I like you. I really do."

As you can see, a great deal of possibility remains, yet the room for a clean break later on is not eliminated. This plan is genius. A breakup masterpiece, really.

Other breakup techniques I have been told about are equally creative.

A list titled "55 Reasons Why You're a Bitch." Way to be direct.

Ceasing communication entirely. No calls. No talking. Pretending as if the other person has died.

Cheating.

Changing your sexuality. Break on through to the other side!

And of course telling the truth. Straight up and to the point:

"It's over between us. It's just not working out. Why? Oh, well [sigh], the truth is that it's not you. It's me. I swear."

9

"**I** BROKE UP WITH Starry," Lisa says, putting down her copy of Kierkegaard's *Fear and Trembling* and rolling over onto my beach towel.

"Finally!" I respond, looking up from my more humble choice of *Bridget Jones's Diary*.

The two of us decided to take the day off from life and do nothing but tan on one of Yale's first truly warm days. I took this to mean easy reading and Amstel Lights. Lisa agreed on the Dutch beer, but sticking with the motif, decided to conquer a Danish philosopher as well. My idea of a great Saturday afternoon does not include exploring the notions of complete obedience to God and questioning one's faith. But who am I to judge?

"What are you connoting by *finally*?" she asks defensively.

"Lisa, let's be honest here, you were dating two professors in the same department. Don't you think that's slightly, I dunno, risqué?"

"Chloe, why live if not for the unpredictable, the incalculable, the mercurial?"

"So why did you do it?"

"Do what?" she asks.

"Why did you break up with Starry?"

"Several reasons. First, I was inspired by your most recent column. I couldn't decide between the two of them, and conducting not one but two relationships this summer seemed unduly portentous. Also, quite frankly, I was getting bored. Stuart spends inordinate amounts of time in the library hoping to write something exemplary enough to publish, while Harry kept on pestering me to have dinner with Stuart and his new girlfriend."

"Uh-oh."

"So I humored him."

"You had dinner with Stuart and his girlfriend? His girlfriend, of course, being you?"

"Yes."

"And what happened?"

"I read them a list of fifty-five reasons why I'm a bitch. Which was hard to come up with, by the way. I got stuck at reason 48, but I pulled through. Then we took tequila shots."

"Oh. So you executed the breaking up for them."

"Exactly. I was briefly entertaining the possibility of a threesome, but being in the same room with both of them for an extended period of time seemed far too mentally exhausting."

"Then what happened?"

"I left the two of them to their own devices and walked out of Richter's. I even bought them their next round of drinks."

"How generous. Are you conducting some type of social experiment?"

"Dating both was not fair to either party," she replies simply.

"Yes, I know, but that wasn't my question."

"How goes your torrid Internet typing romance?" she asks cunningly.

"Can we not call it that?" I ask, embarrassed, lying back on my towel and staring up at the ginkgo tree in the middle of the courtyard that is presently in full bloom.

"And pray tell why not?"

"Because then it sounds like I'm forty-two and fat, and I sit at home waiting for someone equally old and fat and possibly hairy to instant-message me."

"Are you or are you not conducting a relationship via the channels of electronic communication?"

"But the person goes to Yale," I protest helplessly.

"Don't believe everything you read," she replies with a smile. "What do you propose I call this love affair?"

"It's not a love affair, but if you must, that's better than an Internet typing romance."

"Whatever makes you happy, my darling."

Blah. My Internet romance is making me happy, but I can't help but wonder when it will come to fruition—if ever.

"So," Lisa continues dramatically, "what *is* the man behind Courier New really like?"

"He's actually great," I reply sheepishly.

"Look at you, suddenly the embodiment of modesty. I want to hear the gory details."

"I'm not having Internet sex."

"Chloe baby, give me *something* here," she pleads.

"Don't call me *baby*. You sound like Trump."

She looks at me, expectantly waiting for an answer to her question.

"It's odd, actually, I feel like I know him so well. But I don't even know who he is or what he looks like or where he's from, this mysterious Internet dude. He's really funny. I have to forward you some of his e-mails. He asks me all these oddly probing questions."

"Such as?"

"Such as name my top five favorite books of all time. Or who in my estimation was the best president we've ever had—"

"What did you say?" she asks, interrupting me.

"FDR. He has a highway named after him."

"Questionable response."

"Also, who I think is a better actor, Sean Connery or Anthony Hopkins. I mean, how did he know that I'm in love with Sean Connery?"

"Odds are that he doesn't."

"He does now."

"Ha!" she says, laughing at me. "What else do you guys e-mail about?"

"Lots of things. He's sort of like a diary that writes back. You know what I mean? Oh, like the other night after we ran into Veronica? I e-mailed him about it. It was completely out of the blue. And I thought he would think I was a total nutcase, which, you know, I might be. But he wrote back with this very comforting response that was charming and surprisingly comforting. He also told me not to worry, as he had never slept with her, which I thought was funny."

"You mean the wicked whore of the west," Lisa mutters.

"Yeah," I say, nodding sadly. "It's odd, I always sort of wanted to be a little more like her."

"Why?" she asks angrily, taking a swig of her beer.

"Whoa there, calm down."

"To put it candidly, she's a dime-store hooker. Bonnie and Crystal and I knew all along," Lisa says, smugly adjusting her lime-green bikini top and then playing with her charm bracelet. Lisa fidgets when something's upsetting her.

"Come on, Lisa, she's fun and exciting, and funny and confident."

"So are you," she comments pointedly.

"No I'm not. Confidence is in short supply."

"That's only because *you* sell yourself short," Lisa says seriously. She stretches out, moving *Fear and Trembling* out of the way, her slim figure extending as far as her muscles will let her. She points her toes up to the sky and then suddenly springs up with excitement.

"Now, on to weightier things," she announces.

I raise an eyebrow at her. "Yes?"

"How shall we enthrall ourselves this evening?"

"Enthrall? That's a bit of a tall order, don't you think?"

"Nonsense! We need a good solid pick-me-up/pick-you-up."

"How about a pick-someone-up?"

"That's the second order of business. Don't get ahead of yourself."

"We're not going to Gypsy," I say quickly. Gypsy is the graduate school bar, which, if you think Yale is nerdy, makes the undergraduate population look as cool as Madonna in her heyday.

"I wasn't even going to *suggest* it," she fires back. "I think we need something far more stimulating."

"No Red Hot Pony Express either," I add. The last time we had martinis and went over to the poor woman's Chippendales, a male strip show, which comes to Toad's twice a year. The Red Hot Pony Express did not involve ponies but was indeed hot, as the temperature in the place must have been a hundred degrees. Men dressed as construction workers stripped down to their hot pink thongs and shoved their unshaven unmentionables in our faces. Ball sweat does not mix well with four martinis and an empty stomach. We left early and had falafels at Mamoun's instead—New Haven's staple Middle Eastern restaurant.

"Believe me," she says, flipping her hair over her shoulder, "one Red Hot Pony Express was enough."

"It's Saturday. The only thing left to do is Toad's."

"Stale! Soooo stale. I'm tired of La Grenouille."

"Lisa," I say slowly.

"Yes?"

"I think I might really like Post-Boy. A lot."

"You don't even know what he looks like."

"But he gets me. Like you. Or like Crystal. I can talk to him. Or write to him. Or whatever we're doing . . . but I can, and it's great. I don't feel like I'm living up to any expectations—you know? It all just comes naturally with him. I know that sounds silly, but . . ."

"What if he has back hair or . . . or a nipple ring?" she suggests.

"Both fixable."

She smiles. "Risk! Risk anything! Care no more for the opinions of others, for those voices. Do the hardest thing on earth for you. Act for yourself. Face the truth." Then she pauses. "Katherine Mansfield."

"Who's that?"

"My darling, only the most famous writer to ever come out of New Zealand."

"Of course."

"If you want this, take a chance. That's all I'm trying to say."

"Duly noted," I reply. I've already taken quite a few risks on this unknown person. A few more couldn't kill me, I don't think. Although perhaps it's a little easier when he's faceless and nameless. Perhaps it's actually riskless.

Lisa squints in the sun and checks out her quickly chipping manicure while I think.

"Well, what do you want to do, then?" I ask, interrupting the silence.

"I'll think of something. Your task is to be ready at ten P.M. sharp. We are having drinks in your room, so get something good. None of that Dubra nonsense."

"Are you suggesting that it's a Grey Goose night?" I ask.

"Yes," she says gravely, "I am."

IT'S 11:45 AND Lisa and I are on our fourth Grey Goose and soda with three olives and a lemon.

My computer is blaring 50 Cent, and we are partying in the club (my room), bottle full of bub (Grey Goose).

"Shots!" she yells over the music. "We must do shots! Pronto!"

Lisa rushes over to our mini-fridge and pulls the Grey Goose out, nearly dropping it. I, for my part, am shakin' my booty and jumping on and off the couch. Impressive given my choice of foot attire for the evening—a prized pair of green pumps which I think look charming with my jeans, white T-shirt, and large gold earrings à la Barbarella.

"Chlo! Look how much we've drunk. This is terrible," she says, seeming very upset.

"It's okay!" I call back. "Grey Goose makes my heart grow fonder . . ."

"Fonder for whom?"

"For whomever!" I reply, giggling.

"Ooooh. I think tonight is one of those nights," she says, pouring the vodka into two shot glasses and spilling about seventeen dollars' worth on the common room table.

She hands me a glass and raises hers in the air. "Wait! We need chasers. Check the fridge. What do we have in there?" I ask, jumping back onto the couch and nearly pouring my drink all over nubby brown beauty.

Lisa walks back over to the standard collegiate mini-fridge and peeks inside. She is wearing a hot pink bra under a white tank top, about forty strands of pearls, a turquoise blue tutu, and her furry boots. She looks like Brooke Astor meets prima ballerina with a crack habit.

She stumbles a little and looks up at me with a grin. "Hey, schmuck, our choices are V8 or fat-free Jell-O."

For the record, she learned the word *schmuck* from me. Korean-born diplomats do not speak Yiddish.

"All right, all right, Jell-O it is."

Lisa totters back over to me and hands me a shot. She then proceeds to climb onto the table and raise her glass in the air. "A toast!" she exclaims.

"Go ahead," I say, raising my own shot and waiting with bated breath.

"May you be in heaven," she declares, "a half hour before the devil knows you're dead."

"Salut!"

We clink our glasses and throw our heads back, quickly picking up our Jell-O cups and squeezing the artificial flavoring into our mouths for salvation.

A look of panic passes over her face. "What time is it?" she asks quickly.

"Ummm," I murmur, checking my watch, "twelve-fifteen."

"Well, finish up that drink, milady, we are going to be tardy for a thrilling adventure."

"You can't be late for adventures."

"I say we can and we will. Besides, it's about time we did something exhilarating. I fear we are becoming somnolent in our old age."

"Lisa, we are twenty-one."

"I know, life goes by fast!"

"Where are we going?"

"To be determined."

"You don't know?"

"No, I'm just not telling you."

"Fine."

"Fine."

And with that, we both down our drinks, link arms to form quite a pair of drunken idiots, and saunter out of my room as if we own the world. And for a moment, I think we just might.

. . .

WE WALK THROUGH Cross Campus, up tree- and college-lined Elm Street, turn onto Park, and finally arrive at our destination—an off-campus house on Edgewood Avenue.

The music playing inside can be heard from where we stand on the street. I'm excited at the chance to dance and be social. It feels like it's been a while with all the papers that have been piling up.

"You made such a big deal about a party? Lisa, you disappoint me." I shake my head so my earrings make a delicious clinking sound.

"Just you wait," she replies coyly, "just you wait."

We open the door to the house and walk inside. The heat of so many bodies hits us right away, and we find ourselves in a foyer with cracked wooden floors, knee-deep in garbage bags. I look over at Lisa for some clue, but she is just wearing a big grin on her face. Above her head, on the wall, is a messily scrawled sign written in a thick black marker: "Check your clothes at the door!" it announces.

It takes a minute for this information to register, but I quickly figure out where we are. Lisa has rather sneakily brought me to one of Yale's infamous naked parties. Not like Exotic Erotic naked. There, parts are covered up for the safety of others, and though people are scantily clad, they are still to some degree clad. Naked parties are an entirely different story. People are, well, *naked*. Drunk and naked, but *naked*. And I didn't even have time to get my bikini line waxed.

"No, no, no, no, no," I say as I shake my head vigorously, "absolutely not."

"Why not?" Lisa asks, still grinning and peeling off her tank top. The front door opens again and a flood of people I don't recognize barge in and strip down, taking off everything, including their Skivvies.

I, for one, have never been in a Skivvies-free environment and am thus freaking out. Nudity is not celebrated in my house. As far as I know, the Wasp side of the family showers wearing their bathing suits. If my mother knew I was here, she would disown me.

"Lisa," I hiss at her, "what the hell?"

"No, doll, this isn't hell. This is heaven!" she announces, and does a big naked twirl. She's got a cute butt.

I am suddenly feeling quite sober.

"Come on, please?" she begs. "Give it a chance. Weren't we just talking about risks today?"

"You are sneaky. Very, very sneaky. And this," I announce in my sternest voice, "is very wack of you."

"Wack, schmack."

"Remind me why we're here again."

"Because we are naked-party virgins and I decided something needed to be done to change that. Immediately."

She crosses her arms, daring me to challenge her logic. It's hard to take her seriously with one foot turned out tapping the ground in fur-lined boots and pearls bumping against her bare breasts.

"Couldn't you have warned me first?"

"You wouldn't have come."

"I'm not Bonnie. You could have convinced me."

"Well, aren't you convinced?" she asks smugly.

Forced and convinced happen to be two very different things.

"You've got nice tits," I tell her, resigning myself to the fact that we are here to stay.

"So do you. Now take your clothes off," she demands, handing me a garbage bag to put my things in.

"Can I keep my shoes on? Heels will make me look skinnier."

"I think so," she replies.

"Lisa," I whisper.

"Yes?" she whispers back.

"I haven't shaved my legs in two weeks. I've got some deadly stubble going on here. If someone touches my legs, we're in the market for severe injury."

"Don't worry," she whispers, "I have a feeling you won't be the only one."

I take off my clothes and place them neatly in a big black garbage bag, reminding myself that participating in this is excusable because I have had four drinks and a shot.

I turn and follow Lisa's lead down the hallway toward the room where the music is coming from, and where I assume they're keeping all the naked people. As I follow her trim ass, I am silently congratulating myself on my bravery and on the fact that I have been using anti-cellulite body lotion since I was twelve.

We walk past a keg and into a large room with music blaring. This is what college is for, I keep repeating to myself. I am here to be naked. This is *clearly* what I'm paying $37,000 for. And by *I'm*, I mean my parents. This is *exactly* the kind of lesson I came to learn outside of the classroom.

The entire place is a mess of arms and legs and stomachs and backs. And balls. I've never seen so many balls in one place in my entire life. What if I touch someone's ass when I go to get a beer? Or worse, if I accidentally come into contact with a penis? That is the type of activity I usually reserve the right to plan for in advance. What if someone reaches down to scratch something and they miss and scratch me instead? On the upside, the dimmed lights give everyone this lovely cherubic glow.

"Hey, ladies," says a voice behind me.

I turn around and there is butt-ass-naked Activist Adam standing in front of us. He is trying extra hard to look both of us in the face. In fact, his eyes do not drop below shoulder level even once. I look around and notice that no one is checking anyone out. All conversations maintain uninterrupted eye contact. I giggle to myself. More people check me out when I'm *clothed*.

"Hey, Adam," I reply.

"Lovely seeing you two here," he says with a smile. "How are you, Lisa?" he asks, turning his adoring attention in her direction.

To my great surprise, she smiles warmly in place of a quick sarcastic jab in the nuts. "Good. Good," she answers quickly.

Adam's face lights up. He looks as if he's just freed a warehouse of sweatshop workers.

"Really? You are? You're good? That's great. I'm so happy to hear that. I've never seen you ladies at a naked party before," he continues, excessively excited. "To what do I owe this pleasure?"

"We thought it would expand our minds and free our souls," Lisa replies on behalf of both of us. Though the only thing I can assume will be expanded is my chance of catching some weird germs.

"That's totally what this is all about," Adam replies. "It's like about just getting to know who you really are. See, the thing is," he continues, scratching his chin thoughtfully, "is that we all came into this world on an equal, naked plane—and now where are we? All at different levels. We shouldn't let our clothes define us. We should define ourselves."

There is a pause as the two of us just stare at him.

"Can I get you a coupla beers?" he asks quickly, sensing that he has spent the last twenty-four seconds sounding like a complete fool.

"Sure," we reply in unison.

"You were being unusually nice," I say to Lisa when he's out of earshot.

"I tried," she answers dryly.

"And?"

"And I realized that he is still the idiot I always thought he was."

I take another look around the party. Lisa has begun talking to someone else, and I feel the nakedest in a world of naked people.

For the record, a room full of dancing naked people is not the most appetizing of scents. Sweaty naked people don't smell so good. Additionally, there are some people here with odd-shaped body hair patterns. I look down at my legs and don't feel so bad anymore. A guy walks by me with the smallest penis I've ever seen. I know I'm not supposed to look, as it's inappropriate naked-party etiquette, but I can't help myself. It's all just so funny.

I wonder how people pick each other up in here: "My, what a nice vagina you have"?

It reminds me of a comedy bit I saw on HBO once. Chris Rock was talking about being in love. When you're in love, he told the audience, you gotta love the crust of a motherfucker. The crust. You have to love the oddly patterned body hair. The weird-smelling parts. The backne. The unusually large big toe. The funky, lint-infested belly button. My question, then, is how do you get someone to love you if your crust is hanging out all over the place the very first time you meet them?

This party is all about crust. A group of giggling girls run by me and I take a few boobs to the stomach. Awesome.

The boy Lisa is talking to just reached down and itched his bare ass. As a result, the girl standing behind him gets a fist in the thigh. I try not to stand too close to anyone or look at anyone's privates directly. I have gathered from my twenty minutes here that that is *not* cool.

I begin to feel relaxed, but suddenly I am hit with a new, jarring thought. What if it gets too crowded? You could get pregnant just waiting in line for a beer. I'd love to see that conversation go down with my mom. No, actually, I didn't have sex; I just went to a party where everyone was naked.

"Nakeeed?" she would ask.

I would then have to say yes, and that the party got really crowded and some boy stood too close to me and all of a sudden I'm having twins.

"Jeweeesh?" she would ask.

And then I would have to tell her I'm not certain, but I'm pretty sure he was circumcised.

She would love that. I can see it now.

I make my way through the crowd back to Lisa, trying not to actually touch anyone or look anywhere offensive. I am pleased to notice that the hosts of the evening have covered all their furniture in plastic wrap. Smart move.

"Lisa!" I call out.

She looks over her shoulder. "Chloe! I was wondering where your naked self disappeared to."

"I was just taking a look around."

"Anything good?" she asks.

"Uh, define good."

She ignores my comment and turns toward the tall ass-scratcher I spotted earlier. "Chloe, this is Orpheus."

"Hi, nice to meet you," I say, extending my hand, careful to keep it above waist-level. I don't want to shake his penis. That would be awkward.

"Yeah," he says with a smile, shaking my hand. Then he reaches over to the table to grab his beer.

He's got a hairy ass.

"This your first time?" he asks me.

"Yup," I reply. "Yours?"

"Orpheus frequents naked parties a lot," Lisa says, jumping in. "He finds them very enjoyable."

"You must, too," he says, smiling at me. "I love your column."

"Thanks a lot. I love being naked," I add for lack of anything better.

He smiles. "Don't we all."

A girl walks by; her pubic hair is shaped into a heart. This night just keeps getting better. I nudge Lisa, but she is ignoring me, too busy talking to Orpheus about the finer points of Latin American politics.

Left with little to do and not recognizing enough faces to want to stay, I decide to put my naked-party experience (and my naked self) to bed. As Hot Rob said, I can check this one off my list and move on with college life. Hallelujah.

"Lisa," I say, tapping her on the shoulder. Orpheus glares at me. Soon he'll probably find one of his boys to come over here and take one for the team. AKA, entertain me while he tries his moves on Lisa.

"Yes?" she says, turning to me.

"I think I'm gonna go."

"Whoa," Orpheus comments, "sex columnist leaving a naked party, huh? Can't cut it in the nude world?"

The nude world? Who is this tool? And who does he think he is, telling me what I should and shouldn't do? Can't cut it? Here's a tip—trim your pubic hair. That's what you should cut. But I swallow my tongue and smile sweetly.

I turn and look him up and down. "Honey," I reply, "I came, I saw, I was unimpressed, and now I'm leaving."

I turn back to Lisa as Orpheus sulks. "I'm gonna go. Have a great night. Call me tomorrow."

"I'll come with you," she replies halfheartedly.

That line is straight out of the How to Be a Supportive Friend. She doesn't really want to come with me, but she has to offer. If I'm a real asshole, I'll insist that she does, but I think I'm independent enough to leave a party on my own. It won't be the first time.

"No, no," I insist quickly, to Orpheus's great relief. "You stay. I have to get up early and do a ton of reading tomorrow anyway. I have, like, four papers due this week. I'll be fine."

"Are you sure?" she asks, continuing to play by the book.

"Positive," I answer.

Orpheus waves good-bye as I walk away, feeling proud of my attitude and my cellulite-free behind. I am even tempted to do a little finger-snapping, but restrain myself for fear of touching anyone.

I find myself back in the foyer again, knee-deep in clothes-filled garbage bags, but unsure which one is filled with my clothes. They should have a better labeling system. Stay calm, Chloe. Stay calm.

I begin searching through the garbage bags one by one, but it's hard, because bending over in public when you're naked, if you couldn't already guess, is sort of awkward. People are coming in and out of the front door, some naked, some partially naked, some clothed and promptly getting naked. These people have no regard for their personal property, as they leave their things strewn all over the floor for some random naked person to steal. Which apparently is what happened to my stuff because it is nowhere to be found.

As I rummage around, my earrings clink together and the sound I thought was so glamorous earlier is now about as enticing as wind chimes. I want to take them off and put them in my pocket, but then I remember that I have no pockets. *Because I'm naked.*

Now it is time for me to panic. I can't find my clothes, I don't want to rush back in and ask Lisa if she knows where they are, but I need to get home before I have a premature heart attack at the ripe nude age of twenty-one.

I quickly run through my options. I could (a) take someone else's clothes, but that would be a felony, or (b) ask the hosts for something to wear home, but anyone who hosts a naked party is not all there in my book. Besides, I don't even know who's responsible for this charming shindig. Finally I spot a pile of empty garbage bags in the corner. In a moment of genius or something close to it, I grab one and wrap it around my body like a towel. If someone was far away, my outfit could be mistaken for a very short, very tight black vinyl dress. I figure that the dominatrix look is better than the streaker trend, so I tie the bag around my body.

My next problem is making the fifteen-minute walk home. I have a sneaking suspicion that strolling through campus at 1:30 A.M. on a Saturday will precipitate many run-ins and hence many questions that will in turn precipitate many long-winded answers. I am going to kill Lisa tomorrow at brunch. That girl's gonna be over like Jheri Curl.

Since walking home is out of the question, I use the wall phone in the foyer to call the Yale minibus service. I have never in my entire college career used the minibus, but I hear that you can call it at some easy number like 1234 from the little campus blue phones, and it will pick you up wherever you are and take you to your destination. I deduce since I've never taken the minibus that it is likely no one I know has ever taken it either. I quickly dial the number and schedule a pickup.

I now find myself standing on the street outside wearing a garbage bag, two-hundred-dollar lime green heels, and large gold earrings that the saleswoman told me would "glam up any outfit." She clearly did not have this one in mind when she said that.

After I shiver for about ten minutes, the minibus pulls up in front of the house and the driver slides the door open. I run across the street and step inside, making a significant effort not to make eye contact with the bus driver as I mutter my on-campus address. I assume that he's seen it all anyway and won't be overly interested in my unusual attire. All I want to do is get home and get into bed.

I look up to take a quick scan of the seats, noticing that there is only one other guy on it, sitting in the middle. I hurriedly slide into one of the first booths and stare at my thighs. I hope there aren't a lot of other pickups the driver needs to make.

I wish I was wearing underwear. This is completely unsanitary.

I stare out the window, replaying the events of the night in my head, and suddenly begin to giggle to myself. I can't wait to write Post-Boy about the entire ordeal. He'll probably find my adventure quite hilarious as well. I wonder if he's ever been to a naked party. I begin composing the e-mail in my mind as we stop at the first of several red lights. Downtown New Haven is a mess of one-way streets, which makes it impossible to get anywhere by car in under twenty minutes.

"Excuse me," comes a British-accented voice from behind me.

I ignore it and stare ahead. The guy must be talking to the driver. I hope.

"I'm talking to you," he says softly. I am a sucker for British accents. I mean, what American woman isn't?

Giving in to my pathetic weakness, I turn around slowly. "Yes?" I ask.

Sitting behind me is a slim, dark-haired guy. He looks about twenty-five or so, rather pale, but handsome in a Hugh Grant sort of way. He's wearing a crooked smile on his face, and his grin is echoed in his eyes, which crinkle at the corners. His chin juts out a little and his nose is slightly lopsided.

"Well, I couldn't help but notice that it seems someone has thrown you out."

"What?" I ask.

"I don't know if you're aware, but you are wearing a trash bag," he says, smiling.

"Yeah, I know . . . It's kind of embarrassing . . ." My voice trails off, and I'm unsure as to what to say next.

"I'm Colin," he says as he moves forward a few seats to sit closer to me.

"Hello," I say, blushing, "and I don't usually wear trash bags."

"Do you have a name?" he asks.

"Oh! I'm sorry. I'm Chloe," I answer sheepishly. I look up to meet his eyes and they're crinkling again.

"Well, Chloe, I would ask about your unusual attire, but I assume it's a rather embarrassing story, and then I would be forced to tell you why I am riding the minibus and my own horrendous tale of the evening."

"I haven't told you why I'm riding the minibus," I answer.

"I assumed it's because you're dressed like a Dumpster."

"You're right," I giggle, trying to sit in a way that won't reveal too much of anything. This is really awkward. "So . . . are you a graduate student?" I ask, trying to divert attention away from me.

"Yes. Comparative lit. Specifically Latin American. And you? I think I may have seen you at Gypsy once or twice."

"You might have," I say, tickled by his accent. "I'm an undergraduate in the English department. Now tell me why you're on this bus to begin with."

"Well, Chloe, I have just come from the most miserable blind date of my life. And then, to make matters exponentially more horrific, my car was towed. Fucking Americans and all of their parking rules," he says with a grin. "Don't tell me you're American," he adds.

"I'm sorry to disappoint you, I am American—a New Yorker, to be exact."

"Well, New Yorkers aren't Americans. Problem solved."

"So what was wrong with your date?"

"Where shall I begin? She had a bit of lip fuzz. She's a candidate for a Ph.D. in *finance*, and she droned on about futures all night. It was dreadful, we had nothing in common. And to make matters worse, she chewed with her mouth open."

"I've been on a bad date or two in my day," I chime in.

"Your day? You can't be more than twenty-two," he says, teasing me.

"And you," I shoot back, "can't be a day over thirty."

"Of all the gin joints in all the towns in all the world, she walks into mine," he says, feigning an American accent, which, I have to say, is quite good.

"*Casablanca,*" I say, identifying the quote.

"That was before your time," he answers slyly.

"Yours, too."

"Well, there's another thing we have in common," he says, raising an eyebrow at me. "In addition to studying literatures and being stuck on this bus."

"We're three for three."

"That's the green light, then. Can I have your telephone number?"

"I don't give my number to strangers. Especially not European strangers."

"Well then, I have good news. We Brits don't consider ourselves European. We are English—our own entity right in the middle of the Atlantic."

"But you're still a stranger."

"Well then, how can an Englishman, fearful, as are the rest of my people, of overt statements of affection, but with impeccable taste in scotch and neckties, ever be able to get in contact with you?"

I pause and think for a moment. I can't decide if Colin is full of it or just cute. I decide full of it for now, but leave it open to reevaluation.

"You'll have to pass a test," I decide.

"I'm terrible at standardized testing. I barely got through my highers."

"Highers?"

"British tests at the end of secondary school. One needs them to enter university."

"I see. Well, this test isn't standardized. And if you want to get in touch with me bad enough, you'll have to take it."

"I shall, but let me warn you, Chloe, that if I fail, I still want your phone number." He says my name *Chlo-ay*. It's delicious.

"We'll have to see."

"Go ahead, then," he says, spreading his arms out. "Try me."

"Best place for a beer? Or a pint, as you people say."

"The Globe, corner of Marylebone Road and Baker Street, London."

"I've never been."

"Is that good or bad?"

"We'll have to see," I say coyly.

He raises his eyebrows at me. "I'm intrigued."

"Football or soccer?"

"American football."

I'm happy with that one. I hate soccer.

"Favorite author?"

"John Cheever. Oh—and of course that batty American Seuss," he says, teasing.

"I enjoy Seuss, but I haven't ever read Cheever."

"That's a grave, grave travesty. We'll have to change it without delay."

"I thought you were comparative lit. What happened to the Latin Americans?"

"Gabriel García Márquez."

"*Chronicle of a Death Foretold* or *One Hundred Years of Solitude*?"

"*Chronicle*. Indubitably."

"I agree."

"Well, good. Did I do well?"

"Quite."

"Phone number?"

"E-mail address."

"I'll take it."

"All right. It's chloe.carrington@yale.edu."

He nods.

"Aren't you going to write it down?" I ask, panicked, and in a moment of extreme unsuaveness.

"I have the memory of a hawk."

"Do they have good memories?"

"I'm not actually sure, but I thought it sounded convincing. Didn't it?"

"Yes." I smile. "It did."

I look out the window for the first time since I stepped onto the bus. Suddenly we are parked outside of TD.

"Timothy Dwight?" the bus driver calls out in a scratchy voice.

I stand up.

"Yes. Sorry. That's me."

He opens the door, and I suddenly remember my trash-bag dress and my crazy night, all forgotten, or at least briefly put away, because of Colin.

"It was nice meeting you," I say over my shoulder as I hurry off.

"Likewise!" he calls after me.

"Chlo-ay?" he calls, as I'm about to step off the bus.

"Yes?" I answer, sticking my head back inside for a quick second. The bus driver must be thrilled about this.

" 'Never eat apples, peaches, pears, etc., while drinking whisky except long French-style dinners, terminating with fruit. Other viands have mollifying effect. Never sleep in moonlight. Known by scientists to induce madness. Should bed stand beside window on clear night, draw shades before retiring. Never hold cigar at right angles to fingers. Hayseed. Hold cigar at diagonal. Remove band or not as you prefer.' "

I give him an inquisitive glance.

"John Cheever," he replies, grinning.

I kind of like that his chin juts out like that.

The bus driver closes the doors and pulls away, leaving the trash bag princess to walk up to her room in the dark. Under the moonlight, that sometimes, like tonight, induces madness.

THE NEXT MORNING, I find two e-mails awaiting in my inbox. One from Post-Man and one from the Brit. For now, the Brit's seems much more entertaining.

CHLOE,

I thought that after my bad date, things were bound only to worsen, but you proved me wrong and restored my shriveling faith in humanity.

While shaving this morning, I remembered that I had been too nervous to ask you the most important question of all. Will you come to my abode this Friday to partake of dinner with me?

I will toss all pretense of modesty aside. I think friends as we are (or have become), we must make a distinct effort to dispense with any sort of airs. Let us say, con gusto, "The Date of the Century" (always with capital letters).

I hope you can make it on Friday. As a graduate student in a field with little left to be studied, my diluted pleasures in life normally involve a hot pot and a can of beans. Or if I'm extra-fortunate, soup. Of course I'll try to provide something a little more elaborate for our meal together.

From there, we can get to know one another better. What say you?

FONDLY,

COLIN

Fondly? I love the word *fondly*!

I tell myself to remain calm. This is only date one. Hopefully one of many.

I've always held e-mail writing up to an unfair standard. I think it's because all too often I meet fabulously wonderful people in person, only to be grossly disappointed with their e-mailing skills. Nothing is worse than a sparkling individual whose e-mails follow the standard "Hello how are you hope all is well what are you doing tonight" form of complete dullness.

But Colin. Colin has surpassed all e-mail expectations. He may just be the e-mail champ.

I quickly e-mail him that yes, I'll go on a date with him. I had to restrain myself from proposing marriage, but I guess that's what second dates are for.

Spring is here, and somehow things are looking up.

THE YALE DAILY NEWS

SEX AND THE (ELM) CITY
BY CHLOE CARRINGTON

No Matter What the Cost, Keep It Neat, Keep It Clean, Keep It Real

Once a month I get together with my friend Mya. We're not really that close, and often I end up hurling a string of profanities at her before our time together is up. She's usually very good-natured and forgiving about my tantrums, and speaks to me in a quiet, soothing voice reminiscent of the old woman's in *Fried Green Tomatoes*.

At the end of our visit though, Mya and I always end up on good terms. We say our good-byes; usually I tell a joke that makes her chuckle. We hug, then I'm on my way, until I call again four weeks later and the whole process repeats itself. It might seem as if Mya and I have a rather strange relationship, but in reality, we don't—we actually have a great deal of mutual respect and trust.

Mya is my waxing woman, my savior, my knight in shining armor—sort of. When we get together once a month, she pours hot wax all over my body and rips my hair out by its roots, leaving me in incredible pain. Sometimes I'm unable to walk normally for a week.

Which brings me to this week's topic—body hair. I'm

really concerned, not only about my own body hair, but also about the body hair of others. Namely, the removal of it and the necessity for this removal.

Body hair is a rather sticky topic. Its only use is keeping people warm in the winter; otherwise, it usually makes them slightly uncomfortable. "You have a uni-brow" and "What's that hair doing on your lip?" are not ideal conversation starters.

By society's general standards, men are supposed to have body hair. Leg hair is manly, chest hair is manly, but manliness can apparently be expressed only on one side of the body, because according to my sources, ass hair and back hair are unacceptable.

Understandably so. Ass hair is not pretty. In fact, it's funny looking. But ass hair raises an interesting quandary. If ass hair must indeed be taken care of, how is this removal supposed to take place? I would imagine that shaving one's ass is logistically impossible. So what's a guy to do? Where is he to turn? Asking his girlfriend might terminate the relationship; asking a relative, such as his mom, would categorize him as an abnormally peculiar freak of a man; and asking friends is out of the question! When was the last time you got together with your buddies to kick back a coupla beers, watch the game, and pluck hairs from your ass?

As one girl put it, "I think it should be a prime objective of the genome project to work something out where ass hair and back hair are just eliminated."

When in doubt, take it to the pros. Take it to science. Go, genome. Yeah, project.

As far as most girls are concerned, hair removal for men is acceptable as long as it is never mentioned. We prefer to believe that you were born without unsightly hair, silky smooth, and sexy sexy sexy. I briefly dated a boy who revealed to me that he Naired his chest hair. All I could picture was a six-foot well-built man walking into the drugstore and picking up a pink Sally Hansen Hair Cream Remover (with moisturizer), bringing it home, and spreading the pink cream all over his chest, then waiting fifteen minutes before removing it while reading *Glamour* magazine. As soon as stubble began to appear, we broke up.

The big hair-raiser (I'm sorry) was no doubt pubic hair. The general consensus among both males and females was that body hair is not about style or panache, but rather hygiene, and thus the rule of thumb is keep it organized. Pubic hair is like a Filofax. It's no good when little pieces of paper are sticking out of your Filofax; it makes it difficult to fit into your purse. Same goes for pubic hair. Capiche?

For guys, this translates into trimming. I didn't want to be the one to say it, but I just did. I put it out there. Warning: An unkempt crotch may hinder optimal performance.

For girls, although organization is key, the pubic hair question seems to be as complicated as the aforementioned genome project. There are just so many options.

Recently I've noticed an explosion in the woman's pubic hair trend. It ranges from the simple to the intricate. I read in a magazine that the newest New York trend is a complete (Brazilian) waxing of the pubic hair and the application of rhinestones in a variety of designs. Who wants rhinestones on their vagina? This is clear evidence that people who live in New York have far too much money to be rational, normal people. Another pubic hair option that has become en vogue is taking it all off.

One hopeless romantic confessed to me that his fantasy is pubic hair in the shape of a heart.

Another boy said that Mickey Mouse would be hot.

Ummm. That's dirty.

As far as total removal, I was informed that this question is completely reliant upon the vagina (I kid you not). Some people can pull it off, others just can't. "You gotta have the right type. It's gotta be a really, really nice vagina," one seemingly up-to-date gent assured me.

Where am I to go to find out whether I qualify? Do you know any vagina appraisers?

Other guys were completely opposed to the idea of bald pubes.

Disgusted, Rolo, the biggest pimp I know, revealed with a shrug, "It's just gross. It would be like hooking up with a twelve-year-old. And that's just wrong."

What can I say? Rolo knows.

Of course, men were very picky as to body hair standards where women were concerned. They apparently tolerate very little other than a clean smooth shave every time, although they did sympathize with those who waxed. The look of pain that crossed their faces when I described the process was priceless.

One purist insisted, "Girls should not have hair below their eyebrows."

I don't think guys should get action below their waists. Ha-ha. Now we're even.

Moving along, I tried to seek out men who may be a little more lenient with the body hair issue. I turned my attention to leg hair. I, for one, hate shaving my legs more than anything, and although I'm a razor whore in the summer, during the winter months, I do as the bears do and put it into hibernation. Thus, I asked whether, during the winter months, men are willing to be forgiving with legs a little less smooth than buttah?

"Not shaving her legs in the winter? I guess it's okay if she's wearing pants and standing at least ten feet away from me."

Whoa, champ, that's where she will be if you keep making comments like that. I'm not saying do a 180 and go Gloria Steinem, bring in the armpit hair, lose the deodorant, burn the bra. I'm just asking for a little compassion, a little humanity. Body hair removal is among the most irritating things about being a woman. And sure, some of you out there might say, "Hey, don't conform to society's standards, go out there and make a statement." Give it to 'em good, give it to 'em hairy. But what's going to happen to my hookup outlook if my legs look like Pete Sampras's? I'll definitely spark conversation, but forget getting laid.

What's the final consensus?

Keep it clean, keep it neat, keep it real.

I'm sending Mya a copy of this article. She'll be proud.

ℒ 10 ℰ

I AM SITTING IN the dining hall at lunch with Bonnie and Rob, the newly happy couple. My first date with Colin is tonight and I have been prepping for a week. Manicure: check. Pedicure: check. Hair conditioning: check. Thorough reading of *The Stories of John Cheever*: check.

For the record, my e-mailing with YaleMale05 has escalated as well, and we write to each other at least once a day. When I wrote him about my naked party experience, he was thoroughly sympathetic and impressed with my creative post-party attire. He informed me that though he had never attended a naked party, he had once accidentally walked into the ladies' sauna at the gym and could thus identify with my mortification.

"So, guys, I think I'm caught up in a li'l love triangle," I say, pushing some rubbery lasagna around my plate and feeling quite smug.

"Hmmm," Rob replies, unable to muster anything else, as he is chewing on an inordinately large chunk of sandwich.

"Are you really?" Bonnie asks. "I wonder if Post-Boy can count as the third corner of a triangle."

"True," I concede, "but for all practical purposes, it seems as if I am the object of several affections."

"Several means more than two," Rob says, swallowing.

"Fine! A couple, then," I say, sticking my tongue out at him.

"It is exciting," Bonnie adds, "especially this Colin character. I like him. And his e-mails."

Rob shoots her a jealous glare.

"But I don't like him as much as you, of course," she says soothingly.

"All right, you two, I gotta get to class, enough of this lovey-dovey crap," I complain.

"Love? Who said anything about love?" Rob jokes, and now it's Bonnie's turn to be the victimized party. I remind myself never to let my own potential relationships disintegrate into this spectacle.

"Ta-ta!" I call over my shoulder.

"Good luck tonight!" Bonnie yells after me. "Can't wait to hear all about it!"

"Uh, yeah. Me too," Rob adds.

THREE HOURS, SIX outfit changes, four cigarettes, and one V8 (for energy) later, I am standing on Colin's humble graduate student porch, ready as I'll ever be for our date. I take a deep breath and ring the doorbell nervously. The door swings open and he's standing there, as cute as I remember, a big grin plastered on his face. He's wearing a blue-and-white-striped button-down shirt, which is messily tucked into his jeans, a brown belt, and brown loafers.

"Hullo, hullo!" he exclaims. "Welcome to my humble abode," he says, spreading his hands out and stepping back to let me in.

"Hi there," I say, delighting in his accent. I step inside.

"You look positively lovely."

"Why, thank you."

"Come, come," he says, and I follow him into the small living area.

A chipped glass coffee table sits in the middle of the room, a large purple velvet couch directly in front of it, and a comfortable-looking brown leather chair to its right. An enormous bookshelf lined with hundreds of books and CDs is in one corner, while a small television sits on the floor. A faint smell of something burnt fills the air, but I ignore it. The walls are sparse, save for a few framed black-and-white photographs and a huge print of Edvard Munch's *Madonna*. I look at the painting appreciatively.

"Are you a Munch fan?" I ask.

"That depends," he answers.

"On what?"

"On whether you are, and of course on the painting."

"Well, I am, and I particularly like that one."

"Good," he says with a grin, "I am, too. Now make yourself at home while I fix us a drink. Red or white?"

"White," I answer as he disappears into the adjoining kitchen.

I walk over to his bookshelf to check out his selection. He's got just about everything: Tolstoy (two points), Dickens, Shakespeare, García Márquez (of course), Kundera, Milton, Joyce, Rushdie . . . the list goes on.

He walks back into the room, bottle in hand.

"I have bad news," he says, uncorking the bottle of wine. "I'm so completely cackhanded, I have managed to break every single wineglass in my collection this week. I was a bit nervous for our rendezvous."

He was nervous? I like that.

"Cackhanded?" I repeat, puzzled.

"Clumsy."

"Oh, of course. How many did you have?" I ask.

"Two," he replies sheepishly.

"Well, I guess we'll have to drink straight out of the bottle."

"Just like my grandmother," he says, the corners of his eyes crin-kling like they did on the bus.

"So," I begin as we settle in on the couch, "how did you wind up at Yale?"

"It's quite the long story," he says, taking a swig and handing it to me.

"Give me the abridged version."

"I was rejected from Harvard."

"Weren't we all?" I ask.

"Thankfully," he says. "After four years at Oxford, I don't think I would have been able to handle it."

"That's where you did your undergraduate degree?"

"Yes. I got a B.S. in maths."

"Oh, Lord! And you were saying that the finance Ph.D. you went on a date with was boring."

"Well, I quit the math thing, so you can't fault me for it."

"And in between?"

"How much time have you got?" he asks.

"Plenty," I answer.

"Are you feeling peckish?" he asks.

"What?"

"Oh, right. No one understands me here, but I have to hold on to home somehow. Are you hungry?"

"A little."

"Well, I had decided to cook, but, let's just say that didn't work out so well. I ordered pizza. I hope that's all right with you. Next time, I promise I'll study the recipe a little more thoroughly."

Now the smell of something charred makes sense. I'm touched that he's made such an effort, but I don't let it show.

"New Haven does have the best pizza, so I think you did fine," I say instead.

The two of us spend the rest of the evening sitting on his funny purple couch, gorging ourselves on pizza and wine, and getting to know each other. Colin tells me about his childhood growing up in a working-class section of London. His father is a welder, and his mother died when he was very young. I tell him I didn't know that welding was still a profession, and he laughs, telling me that I'm refreshing. I talk to him about my love for *Anna Karenina*, my weakness for shoes, and my own crazy parents. I finally tell him the reason I was on the minibus the night we met. He howls with laughter and recounts stories of life after he finished his undergraduate degree, traveling around Southeast Asia and Latin America; then returning to London, working odd jobs to make money, and traveling again.

"After a while," he says, "I realized that I was in love with books, and so here I am. I'm the maths major who didn't even give numbers a shot."

"Who needs numbers anyway?"

"Not you or me," he answers.

And then he kisses me. It is the most wonderful kiss I've had in a long, long time. Possibly ever. No Black & Decker tongue, no excess spit; it's just good. I will it to last forever, but of course it doesn't.

A little after midnight, I tell him I should get going. Though he asks why in the world I would do a thing like that, he lets me. He walks me home and kisses me again.

"Thank you," I say softly. "I had a great time."

"Me too," he answers, and then "I have something for you."

Out of his coat pocket he pulls *The Wapshot Chronicle* by John Cheever.

"I thought you might like this for bedtime reading, in case you tire of thinking of me."

"I probably will," I answer nonchalantly.

"I'm not surprised. But you know, this man is a genius. Words to live by. I promise."

"Better than *Anna Karenina*? I don't know. I'll be the judge of that."

" 'Fear tastes like a rusty knife, do not let her into your house. Courage tastes of blood. Stand up straight. Admire the world. Relish the love of a gentle woman. Trust in the Lord.' "

"Don't you have any of your own material?"

"No. And he's right about all of it, especially the part about women. Although I think you can ignore the rubbish about the Lord. I don't trust anyone I haven't met."

"Good night, Colin."

"Good night, Chloe."

STILL ON A high from my evening with Colin, though it's been about three days, I bound toward the *Yale Daily News* building at the speed of light. Or at least something close to it. I think that being in the beginning of a relationship burns a lot of calories. I have run everywhere over the last several weeks, and have found myself on time to almost every one of my engagements. I'm in such good spirits that I'm even looking forward to seeing Melvin tonight. Our relationship has become cordial since the last fallout, and I'm even toying with the idea of forgiving him.

When I arrive at the *News*, I am the only one on time, as Melvin is customarily nowhere to be found. Due to my super-calorie-burning skills, I allow myself a slice of pizza from the night's delivery and make my way up to see Brian Greene. He and I haven't spoken in a while, and despite our checkered past, he's been a good friend over the years. I rush up to the two-room, which is looking unusually calm this evening.

"Where's the drama?" I ask him, tapping him on the shoulder.

"Hey, Chlo!" he replies excitedly. "Surprisingly, we've had none this evening. We might just get the paper to the printer on time," he says, casually leaning back in his chair and folding his arms.

"On time? That can't possibly be!"

I don't think the paper has been promptly delivered to the printer's since the Kennedy administration.

"It's happened the last three nights in a row," he says, smiling.

"Congrats," I say. Brian Greene gets it done. Well, at least out of the bedroom.

"So what's new with you? Your column's been great lately. I've been meaning to tell you."

"Thanks," I reply, beaming. "You know, not much to tell. Just a few exciting tidbits here and there, but nothing to write home about."

He notices the smile right away.

"Are you telling me that our prized sex columnist might be taken?"

"*Taken* might be a little preemptive, but I may be headed in that direction."

"Well, don't let the columns slip. Being coupled is no reason to lose that thing you do so well."

"What thing?" I ask, raising my eyebrow flirtatiously.

"You'll never change," he says, "but I meant the writing."

"*Sure* ya did," I tease him.

"Ha-ha," he says sarcastically.

"So have you thought about what you're doing this summer?" I ask him.

"Internship at *WSJ*," he says proudly.

"Really? That's amazing!"

"Yeah, I'm excited. On the business desk, which I know nothing about, so that's sort of nerve-racking."

"You'll learn. You always do."

"I just hope I don't disappoint anyone. Do you know what you're doing?"

"No. I haven't even thought about it. I've been so bogged down with work and . . ."

"Looove," he says, teasing me.

I ignore him.

"Speaking of disappointing, where's Melvin?" I ask.

"I actually have no idea," Brian says in a rare moment of mis-management. "He's been acting weird lately. I've barely seen him at any of the *YDN* happy hours, and he just seems sort of nervous all the time. Do you know what that's about?"

"No. I have no idea. We're not really on speaking terms."

"You should talk to him," he says seriously. "I think he misses you. Besides, you've known him for so long. There's no point in trashing the friendship over the poor guy's general ineptitude. Anyways, he is so clearly in love with you it's ridiculous."

"It's just an old high school joke," I reply, "nothing to be taken seriously."

"Whatever you say," he replies doubtfully.

"Anyway, I better go see if he's there. Good to see you."

"You, too." Brian turns back to his work, diligent as ever.

I rush down to Melvin's editing station, and surprise, surprise, he's still MIA. Taking advantage of the delay, I decide to slip into his seat and check my e-mail. Perhaps my Post-Boy has written me in the last few hours.

Quite frankly, I don't know how Lisa did it with two boyfriends. One live man and one cyber man is more than enough for me to handle.

Melvin's Internet has already been opened, so I click on the page he has up. At least this is a clear sign he hasn't been gone for too long, and is thus bound to return soon. I click on the address bar and type in my Yale Mail (yalemale . . . ha-ha) address. As I'm about to press Enter, I take a quick look at the page Melvin had set up.

I gasp. Oh, my God. This can't be true. No, no, no.

The page staring back at me on the computer is a hotmail account for one illustrious YaleMale05.

I look over my shoulder to see if anyone is looking my way, or to see if Melvin is around the corner and on his way back. No one is interested in me, too occupied with their own impending deadlines.

I scroll through his inbox. Message after message is from me. There's the one about Veronica. The first one I ever wrote. Casual midday hellos. Forwards of funny articles—even the one about gay penguins at the Bronx Zoo. There must be thirty of them. But I am the only name that appears in the "from" category. No one else e-mails him at this address. He set it up just for me. And to think that this has been going on for months, *months* without my knowledge.

I can't breathe. Melvin? Why does it have to be Melvin? Why was he such a dick on our date? What is going on? I can't figure him out. He betrayed my trust by e-mailing me incognito. My eyes well up with tears, partially due to disappointment and partially because of shock. I blink them back, willing myself not to cry. Not in public.

I feel someone standing behind me. I turn around and there is Melvin, a look of sheer horror spread across his face.

"Chloe," he says softly, "I can explain."

"Why?" I ask. It's all I can muster.

I need to get out of here. I need to get out of here now. I need to digest this information. I tell myself not to make a scene. Don't lose control. I stand up and gather my bookbag and all of its contents, which with my luck have spilled all over the floor under the desk.

I crawl around on my hands and knees, picking up pens, gum, cigarettes, and class notes. I feel humiliated and exposed.

"Chloe, wait. Please wait," he says, taking his glasses off and rubbing his tired eyes. He looks so sad and apologetic, but all I can think of is what a bastard he is.

Finished gathering my belongings, I grab my bag and begin walking away. Melvin follows me. I run down the curved staircase past the publisher's office and past the reporters' room. I push the heavy wooden door open and rush outside. A cool breeze hits my face and quickly dries the tears that have escaped down my cheeks.

Melvin is behind me, but I don't stop to turn around or look at him. I stride away, leaving the *Daily* behind me. I can hear his footsteps as he trails behind me. I quicken my pace, and he quickens his, too.

When we arrive outside of Timothy Dwight, I turn around to face him. I feel as if my fantasy has been splayed all over the ground, its guts laid in front of me as if by a horrible car accident.

"You know," I say in an even voice, "it's true that I came to the paper tonight to edit, but I also thought, why not patch things up with Melvin? Why not become friends again?" I swallow hard and remind myself to hold on to some poise. "I've known you for seven years, and in that time you have done some pretty shitty things, but play with my mind like this? Invade my privacy? How do you explain that? What the fuck has been running through your head for the last six months? How long were you planning on continuing this charade?"

He just stares at me, his mouth slightly open, looking ready to answer but not sure where to begin. "Chloe, you wouldn't take me seriously otherwise," he finally says slowly. "I tried, I tried on that date, but I just didn't know how to talk to you."

"Melvin, what has changed between high school and now? Nothing. I'm the exact same person I always was."

"But, Chlo, you're not. Well, you sort of are. I understand now that you are. But you're also this sex columnist, you are so confident and together . . . I just . . . you never take me seriously—"

"Melvin," I say, interrupting him.

"Wait," he says raising a hand, "wait just a second. Please. But after our date I realized that you weren't that different. Granted, older and more mature, but still funny and brilliant and interested in all the same things you've always been interested in. Literature and . . . and . . . fashion . . . and art . . . and I just, I just wanted to tell you that I understood you, but every time I tried talking to you in the same way I always had, you wouldn't let me. So I thought I'd become what

I thought you wanted—like the guys I thought you wanted to date. The Toad's-going guys. But then I realized that you didn't want that either."

"So you decided to invade my private life?"

"I couldn't resist. It was the only way you would talk to me again. It was the only way you'd let me in."

"Why did you start posting to begin with? Way before we even started e-mailing?"

"To make you better. You were always great, but I knew that you reacted strongly to criticism, and you would take a recurring critic seriously. That's why I told you that your critics were just fans in disguise. Remember? Remember that e-mail?"

"I have a headache. I need to go upstairs. I need to think," I say, not wanting to respond and tell him that that e-mail made me feel a million times better.

"I'm sorry, Chlo. I really am. I'm so sorry."

"But Melvin, Post-Boy wasn't you. Isn't you. Whatever."

"It is me," he says quietly. "You just didn't want to see me. You've never wanted to."

"I gotta go. Don't e-mail me. Just leave me alone, okay? Please."

He nods and slowly walks away. I watch him for a little while, seeing his back hunched a little, his glasses in his hand. He shakes his head slowly.

It all sort of makes sense now. The Sean Connery. The echoing of my speech at TK's. Then again, it seems to make no sense at all.

I can't really swallow what these recent events mean. It's so much harder now. Post-Boy is Melvin. MELVIN. Nerdy high school Melvin. But if he has allowed me room to grow, why can't I let him? Why can't I take him seriously? Have I hurt him so badly that he can't be himself around me? Much like I couldn't be myself around anyone? Well, until Post-Boy. And then Colin.

I trudge up to my room, far more confused than I left this morning.

When I get there, the lights are off and no one is home. I sit in the dark for a couple of seconds and pull my cell phone out of my bag.

I slowly dial Lisa's number.

"Hello?" she answers after two rings.

"Hey. It's me. You'll never believe what happened."

"Try me," she answers.

"Post-Boy is Melvin."

There is silence on the other end, and then she coughs. "I'm sorry, Chloe, I think I was caught up in a peculiar reverie. What did you say?"

"I said that Post-Boy is Melvin. Melvin is YaleMale05."

"Oh." More silence on the other end.

"Lisa! Say something. What the hell am I supposed to do? How do I react to this?"

"I don't know," she says quietly. It's the first time I have ever heard Lisa utter those words. She always knows what to do. It may not always be right, but it's something.

"That's not gonna cut it. I need help," I wail in a panic.

"Well," she says slowly, "I think . . ." and then she stops.

"LISA!"

"I think," she starts again, "that as long as I've known you, you solve things by writing. You've grown through writing the column, and whether you like it or not, you've grown through writing to Post-Boy— I mean Melvin. Maybe you should . . ."

"Write?" I ask.

"Write," she says. I can almost see her nodding her head thoughtfully and absentmindedly chewing on a piece of her hair.

She wishes me luck and we hang up.

All year long I have written a sex column, and suddenly I am faced with something deeper. Something far more than sex. I wouldn't quite call it love—but something has happened to me with Post-Boy *and* with Colin that has never happened with any other man before. I've taken a risk—the risk of exposing my true self. The part that analyzes and thinks. The part not for public consumption. The vulnerable part. Perhaps the best part. I have exposed only a little bit of the truth, but it was far harder than taking off any article of clothing. I let down my guard, and unlike sex, it's not funny at all.

Thinking that he could win my heart by disguising himself, Melvin has exposed me and has allowed me the confidence to perhaps one day give my heart to someone else.

With this in mind, I walk into my room, light a cigarette, and erase the column I had written for this week. I begin, at Lisa's advice, to write something completely different from ever before.

THE YALE DAILY NEWS

SEX AND THE (ELM) CITY
BY CHLOE CARRINGTON

What's Love Got to Do with It?

When I was in kindergarten, I was the only girl allowed in the no-girls-allowed boys club. But I couldn't wait for grade school because all the boys were cuter there. Plus they didn't play with themselves in public. And when I was in fifth grade, I had a crush on an eighth grader because he was far taller than any of the shrimpy boys in my class—that is to say, he was my height. Then I got to middle school, and all I wanted to do was get to high school so I could sit outside on the lawn smoking and kiss guys and go on dates. But not necessarily in that order (smoker's breath, ew). But in high school I discovered that guys got zits and the lawn was itchy.

So I couldn't wait for college because everyone told me

I would meet the man I was going to marry. I was going to fall in love.

It's been three years, and I'm still waiting.

But in all seriousness, it seems I've considered love and sex to be separate entities. There's been no discussion of love, no roses and romance. Yale, we've rounded the bases together, with not a single profession of "I love you."

What makes sex funny and love not? There are no jokes about people falling in love, but there are plenty about people getting laid. Is love just too close to home? Have we indeed done the unthinkable and separated sex and love in our minds so that one is almost completely distinct from the other? Do the three rabbis in the bar only have sex? Do they never fall in love?

With people we really like, we take it slow sexually—at least at the beginning. We don't say "I love you" for ages, either; we have to wait until we're absolutely sure. Insurance companies should begin insuring love—if it doesn't work out, you're compensated. Get love insurance at the beginning of a relationship, when you think things might get serious. Ten bucks a month, and if you love him and he loves spending time with you, you're insured. Your insurer will find you someone else who'll reciprocate the deepest emotion in the human repertoire. It's a beautiful idea, really.

Sex and love both leave us vulnerable, and there is little that is funny about vulnerability. Yet we are vulnerable in different senses. That's why our hearts are on the inside and the sexual organs are on the outside. To be physically naked and to be emotionally so are quite different things.

Nudity is inherently humorous. The body is beautiful, of course, but the things we do with our bodies in the sack are plain weird. What about the 69 position? That could be done away with entirely. It's the position in which you are able to see your partner at the worst possible angle in the entire world.

Furthermore, the things we say in bed are atrocious. The sounds we make. Have you ever heard your roommate having sex? It's embarrassing.

The fetishes we have are ridiculous. There are magazines devoted fully to sex. How to have sex, where to have sex, with whom to have sex. Sex is full of odd details that end up being really just silly. Love, on the other hand, makes us act silly or stupid, but it does not make us bark like a dog or want to use whips. I mean, uh—if that's your thing.

I don't mean for this last column of the year to go off the philosophical deep end, or even to ask you to question your souls—to reach down and come up with something ingenious, to rediscover, or to reflect. I'm not asking you to go out and find that one person and reveal to her your deepest, darkest secret, that—gasp!—you are IN LOVE with her. (And this is a dark secret—trust me.)

I merely ask that every once in a while when you are getting laid or thinking about getting laid or hoping to get laid, you think about love. And when you find it, you clue me in on how exactly you were able to do so. Perhaps give us all a little insight into what makes that person the one, or the one for right now. Also tell me how the sex is. It might be interesting to discover what happens when sex and love meet halfway.

Then again, perhaps I'm thinking too hard, because as I sit here writing this final column, Fat Joe has just come on to the radio and he's presently asking me: "What's love gotta do with a little ménage?"

Joe, I don't know. What *does* love have to do with a little ménage?

Have a good summer, Yale. I hope we can continue this long-lasting and wholly physical relationship next year. And who knows? Maybe this summer I'll fall in love.

ᕬ Epilogue ᕬ

ℛECENTLY, ONE LAZY SATURDAY afternoon, I found myself in a bookstore cruising the aisles in search of some light summer reading. I spotted a book of well-known quotations, and as I'm drawn to wisdom dispensed quickly and easily, I picked it up and perused it for a few minutes. Finally I came across a page devoted to the uncensored insights of Andy Warhol, where two quotations in particular caught my eye: "Sex is the biggest nothing of all time." And, "Everybody winds up kissing the wrong person good night."

The first thought that came to mind was that if sex wasn't such a big deal after all, why had I spent the last year writing about it? And a large part of my short adult life thinking about it?

The second was that I was fortunate enough to have begun kissing the *right* person good night.

After my final column of the year was published, I wrote again, this time to Melvin, at his real e-mail address. I told him that he had done more for me than I had ever given him credit for, and I apologized for never showing him that I recognized the good that lay beneath his surface. While he had allowed me to let my true colors shine through (to borrow a line from Cyndi Lauper), he had to hide his own to do it. We got together to talk and concluded that we were simply better off as friends.

Two months later, Melvin, while interning along with good old Brian Greene at *The Wall Street Journal* in New York, met a girl named Sophie. She, two years his junior, was working at the Lifestyles desk and asked him out to coffee. Coffee turned into dinner and dinner turned into drinks.

From what I gather from his frequent e-mails, she has done quite the job of updating his wardrobe, while he says proudly that he has taught her a thing or two about sex.

I, on the other hand, went on several more dates with Colin. And then several more. I am living in London this summer, interning at *FHM*, a British men's magazine, writing a sex column, and occasionally infusing it with a little love. Colin is here, too, happy to escape from those "damned Americans" and working on his dissertation, which he hopes to finish some time "in the next bloody century."

Though he's not "Jeweeesh," my mother has learned to like him nonetheless, and my father, appreciating Colin's Protestant roots, has managed to show him a little affection as well.

And just for the record, I have taken this summer to fall in love.

ℛ Acknowledgments ℛ

To Christopher Rovzar, the *Scene* editor who planted the seeds for this book by calling me one September evening and asking me to write a little column in the *Yale Daily News*. Chris, I thank you for seeing the potential in my writing, and for making every column I wrote much, much funnier.

To my friends and roommates, without whom there would be no material to write about. Thank you for putting up with late night phone calls, tears, and finally for sharing in the celebration. You have opened your hearts and your lives to me, and I am forever indebted to you. This, of course, does not mean you get free books.

To my best friend Darius—there are no words.

To my darling brother, Daniel, for keeping me in check and never failing to make life interesting.

To my forever fabulous agents, Joni Evans and Andy McNicol, who were crazy enough to trust a twenty-year-old kid and who always, always tell the truth.

To the wonderful people at Hyperion—you have made this process a true pleasure. Thank you for granting me this amazing opportunity.

To Leslie Wells, my (very) patient editor, who has read this book countless times and who has made it better every step of the way. It was an honor to work with you.

To Dean Loge, my taskmaster. You were unbelievably tolerant of my nervousness, and never failed to provide thoughtful criticism. For these reasons and many more, I will miss our Tuesday meetings.

To Steven Brill, a wonderful writer, journalist, and teacher. I have learned a great deal from you. Thank you for your generosity.